LOVE AND CHALKDUST

LOVE AND CHALKDUST

by Paul Francis

LIBERTY BOOKS

Published by Liberty Books:
7 Swan Meadow, Much Wenlock, Shropshire TF13 6JQ.

Further copies can be obtained from that address,for £8.00
(inc. p.and p.), payable by cheque.

ISBN 0 9520568 1 X

British Library Cataloguing-in-Publication Data
A CIP catalogue record for this book is available from the British Library

Design and production by Dick Richardson, Country Books, Courtyard Cottage, Lttle
Longstone, Bakewell, Derbyshire DE45 1NN

A NOTE ON THE AUTHOR

Paul Francis taught in four comprehensive schools, from 1967-1998. He is an consultant and freelance writer, who has performed in festivals at Ledbury, Telford and Wenlock Edge, and won first prize in the OUSS "Sonnet at the Millennium" competition, 2000. He is the author of the following books:

Education:
Beyond Control?
What's Wrong with the National Curriculum?
Woodhead on the Block ?

Discussion materials:
Working Talkshop
What do You Say?
Boys will be Men
(And, with Richard Bain and Richard Matthews)
Talking to Learn

Collections of plays:
Power Plays
Under Pressure
Looking for the Moon

Collections of poems:
Our Class
Frozen Flashbacks
Nuggets from the News

He has also, with Gill Murray, edited two
anthologies of short stories for KS 3:
Myths and Legends
Survivors

DEDICATION

To all teachers,
great and small,
with whom I have worked.

LIST OF CHARACTERS

Don't panic – this isn't "War and Peace", but it is set in a comprehensive, which means that there are a lot of people involved.

STAFF at RAB BUTLER SCHOOL:

Colin Parnaby, head teacher
Joyce Davies, his secretary
Rod Spencer, deputy head
Chris Macdonald, deputy head

Terry O'Mara, English and drama
Jackie Grabowska, English teacher
Jill Williams, English teacher
Brian Summers, head of English

Mick Wall, head of technology
Sylvia March, languages teacher
Marion Harper, geography teacher
Pete Wrench, PE teacher.

SCHOOL PUPILS (in school years; 11 are aged 15-16, 8 are 12-13):

Dale Adams (11)
Muptaz Singh (11)
Tina Clark   (10)
Emma Sheargold (10)
Dennis Waite (9)
Sharon Collier (8)
Valerie Jones (8)

OTHER ADULTS:

Mrs. Chalmers, chair of governors
Linda Jones and Elsie, cleaners
Martin Walters, head of Priory Hall
Eric Higham, head of King Edward's
Rick McManus, teacher at King Edward's
Philip Rowley, English adviser
Mary Prendergast, inspector
Phil West, inspector
Mark Hutchings, parent
Sheila Thorpe, parent
Janet Smart, headship candidate

Chapter One

SEPTEMBER

This time, Van Morrison might not be enough. Van the man had seen him through till now, but Terry was a year older, had gone through two false starts, and it was this job or the dole.

His rusty Morris Minor crawled across the car park, and he looked warily for the labelled spaces, white paint on tarmac that the peasants must respect. His tapedeck rumbled on. "Bright Side of the Road" chirped away, in its jaunty defiance of reality, routine. With a slight pang, Terry turned it off, stopped the car, got out, and looked around.

Rab Butler was the second-best school in Shellworth. Or the worst. King Edward's, tall grey stone and steeped in history, climbed out of the middle of the town, asserting tradition, quality and academic standards, and a term there had been more than enough.

Rab Butler was tattier, more modern, down to earth. Post war, when the important land was already occupied, it had been built on the outskirts of the town, with playing fields that spread past the tights factory into open countryside. The school was an anonymous clutter of rectangles, panes of glass, white woodwork, grey, flat roofs. Dull, unexciting conformity, like the squares on a timetable. But Terry wasn't after a thrill; boring, regular employment would suit him fine.

Joyce Davies worked at her desk, humming along to the flute and harp concerto. More ambitious secretaries would have demanded sacred space, a room of their own, rather than this bastard territory guarding the Head's domain. Poised between Parnaby's office and the open corridor Joyce could well be receptionist, typist, agony aunt and reprographic slave, all in the space of an hour, and that was what she liked.

A few years back, when revamping office space was all the rage, Colin had asked about a change. Joyce had said "But I thought you were short of text books?", and they had settled for the status quo. The status quo included Rod Spencer, who now bore down on her with a purposeful gleam.

"Ah, Wolfgang Amadeus."

"It's James Galway."

Spencer was so thick-skinned you couldn't hurt him. The horn-rimmed glasses were inoculation, a barrier against the signals that human beings gave out. All Rod gave out was the wearing odour of conceit, somehow more potent at the start of term.

"Is the head around?"

"Maybe he's in the Science labs. He's not here."

"But it's urgent that I see him."

She watched him fret, the eyes blankly searching, the hand needlessly straying over his flat, black hair. Was this the sole surviving purchaser of Brylcreem ?

"Or he may have seen the exam results. In which case he'll be hanging from the wallbars in the gym."

"That's not fair, Joyce. I've analysed those results myself and I think they can be interpreted in a very favourable light."

"I'm sure they can. When you've worked on them. But I'm afraid I still don't know where Mr. Parnaby is. It is only half past eight, and term doesn't start until tomorrow."

"It's all right. I'm not complaining." A nervous laugh. "After all, we're on the same side."

Joyce's snort might have been a sneeze. Or not.

"I beg your pardon?"

"Don't worry about me. Just ancillary, I am"

"Oh no. The head's PA – you're the most important person in the school."

"PA? I thought that was a megaphone. Morning." Parnaby ambled towards them out of the corridor. Joyce watched him with affectionate pity. His suit was shabbier than Rod's, his bearing stooped, his gait less dignified – so why did she love him, and hate the other's guts?

"Colin - good to see you back."

"You sound ominously keen, Rod. Have a good holiday?"

"Fine, thanks. Could I have a word?"

Parnaby leaned against Joyce's desk, and smiled. "Help yourself. What do you fancy – Targeting? Marketing? Zero tolerance?"

"In the office?" Spencer's keenness was already looking frayed.

"All right. Sorry, Rod. Start of term blues." With an effort Colin Parnaby, head of Rab Butler Comprehensive School, reconciled himself to the start of term. "You'd better come in."

If you want to make the big time, get the boat. That much was common knowledge – George Best, Van Morrison, Kenneth Branagh. Terry was just the latest on the emigrant conveyor belt. The difference was, they had talent.

Through the windows it looked like any other school. Smaller and scruffier than King Edward's but then most schools were. He'd never been happy with trying to look smooth. More to the point, they had tried him, and they didn't want him to stay.

So he shunted on, a move at a time. Nobody else had a career plan these days, so why should he? Right, so the departure from Belfast could have been better planned and his CV had a vandalised look, but he could still end up OK. Shellworth was a nothing sort of town in the middle of nowhere, but he'd come last Easter because his Aunt Teresa was there, and found himself a flat. She had given him the battered Moggy and her blessing, and had then gone off to New Zealand, but he'd coped, and now he'd cope again, maybe.

Once again he stood, looking up at the chalkface. Trials of nerve and stamina, tests of his resolve, ninety termly pitches stretching out of sight. A prospect all the more daunting for the fact that he had already failed twice. Well, one dramatic fall, and a slither to the ground, but neither did much for his confidence. And now Terry, like a seasoned climber, like a kid learning to ride, must summon up the courage to take the risk again. He stood at the foot of the face.

Parnaby's office was in two halves – work at the desk, with a couple of hard chairs and his throne behind, and the social end by the window, with four soft chairs and the table. Joyce had brought in some flowers, but otherwise it was just the same. When he had a head's office, Rod would be in every August, and the evidence of a fresh start would be there for all to see. Parnaby headed for the social end, and waved Rod to a chair, any chair. He sat, and made his move.

"You heard about Walters?"

"Yes. Poor old Martin." Parnaby's gaze swivelled mistily around the room, as though watching footage of his former colleague, on a range of different screens. "He and I were talking last term, about retiring. Getting the timing right. Now the blighter's hardly got his fishing tackle out and he pops it -" and he was off on a private track. Plenty of time to retire, he'd thought. But so had Walters.

"Yes. Er – "

"You only met him once, I think. You weren't impressed."

Spencer adjusted his glasses, trying to look fair.

"I may have been hasty."

"No, I don't think so. Martin Walters wasn't that bright. Just a decent bloke, fallen among educationists."

"I thought I might apply. For Priory Hall. The headship, I mean."

Of course. How could he not have seen that for Spencer the death of Martin Walters would be not a warning, but an opportunity?

"Well, er...yes."

"If you think it's wise." The effort of self-effacement did not come naturally. Parnaby could have sworn he heard the muscles creak.

14

"You've got a lot of ideas, Rod. They seem to like that. What about Chris?"

"I haven't told her yet."

"What I mean is – will she apply?"

He would have got the same effect by stripping naked. Parnaby was a kind man, but he couldn't help enjoying the spectacle of Spencer straining to conceal his injured pride.

"Oh...Well, I don't know. She might, I suppose. I'd assumed, because I was senior deputy, that she'd wait a bit – "

"She was only appointed three months after you. It's not a massive gap. Less than one rung on the ladder...."

"I hadn't thought of that."

At last, Terry found a door that opened. He couldn't be sure if this was the main entrance, but at least he had got in. It wasn't the cinema foyer approach, with glossy photos of local industrial leaders visiting the school, and blown up photocopies of news cuttings squeezed from the previous thousand issues of the local rag. Like a prospector working to rule, a faded caretaker was sweeping piles of dust from one corner, and tattered notices hung from the wall, each suspended by a single staple.

Beyond this space was the entrance to a large hall, which would certainly do for drama. King Edward's had its own theatre, but this was a different league. Terry knew he couldn't be choosy. He was English and Drama, and nobody so far had said how much of each, but he'd take what he was given, and teach in a corridor if he must. Unqualified beggars couldn't be choosers.

From the far end of the corridor, Joyce watched.

"I think he's arrived."

"Who?"

"Your reject from King Edward's. Mr. O'Mara."

"Don't be like that. Eric speaks quite highly of him." Parnaby liked to be fair. He might be slow, anxious and tired, but it was important to do the decent thing. As Joyce would have insisted, in his defence, to any potential critic. But still it drove her mad.

"But Mr. Higham hasn't given him a job."

"You know King Edward's. Stuffy lot, their governors. Never did have much time for drama. I think he may be just what we need."

"He seems scruffy to me."

"Joyce, he's not a model, he's a teacher."

"We'll see. He looks a bit lost."

"Can I help you?"

Terry turned to face a double act. One short, ginger, lively, the one who spoke. Her mate was tall, black, stately - either an intellectual rock star or an athlete. It was no good. Talent-spotting, the hobby of a lifetime, wasn't going to slip modestly away. Deliberately, as if reviewing resolutions on January 2nd., Terry went through his vows.

Just the job, no women, play safe.

"Er, right. Thanks...I'm looking for Mr. Parnaby's office."

"Down to the end of the corridor. Turn right through the double doors. It's on the left."

"Brilliant. Ta."

The ginger one smiled easily, and pointed, watching long enough to ensure that he found his way. Then she was off, chatting with her sidekick. They looked like they belonged.

"Mr. O'Mara?" A pleasant, fiftyish lady, in cardigan and glasses, like his Aunt Teresa, had walked down the corridor to meet him. "I'm Joyce Davies, Mr. Parnaby's secretary. He's expecting you."

At King Edward's the woman had made a big thing of being the Head's *private* secretary, as though there were ten public ones below her. Moving downmarket was just fine. She escorted him down to her desk, in an open work area surrounded by photocopier and piles of paper. There was a cheerful, balding uncle figure, with a paunch, standing by an open door.

"Come in, Mr. O'Mara. I'm Colin Parnaby. Pleased to meet you."

It was a small office, a bit messy, with a lot of kids' stuff on the walls. No computer, no executive games, but lived in. At King

Edward's they laughed at Parnaby, because his suits were crumpled, his exam results were worse, and he was knocking off his secretary. Not this one, surely, this cuddly little aunt? Tea and crumpets looked like her limit. Still, you could never be sure. Lavinia had looked prim and boring, once.

"Eric Higham speaks very well of you. As you'll be aware, there are differences between King Edward's and ourselves. One of them, I think, is that we have the freedom to value drama rather more highly than they do. Please, sit down."

He gestured towards the soft chairs by the window. Terry sat down carefully, trying not to slouch.

"Right. Fine." Empty platitude time.

"Although we shall be asking you to do some English as well."

"Sure. I'll be glad to. I did some last term, and back in Belfast. I'm sure you'll have people to keep me on the right lines."

"Oh, we do. We're grateful that you could fill in for us at such short notice."

Come on, then. How much English, how much drama?

There was a pause. Terry could have sworn that this headteacher was also stuck, as tongue-tied as himself. Just a wet, helpless smile. He's waiting for me to speak.

"It suits me. King Edward's only had a short-term vacancy, otherwise...I'd be..er, out of a job, you know what I mean?"

Face it. You're desperate, he's desperate. That's why you're here.

"And I take it you have not yet completed your first full year?"

The hard bit. Why, precisely, Mr. O'Mara, did you leave your first job and run away to England? What bizarre circumstances could make someone like you settle for this mediocre compromise, this stretch of the midlands that is neither north nor south, town nor country, suburb nor slum ?

"No. That's right."

"But I don't see why that should be a problem. As you know, this is a temporary post, for this school year, but if you're still with us in July, and everything's satisfactory...well, who knows?"

"I'll certainly do my best."

17

"We can't ask more than that. Well, Terry – we use first names here, if that's all right with you?"

He nodded inanely.

"Welcome to Rab Butler. Rod Spencer, my senior deputy, will fill you in on the timetable. The staff meeting starts in a quarter of an hour." Wearily, Parnaby got to his feet and opened the door. "Joyce, could you show Terry to the staffroom please?" She nodded, a bit coolly, and he followed her.

They passed two teachers talking: a tall, earnest chap with shiny black hair and horn-rimmed glasses, and a fierce woman with short hair, in a grey power suit. Terry had resolved to smile and get on with everyone, but he got the impression that neither of these two had made a similar vow.

Back in the reckless past, when teachers developed the curriculum and took nicotine at break, the staffroom had a smokers' corner. Now it was purged of smoke, but the name remained, and the shabby chairs in the corner still acted as a magnet to the older, grumpier, disaffected male staff.

Jill Williams didn't care where she sat. She put down her bag, and looked briefly round. There were a few changes – new headings on the noticeboards, less rubbish on the floor – but nothing much had changed.

"Hello, Mick. Good holiday?"

"Morning." Mick Wall, tubby and familiar, made her feel at home. He'd started off as Woodwork, Scale 1, and now they called him Head of Technology, but he wasn't fooled. "Ready for the fray?"

"I'll tell you tomorrow."

"You're bluffing." He poked around in her bag, prodding the pile of marking, the folder of worksheets she'd prepared. "While I've been polishing my sun tan you've been preparing lessons. Go on, admit it. You organised women make me sick. How about you, Sylvia?"

"No, I'm not sick, thank you. But it was nice of you to ask." She looked serene, dressed for a private view rather than a training day.

Jill nodded a greeting. "Nice holiday?"

"Oh yes." Sylvia March, head of French, enjoyed her summer holidays. Five weeks of French food, wine and conversation. And now she was in England again, about to teach, again. Everything had to be paid for.

"I fear I'm going to regret it."

"Not as much as you're going to regret this." Mick nodded towards the end of the staffroom, where the management team were arranging their chairs, before addressing the staff. One day – a Professional Development day - in which to prepare for kids.

"Well, then, colleagues, if we could make a start..." Chatter subsided, latecomers crept in, and forty daydreams continued for as long as reality allowed.

"And I'd like to welcome Mr. Peter Wrench to the PE department..."

A young lad in a green tracksuit looked round the staffroom anxiously, smiling a welcome. Fresh from college, fit and keen, unmistakably innocent.

"...and to teach English and Drama, Mr. Terry O'Mara joins us, after a term at King Edward's."

There was some brief, light-hearted hissing, in honour of the local rivals, followed by exaggerated smiles aimed at Terry, as if to reassure him they wished him well. Any teacher was welcome these days; the alternative was gaps on the timetable, cover lessons for staff, less free time. Terry, hair uncombed, lessons unplanned, tried for his modest-but-capable look.

Parnaby gave a pointless little cough, the embarrassed prelude to his message for the staff. "Well, colleagues, over the past few years we've all heard more than enough about opting out. But so far as I am concerned, this school is opting in. Whatever the external pressures, and they are considerable, we at the Rab Butler are committed to education for all, in the widest possible sense; in each subject of the curriculum, in lessons and beyond, our concern must be for the fullest possible development of each individual child."

There was a pause. A couple of older heads nodded, while

others gazed at the floor. Uncle Colin was showing his age, again. Terry, looking for clues as to how he should respond, scanned the room. Not much to go on. Not much talent, either. Though just in front of him there was a thin woman in a red jumper, with long blonde hair. The Meryl Streep type, maybe, though he couldn't see her face. He wasn't on the pull, but if he had been she was where he'd start.

Parnaby, relieved to have said his piece, flapped a hand in Spencer's direction, and sat down. Rod leapt to his feet. This, after all, was what it was for: the late nights, the boring courses, the struggling with paperwork, these were the price you paid for privilege. Decent pay, his own office and – sometimes best of all – the chance to address the staff.

"You'll see that we've had to extend the noticeboards devoted to assessment arrangements and financial management. I'm sorry about the posters for teacher unions and staff social events, but we'll find a suitable alternative. You may also notice that the staff workroom has been updated, so as to provide an updated resource bank for developing our response to the demands of the National Curriculum."

Within seconds the meeting was glazed over, covered like a cake. The phenomenon of Rodspeak blurred the senses, although on his own agenda the climax was still to come.

"And now, I have something to say about the timetable."

Forty possible responses lingered in the air.

"The print-out was in pigeonholes at the end of last term, and the programme's built-in consistency check means that the possibility of errors is excluded. Should you have any queries, please put them in my pigeonhole by the end of this week."

Chris Macdonald, the short-haired deputy in the grey suit, stood up.

"If I could just – "

"And finally…" Rod turned, with exaggerated caution, to look at Chris, who seemed not to know her place.

"Oh, sorry." She sat down. Rod smiled, gratefully. Fifteen – love.

"Just a quick word about our promotion campaign. I don't have to stress how important it is that we present ourselves in the best possible light to prospective parents. After all, our jobs are on the line..."

Not his, surely, thought Terry, who had never known a time since college when his job was *not* on the line.

Chris Macdonald, thwarted, reviewed the scorched terrain, site of last year's battles over what Rod was pleased to call "the commercial imperative." It had started from apparent trivia – a snack machine, by the toilets. Well, why not, if it brings in revenue? Answer, because it totally undermines the school's policy on healthy eating, drafted by Chris, broadcast to the staff, and enshrined in the school's tutorial programme. But not, it would seem, in Colin Parnaby's skull.

So that battle would have to be refought, Chris mused, only this time she would keep her cool. With a mix of excitement and embarrassment she recalled the peak of last year's row – "So where does it stop, Rod, this commercial imperative? Do we sell cocaine to the kids, or hire them out as tarts?" That had been too much for Colin, and it hadn't gained her anything, except the warm glow of seeing Rod discomfited, and the satisfaction of relieving her feelings. Which was a rare enough experience, these days.

And still Rod was droning on.

"We've now published this excellent magazine, for which I'm very grateful to the English department, and Jill Williams in particular" – a formal nod to the tall woman with frizzy hair whose friend had given Terry directions. The friend was nudging Jill, whispering a joke which was not to be shared with the interminable Mr. Spencer.

"During the next few days I'll be approaching some of you with ideas I've been knocking together over the summer. But please feel free to come up with your own suggestions for selling the school."

"I can't imagine who'd wish to buy it."

It was Meryl Streep, turning round, with a conspiratorial mutter and an encouraging smile. Was she lining him up, like he had lined her up, before he thought better of it? He could make resolutions, but he wasn't a saint.

Spencer, having established his place in the pecking order, treated his fellow deputy to an ingratiating smile. She rose, briskly, unperturbed. The grey suit was armour, and the brief interruption to her blank expression registered irritation rather than hurt. Chris Macdonald had met a lot of condescension in her time.

"This term's tutorial topics are outlined on the noticeboard, and tutors have a programme in their pigeonholes." She stood confidently, but the voice was dull and strained, competent but cool. "We have a range of visiting speakers and videos booked, but feel free to add suggestions of your own. Please see me if you have a problem."

A stage whisper. "Ooh, that sounds promising."

"Mick?" The tall, black woman turned round to face him.

"Yes, love. What can I do for you?"

"Grow up. Please?" The meeting was breaking up around them.

"Oops. Another blunder." Unrepentant, he winked at Terry, and came across to shake his hand with a grip that would pulverise nuts. "Hi. Mick Wall. Welcome to Stalag Luft. Terry, is it?"

"That's right."

"Meet Jackie and Jill, the Little and Large of the English department."

"Thank you, Mick. No new jokes this year?" The short, ginger one grinned at Terry. "Hi. Jackie Grabowska. Do you know where the English meeting is?"

"Not a clue."

"Come along, we're just going." Jackie was taking him in hand.

"Joyce, is Colin in?"

"I think he's on the phone"

"Could you check, please?"

"Certainly, Miss Macdonald."

22

The rules were clear. Neither party would be rude, Joyce would call Chris *Miss* Macdonald (despite repeated requests to use Ms.) both would carry out their respective duties with identical efficiency, and between them would flow a seething, subterranean current of mutual dislike.

Joyce played on the switchboard with what seemed to Chris like excessive care. "He seems to have finished now. Would you like to go in?"

"Thank you."

It was the merest, minimal acknowledgement as she swept through the door and closed it behind her. Parnaby was at his desk, and started to rise.

"No, don't get up. This won't take long."

"Chris, good to see you. How was the holiday?"

"Fine, thank you."

"Now, what can I do for you?"

"I am considering applying for the Headship at Priory Hall."

"Yes?"

"What do you think?"

God, what did he think? What he thought was that he was too old to cope with people like Chris Macdonald. She was very good, would do very well, had read three times as many educational books as Colin had heard of. They lived in different worlds.

"I can't see any objection…"

"And if Rod applied?"

"I'm sorry. I don't follow you."

"If you were asked to supply references on us both, would you do that? Or would you automatically favour Rod, because of seniority?"

What must it be like, to think so clearly? To have the alternatives defined in some mental computer programme, dispassionately laid out to view? On this day before the start of the Christmas term, Colin Parnaby's brain felt no clearer than it had at the end of the summer term. Joyce was right: he should have gone then.

"No problem. I'll happily write references for you both." Cunning, he added his own layer of qualification. "If required, of course."

23

At the English meeting Brian Summers, head of department, seemed neither horrified nor delighted by the addition to his team. Jackie and Jill supplied the energy, bristling with paperwork, flicking confidently through ring-binder files and minutes of previous meetings. There was a lot of paper around, but they were English and Terry was Drama, so he didn't let it get him down. They could scribble in their files, but he could perform – to each his own.

English was books and writing, syllabuses and making corrections. Critical essays, Victorian novels that cranked slowly into action, comprehensions where he couldn't understand the passage, let alone answer the questions. Drama was freedom, moving around, making up your own lines, seeing where it led. As a kid, Terry had got his buzz from drama rather than English, and his bet was that kids would also see it that way.

But he wasn't encouraged by the timetable which Spencer had thrust into his hand on his way to the meeting. Lots of English, not much drama, so he'd better listen to what they said. It was at least livelier than King Edward's obsession with exam results and test scores. Jackie did most of the talking, enthusiastic but inviting, trying to involve others in the discussion. There was an older bloke in the corner who grumbled a bit, and a lady part-timer who seemed mildly interested without saying much. Jill said little, but seemed to know a lot. Watched, listened, followed each face in turn, and took notes.

He didn't want them all brilliant, or they'd show him up. But if they were all useless, he'd be stuck. So this mixture of boredom and energy, thinking and routine, should end up about right. Besides, nobody was paying him just to get a buzz. He had a few drama lessons, and he'd do what he could to liven up the English, but if he was going to get through till Christmas, he'd have to follow what was going on. Act interested, ask for help, and not chat anyone up. Meryl Streep would have to wait. Lavinia, where are you now?

The kids weren't in yet, so there were no school dinners. The poor, the mean and the elderly staff brought sandwiches, but the more sociable adjourned to the local pub. The White Horse offered a country and western juke box at excessive volume, but reasonable food. To the accompaniment of Johnny Cash and the Orange Blossom Special, Mick Wall attacked a steak pie and a mountain of chips.

"There you are, Mick", Sylvia announced, placing a glass before him. "One pint of best – or so the barman says. Just look at it."

"Cheers, Sylvia." Mick supped the bitter, slowly. "Tastes all right."

"Not the beer. The ambience."

"Ambience. Don't tell me. French for walking?"

"Lifestyle. The decor, the food, the music – the whole quality of life. You really notice the squalor, after a month of civilisation." She raked the pub with a dismissive stare, and sat down.

"I didn't know you went to Bridlington."

"Not Bridlington, Michael. France. Where they know about food and treat you like a human being."

"You'll be emigrating, then?"

"I wouldn't mind. No more covering for absent colleagues, go out of school if you're not teaching, decent wage packet at the end of the month – oh yes, I could be tempted."

"What about the dogs?"

"They've changed the rules now. Should make it easier."

"Well, they can't stop you dreaming."

"How about you, then, Mick?"

"Me? Oh no, Jackie. I've got different dreams."

Jill, tapping to the music, mimed alarm. "I don't think I want to hear this."

"Fame and fortune. I've got this lovely little idea lined up." Mick leaned forward, warming to the theme, binding in his hearers with a plotter's grin. "Burglar alarms. Neat, simple, cheap and one hundred per cent reliable. Sometimes I just lie there in the middle of the night and the sheer beauty of the idea knocks me out."

"And then you wake up."

"No, Jackie, it's real. There's a market out there. I can taste it."

"Give it to Rod. Rab Butler PLC can sell it for you."

"Don't talk to me about that man. Have you seen our timetable? My two year old daughter could do a better job. I tell you, that man has to go."

Terry watched, amused, appalled. Mick was a riveting performer, but which bits of this did he mean? And how could you possibly tell ?

"You are following all this, lad?"

"Mmm."

"Right, son, bend your ears back. Mick Wall's personal guide to the staffing situation at Rab Butler, soon to be available on video at your local music store. Uncle Colin is in charge. No, I'll rephrase that. He's the head. Decent bloke, cuddly, lovable and at least ten years behind the times. But nice with it."

"Nice with Joyce, too."

"You don't know that, Jackie."

"Come off it, Jill. Don't be so tight. Everyone knows that."

"And then we have our two deputies, Rod Spencer and Chris Macdonald."

"The ones who spoke at the meeting?"

"Right. In the red corner, I give you Hot Rod, king of the timetable, finance and links with local industries. Almost anything, really, as long as he doesn't get near kids."

Jill was scathing. "He's also a sexist, careerist slob."

"Yes, that too. And in the blue corner – "

"Not Chris. She's in the red corner."

"The lovely Chris Macdonald." Terry was struck by the feeling in Mick's tone, lyrical yet bitter, while Jill was simply outraged.

"Now that is sexist."

"He's still crazy for her, after all these years."

"Jackie, you are supposed to be my friend. Anyway, Terry, if you have problems with sex, money or personal hygiene then Chris will sort you out."

"What about my car?"

"Sorry?"

"What if I have problems with my car? There's something going funny with the clutch."

"No, I wouldn't take your clutch to Chris Macdonald. I'll have a look at that for you, son. In good time. But first, get the hang of the paper. Not colourblind, are you?"

"Don't think so."

"Right. Yellow is internal memo, pink is special information for all staff, and green – well, green is cover. Filling in for absent colleagues. Got all that? The first test will be tomorrow, starting at nine…"

In a blur that was only partly Guinness Terry watched the faces and the chat and the paper swirl before him, pleasant, welcoming and confusing all at once. This would be his world for the next twelve months, and tomorrow came the kids.

Meanwhile Joyce and Colin munched their sanwiches, at the social end of his office.

"You don't suppose that anyone will mind?"

She was amused, rather than angry. He was divorced five years ago, his ex-wife was with her new husband down in Cornwall, the staff speculated freely about the two of them, yet still he sought to conform to a propriety that was his alone.

"Eating shortbread, Colin, is not an offence. Besides, tomorrow the kids will be here and you'll be back on duty. It's our last chance till half-term."

"You're right. I'm sorry. I can't help thinking about Martin."

Joyce munched an egg sandwich, wholemeal, thin-sliced.

Colin had stopped eating. "I knew it at the time. You've never got as much time as you think."

"He was older than you."

"But not by much. And I want more retirement than him."

She shrugged. Her mother, she might have said, was twenty years older than either Walters or Parnaby, and she was still alive.

"They're both going to apply."

"Sorry?"

"Rod and Chris. They're both going after Martin's job."

She thought for a bit, then wrinkled her nose in distaste. "I suppose I'm not surprised."

"You don't like either of them, do you?"

"It's not a question of like. But no, if it was, I don't. They're both out for themselves."

"Isn't everyone?"

She stopped to look at him, hurt.

"No, Joyce, not you. Not us, but we're the old generation. They do it differently now."

"You mean you've got to be selfish, ruthless and egotistical before they'll make you a head?"

He took a bite of his apple, and paused, to ponder the hypothesis. Set against recent appointments, it seemed to work. When he thought back to his early days in the job, it was like a black and white film. Lost innocence, the sense of running things. And now, each day's post brought him glossy, unreadable reminders that these days he wasn't running anything but scared.

The slow walk through the door, surveying the wreckage within. No comment, no reaction, save the first utterance for as long as possible…

"I'm Terry O'Mara, and I'm your English teacher." Loaded pause, and a welcoming smile.

CRASH! "The name's O'Mara, and you'd better get it right."

Saunter in, and sit cross-legged on the table. "Hi gang, now let's do it…"

There were many ways of getting it wrong. Terry hadn't finished much, but he'd made a lot of starts. Two dollops of teaching practice, the job at Stranmillis, the abortive term at King Edward's…this wasn't the first time he had started to teach. It was like the opening of a play: the best time, maybe the only time, that you could confidently plan. What is the first impression we get of this central character, the teacher ? How does the story start? Whatever you say, say nothing. Hold it back, give little away, play safe.

And he'd survived. Well, it was only a double lesson with his year 10 tutor group, but that at least was over. Some very mature, very charming girls, a handful of lads who looked as though they might be dodgy later on, and an amorphous clump in the middle he couldn't sort out. But so far, nothing he couldn't handle. Terry fought his way through the crowded corridor, hoping that this was the way to the staffroom.

"Excuse me, but I work here. Thank you."

Like the kids, he made way for the imperious tone. A smart woman in a brown suit and scarf swept through the crowd, smiled faintly as she passed and left him to grab the staffroom door before it closed. Somebody March, who spent her holidays in France. Inside, there was Meryl Streep, who turned out to be called Marion Harper and to teach Geography. She was talking to Jill Williams, the tall, black woman from English.

"Jill, there's a girl asking for you outside. That pushy year 8 kid, something Collier."

"Sharon. Thanks, Marion."

"It's been a long Tuesday morning. This term's really dragging."

"Yes, Mick. And then you say 'It's as though we'd never been away.' "

"What's up, Jackie? Don't you like my dialogue?"

"Always did. Well, the first three times, anyway. For a soap it would be fine. I just don't want to live with it."

"I didn't know I'd offered. I'll tell the wife. You got any sugar?"

"OK, Terry?"

Jackie nudged him matily, as he hovered in the queue for coffee, trying to balance modesty and thirst.

"Er, yeah. Fine so far, thanks. Only fifteen weeks to Christmas, is it?"

"Great. Another idealist. Welcome to the club, son."

Outside the staffroom Valerie and Sharon were waiting as Ms. Williams emerged, mug of coffee in her hand. Sharon, tall and composed, was the usual spokesman, so Jill was surprised that Valerie spoke first.

"You said it would be in, miss. My poem."

"Yes, Valerie. What makes you think it isn't?"

"Sharon's got the magazine, miss." Shyly, Sharon surrendered it. Jill flicked through the familiar pages, silently fuming.

"Where did you get this from? I haven't got one yet."

Sharon was back in charge. "Mr. Spencer gave it to my dad last Friday, miss. At one of those lunch thingies."

And as Jill flicked through the pages, Valerie burst out – "It's not there, miss. It was on that page, there, opposite the elephant story. You let us see the proofs."

"That's right. I remember."

"That advert, miss. FLATPAK SUPERMARKET. That's where it was."

"You're quite right, Sharon. I'm sorry, I don't know what happened. I'll have a word with Mr. Spencer. Is it all right if I borrow this?"

Sharon nodded confidently, while her friend felt an unfamiliar tremor of despair.

"I thought you liked the poem, miss."

"Valerie, I did like the poem. I still like it. If it's not in the magazine I shall make sure we put it in the middle of a wonderful display. But for now, just leave it with me? OK?" The two 12 year old girls, trudging off forlornly, are replaced by two 15 year old boys, both in belligerent mood.

"Is Mr. Wall in, miss?"

"I'll have a look."

The door closes again. Inside, frantic swilling of coffee, gathering of bags, drawing of breath. Outside, clusters of bored criminals, anxious supplicants, patient seekers after truth.

"Sir– "

Mick Wall, coffee in one hand and briefcase in the other, negotiates his way out of the staffroom door. The two boys close in. Muptaz is polite and immaculately groomed, while Dale is rougher, more shifty looking, but they are united in a common, angry cause.

"Sorry, Muptaz. I'm teaching."

"But it's urgent, sir."

"Yes, Dale, I'm sure it is. See me in the lesson."

"That's not till Thursday, sir."

Mick throws him an unconvincing smile as he drains his coffee, and stuffs the empty but dripping mug into the recesses of his briefcase.

"Well done. You know your timetable already. Thursday, Dale."

Acting definite, running scared, exit teacher.

"If we did that, we'd get done."

"I told you he wouldn't listen."

"He's got to listen, one day. He can run, but he can't hide."

"I'll kill him, Muptaz."

"No. I've got a better idea."

Terry's early lessons went by in an anxious, competent blur. No showing off, no casual jokes with the kids. What was it the old hands said ? – "Never smile before Christmas". Formal, organised, restrained; he was bored out of his skull, but it was good and safe.

Jackie was a big help. Cheerful, open and generous, she was ready to share everything – good ideas, lesson plans, duplicated sheets.

"How's the marking?"

"Oh, you know. A necessary evil."

"Don't let Brian catch you saying that. What you write at the bottom of a kid's book, that's what shows you're a teacher."

"Yeah, but not every time, surely?"

"Well, see how you go." She grinned, winked to soften the blow, and then went through his lesson plans, adding suggestions, oozing enthusiasm. She was bright, positive and helpful. She was also very married, very Catholic, and that hurt. Terry, like Van, was a loner, vulnerable and tough, wanting the moon but also missing the warmth of a three bedroom semi-detached.

Mick Wall surveyed the staffroom annex with disgust.

"Sylvia, have you seen what they've done to the workroom? "

"At my stage of life, nothing would surprise me."

"It's Rod. He's filled it with ring-binder files and pretty wallcharts about the National Curriculum."

"You just watch. Standards will soar."

"But where do I go for a chat?"

"Your problem, I'm afraid." She crossed to the grid of teachers' pigeonholes, and flicked rapidly through the messages. "We can't waste taxpayers' money keeping you happy. Anyway, why don't you empty your pigeonhole for a change ?"

He looked, without enthusiasm, at the grid. Later on, fruit would fester, piles become wedged, and dust would accumulate on the missives aimed at long-term absentees. But now, the paper was new, bright and threatening. Mick went gloomily through the assortment aimed at him.

"She loves me, she loves me not, she loves me....Ooh, look. A billet doux from the gorgeous Chris Macdonald." A brief glance at a yellow sheet of paper, followed by a longer, harder look. "It's a forgery. Somebody's winding me up."

Terry walked past, collecting his own mail. "What's up, Mick?"

"Personal hygiene. Chris says my kids are doing personal hygiene."

"Not before time, if the way they smelt yesterday is anything to go by."

"But Sylvia, I'm supposed to do it with them."

"Like I said, not before time."

"Never mind, Mick. It's nothing personal. Hey, that's good. Nothing personal, get it?"

"All right, Terry, very funny. Just decide whether or not you really want me to fix your car, yeah? Chris Macdonald, that's who I want – "

"Well, so long as it's mutual."

Terry chuckled, and looked through his post. He too had a yellow sheet from Chris Macdonald. Tutorial topics for this half-term: racism, handling money, and drugs.

Out in the playground, a tall, awkward girl approaches a boy. He is a year younger, black, burly and burdened with suspicion.

"Hey, Dennis."

"What?"

"Tina wants you."

"So?"

"So you'd better go. She fancies you."

He doesn't understand. He would think about it for longer, if thinking would help. But it seldom does.

"Maybe I'm not interested."

"If you don't, she'll beat you up."

Dennis' brain met many challenges during a school day. To be faced with sexual attraction this early in the term was unusual, but the prospect of a fight he could grasp. Slowly, he followed the girl across, to where Tina stood, leaning against the wall. She was a tough, streetwise blonde, who smiled as he approached.

"You want me?"

"That's right, Dennis. Got it in one. OK, Mandy, you can leave us to it."

Obediently, her message delivered, Mandy moved away.

"Hey, what's going on?"

"It's all right. I'm not after your body. Well, not yet."

"What you want?"

"Dennis, I like you. I'm on your side. Got a fag?"

"Yeah."

"So, give us one. If we're going out we're going to share things, right?"

He fumbled a packet of cigarettes out of his pocket. As she took one, her fingers brushed his hand.

"We're going out, are we ?"

"Yes, Dennis. That all right with you?"

"Dunno. S'pose so."

"That's all right, then. Come on."

Jill stood waiting, scanning the bare walls of Spencer's office till he deigned to notice her. He scrolled through another table of figures, and then looked up.

"Jill. What can I do for you?"

"You can tell me about this." She handed him the magazine.

"Yes, yes, of course. Do sit down, please." She sat, and he went to close the door. Then back, behind his desk, to safety. She looked at him, but his gaze was travelling, across and around the surface of his empty, polished desk. All the time, a voice in his head muttered that he was the Headteacher designate at Priory Hall.

"I'm teaching in five minutes, but – "

"Look, there. Isn't that Waite with…um..what's her name?"

"Tina. Tina Clark."

"Yes. She's 10A4, he's 9C. I don't like the look of that."

"I can come back if you like."

"No, sorry. The magazine…" He stared at his family photo as if for the first time. He shifted in his seat, and crossed his legs. "As I said, I do think it's good."

"I don't mind not getting my copy first, but – "

"No, it was remiss of me." A Spencer apology, something of a collector's item. If he had edited the magazine he would have been mortified not to get the first copy.

"What about Valerie's poem?"

"Valerie?" The database was blank.

"Valerie Jones. Year Eight. She wrote a poem about a drug addict."

"Well, that was a bit tricky….um…are you teaching now?"

"Yes. But I can wait."

"I don't want to keep you."

Fighting her instincts, Jill stayed. And waited.

"I had this ad in from FLATPAK. A bit late, but they'll be a useful contact. MD might come on the governors."

"So you chopped the poem?"

"I did have some doubt about it, to be honest. It's a good poem…"

"Why didn't you say?"

"It was the holidays and…well, you know how it is."

"No, I don't. How is it?"

Professionally, this wasn't helping , but her rage would not lie

34

down. With every second that passed her class was unattended, she was vulnerable and he was one step nearer safety. As he clearly saw. He gave her his concerned look.

"If there's something I could do?"

"Perhaps you could explain to Valerie why the poem has not ended up in the magazine, after I promised that it would?"

His eyes followed his right hand as it toyed with his wedding ring, and then back to face her. She had not gone away.

"Yes. Yes, of course. Could you…um..leave that one with me?"

She didn't quite slam the door, but near enough.

Terry had them spread across the hall, on all fours, totally quiet. Every face in his direction, the drama teacher's dream.

"Bog off, Adams!"

"Bog off yourself – oh, sorry, sir."

Two lumpy year 11s in PE kit had waddled into the middle of his space.

"What are you doing here?"

"PE, sir."

"No you're not. I've got a lesson in here."

"All right, get in there and line up by the stage!" Pete Wrench's powerful frame surged through the doorway, a second after the booming echo of his voice.

Then he saw Terry and his class.

"Oh, sorry."

"No problem."

"We got rained off. It's like a paddy field out there. Gerry said it would be OK to use the hall."

"I'm supposed to have a drama lesson here."

"Sorry. I didn't know. "

Impasse. Two young teachers, new to the game. Year 11 against year 8. Boys in PE kit; kids fully dressed. Terry saw that if anyone was going to be trailing round the school, searching for space, it would have to be him.

"OK, my lot. Over there by the door."

"But, sir – "

"I said, over there! "

Pete was effusive – "Are you sure? I feel terrible. I know you need the space almost as much as I do…"

What did he mean, almost?

"That's OK. I'll take them out sunbathing in the summer, and we'll muck up your cricket."

"Yeah, sure. Fine. Er, thanks again."

A pleasant, polite PE teacher. Terry remembered Mr. Monaghan, the Goliath of his own schooldays, who prowled the gym, slipper in hand. If Monaghan could see Pete Wrench, it would send him spinning in his grave.

Two hours later, the school was empty and calm, except for the hum of hoovers and the cleaners' chatter. As the evening walkers and their dogs savoured the September sunset, Rod Spencer sat in his study. The blinds were shut.

He was composing the statement which would accompany his application for Priory Hall. He had most of the sections planned, ready stored on his pc – local management, marketing and the use of league tables in the raising of standards. What he needed now was a title, a heading that would indicate the balance of progress and tradition, consolidation of academic standards with vibrant advance. Chris Macdonald would be waffling about young people's awareness and equal opportunities, but she wouldn't be able to offer so sweeping a vision of the world to come.

Then he had it. It was so simple he wondered that he hadn't thought of it before. With a heady sense of triumph, he zipped the cursor to the top of the screen, called up CAPITALS and **bold** and underlining, and the legend was inscribed;

EDUCATION FOR THE NEW MILLENNIUM.

CHAPTER TWO:

OCTOBER

Mick Wall stamped his feet on the cold tarmac of the playground.

"Well, Ms. Williams. Have you checked the girls' toilets for smokers, illicit substances and obscene material?"

"It's break duty, not a vice squad raid."

"There are days when it's hard to tell the difference."

But this wasn't one of them. As they watched, most of what they saw was civilised. Games of football, circles exchanging gossip, a few shrill boys chasing each other around. No protection rackets, no flick knives, no injuries. And therefore, no accident forms.

Mick hunched his shoulders and blew on his hands.

"Who are you backing in the leadership stakes, then?"

"Sorry, I'm not with you." Jill, smart enough to bring her coffee with her, hugged the mug with both hands. He liked talking to Jill. Partly, she was good company; partly, she had this gorgeous deep voice, like Bessie Smith, almost like a bloke, yet not like a bloke at all. If it wasn't for Karen, he might fancy her. But those days, like his fitness and much of his hair, were gone.

"All the deputies, lining up to be head at Priory Hall."

"Is that where Walters was head ?"

"That's the one. Dropped down dead, on his summer holidays. Makes you think, eh?"

"Makes you think what?"

Mick shrugged, in a reflex of self-effacement.

"Don't ask me. I'm just a chippy."

"Head of Technology, I heard."

"That's what it says on the door. Today, anyway. God knows what it will say tomorrow. I'm just a woodwork teacher, me."

"So who's up for this job?"

"Just about every deputy in the county. Both of ours, for a start. Who do you reckon – Hot Rod or,..er, Chris Macdonald?"

"I thought you and Chris used to be mates?"

"Yeah, better than that." And if it hadn't been Mick, noted staffroom comic, Jill could have sworn a cloud of grief drifted across his face. "But not any more. Now she sends me little notes about personal hygiene, and I can't even get to see her. Now, in the old days, when she was Home Ec. – "

"And you were just a chippy –"

"Happy days, eh? Don Cuthbert was head of metalwork, when Parnaby first came. He sent over once, asking for a bit of metal as a key ring. Don sent him back this hulking great sheet of steel, with his keys dangling from a hole in the corner. It took three kids to carry it." He slapped his arms round his sides, looked across the playground, and shook his head. "We had some laughs."

"You're showing your age, Mick."

"Yeah, well. I remember games of cricket in the staffroom. It wouldn't happen now. Now Chris Macdonald is looking at headships, and we're freezing to death out here. It's a funny old world, all right."

Tina brushed a quick hand through her hair, scanned the snaking queues, and grabbed at Dennis as he passed.

"What you got next, Dennis?"

"Maths. I think."

"You don't want to go to Maths."

"So?"

"So come with me."

"Where we going?"

There was something about all this that Dennis still couldn't believe. He stared open-mouthed at Tina, but she just grinned at him.

"Look around. See what's in the car park."

"Tina. I got done for that."

"I know, Dennis. That's why. You know what you're doing." She flashed him an exciting, encouraging smile, big lips, open mouth, and took his arm. "Like they say in the ads, consult a specialist."

He went with her, puzzled, till she stopped.

"Watch out. Wally and Williams. Wait till they've gone."

"They'll see us. Bound to."

"No they won't. They've got lessons to go to, same as us. Come on, this way."

The sound of the "Eastenders" signature tune, slightly too loud, wafted across the hall, and was then abruptly cut off.

"No. Just for once, you do without your soap, and you listen to me." A young voice, angry but controlled, compelling. At the far end of the hall, Parnaby saw the outline of a tall, thin girl, with long straight hair, who stood uncannily still. "I'm not staying. I'm getting out, and I'm going to look after myself. OK, so I don't know much, and I haven't got a job, but at least I'm going to try to be alive. I'm not going to sit here and rot. Bye, mum, I shan't be back."

The clack of her heels across the polished floor was accompanied by enthusiastic clapping – from one pair of hands.

"God help us – who's that philistine ?" Terry screamed.

"Sorry, Mr. O'Mara, my mistake."

"Oh, Mr. Parnaby. I'm sorry. I didn't see you there."

"That's quite all right. It's the risk I run, poking my nose in. You don't clap, then? That was very good, Emma ."

"Thanks, sir. It's drama, not theatre. Theatre you can clap."

"I'll have to be more careful."

"Did you want me, Mr. Parnaby?"

"No, just passing through. You carry on."

Terry glanced at his watch.

"It's packing up time, anyway." He raised his voice. "OK, let's get these chairs straight. Furniture sorted, bags collected and you lot in a line by the door, but pianissimo, got it?"

They had got it. To his relief, this routine was established, and he was in control. Which was just as well, as Parnaby had stayed, even after the bell had rung.

"She's good, isn't she?"

"Emma ? She's not good, she's magic. The Jane Horrocks of 10A4. OK, you lot, you can go – but walk." They went, more or less calmly, while he and Parnaby watched.

"Drama does a lot for these kids, Terry."

"It feeds the animals. At least with me they can pace around the cage."

"No, it's better than that." Parnaby, a believer, would not be swayed. "You can see they're involved, they're gaining confidence."

"Yeah, but drama, in the National Curriculum..."

"It's there. Look, I don't know if you're interested, but Philip Rowley's running this course in November, drama for English teachers. Might suit you. And anyway, it shows there's still a place for it. Really, it's there."

"It's there in spirit – like the ice cube in the whisky. Look again in five minutes and you wonder where it's gone."

"You're not losing heart, I hope?"

"It's an occupational hazard. All over the country there's drama teachers, looking for some heart. We're watch repairers in an age of quartz. "

"Well, you're safe until the summer." He paused, trying to balance reassurance with caution. "Maybe longer than that." And hurried off, worried that he may have said too much.

Terry watched him go. Nice enough old chap, in his way, but how long was he going to be around?

Sharon scampered to catch up with Valerie, as she walked out of school. She ran neatly, comfortably, knowing she would catch her slower friend. Around them boys swirled wildly, a different species on alien ground.

"Valerie, what homework have we got?"

"History, bit of Maths. Well, that was different."

For Valerie, a dumpy intellectual, PE was less of a challenge than a threat. At least innovation gave her something to think about. Sharon, a fitter, leaner competitor, was not so keen.

"What's different about it? Didn't you know boys were clumsy and rude?"

"It makes a change. And he's nice."

"Who, Mr. Wrench?"

"He's ever so young. I thought men PE teachers had to be hairy and shout, like Mr. Thomas."

"Compared with Thomas a rottweiler would be an improvement."

"Perhaps he's one of these New Men they keep on about. Do you want to come back for some tea?"

Sharon stopped to think, calculate TV programmes, guess what her mum was doing.

"OK. Hey, have you see Ms. Williams' display?"

"The advertising one?"

"No. For your poem. It's ace. She's got all these gloomy drug posters round it. Looks dead scary. And the poem's all blown up, big print and everything. You'll be famous."

Sharon's enthusiasm, the smile, the hand on her arm, were all to cheer her up. They didn't work.

"I'm not in the magazine, though, am I?"

"What did Williams say about that?"

"She said Spencer would explain."

"Mr. Spencer ? He's not an English teacher.".

"I know. Apparently, he runs the magazine."

"So, did he talk to you?"

Her facial muscles tightened as Val, the thinker, put in over-time. But still, it made no sense.

"Well, sort of. He sounded dead embarrassed, or busy, as if he'd rather be somewhere else."

"And what did he say?"

"Leave it with me. That's what he said. What's that supposed to mean ?"

41

Linda Jones was nice. Of all his relationships with the opposite sex, Linda was the one he found easiest. Maybe it was the ready smile, the chaotic wavy hair, the warmth – or just the coincidence that all of these reminded him of his mum.

"I don't know how you do it. "

"Make such a mess, you mean ?"

"No. Put up with them. Two of them for six weeks does my head in, but you've thirty of them, all day."

She always talked as she worked, sweeping, wiping tables, while Terry reshuffled the piles of marking which strayed across his desk.

"I'm getting used to it."

"Don't worry. You're doing fine."

He looked at her sharply. How did she know ? She was in before school, back after school – was she squatting in a cupboard in between ?

"It's all right, don't panic."

She was picking at a particularly stubborn blob of chewing gum, but had still picked up his unease. "Messy little beggars. No, my kids are here. Believe me, there's teachers a lot worse than you."

It wasn't the most ringing endorsement he'd ever heard, and he restrained himself from asking for details of the teachers who were worse, but the marking was a couple of ounces lighter as he piled it into the plastic bag.

"There is one thing, though." She looked up from the chair she was holding.

"Yes?"

"Could you get them to put up their chairs ? You know, on the tables, in the last lesson?"

"Oh, sure." The relief swept through him, and carried him and his plastic bags across the car park. By the time he parked the Morris outside his flat, he was a successful teacher - and he hadn't even reached half-term.

As Mick came out of the workshop they were waiting for him. He tried to breeze past, but Dale blocked his way. Only 16, and small for his age, with a weaselly look, but today he was more than a kid.

"Sir, this is important."

He was keen, a bit of a mouth, but he could be bluffed.

"Look, you can see I'm busy." Exaggerated mime – just look at my overall, the glue gun in my hand. How could you have the heart to pester me now? "You've done a very good project, and I've told you you'll both get good marks. Don't be in such a rush."

"But if we don't patent it, sir, someone else could pinch it."

"So you know about the patent laws, do you, Muptaz?"

"A bit, sir. My sister's doing law." He was the scary one. Always calm, always polite. How did a teenage kid get to be that cool? "She's got to find out if we're too young."

"Yes, well, you don't want to rush things. It's the exam you should be thinking about now. When you've left school there'll be plenty of time to make a fortune, right, lads? " The cheery nod, the nervous smile, the hand brandishing the glue gun – all said everything is fine. They weren't convinced.

"You won't show it to anyone else, will you, sir?"

He was shaken, and it showed. They watched him closely.

"I beg your pardon?"

"He didn't mean it, sir. Come on, Dale."

"Are you suggesting I might be indiscreet with your GCSE coursework?"

A pause. Too long a pause. Three still figures, in a workshop landscape, suspended in time. And the oldest, the bulkiest, was not in charge.

"Er, no sir."

"That's all right, then. Run along. I'll see you Monday."

As Mick retreated back into his office, both boys turned back and stared at the closed door.

"I told you. Guilty as hell."

"So what d'you reckon?"

"Plan B. It's got to be."

"Who's going to ring?"

"I'll toss you for it."

Chris Macdonald read slowly through the application again. She was impressed. Biased, too, since it was her own application, but she made a persuasive case. Made it on her own, she noted tartly, since Simon seemed less and less interested in the progress of her career.

He had his reasons. Being an LEA adviser looked less and less like a smart move. In the old days it was hierarchy, moving up the ladder of suits and mileage allowance, hands on the levers of power. But there wasn't much power in the LEA now, and the mileage kitty was shrinking by the day. Simon's own future was a lot less secure than it had been, and they kept giving him details about training to be an inspector.

"Do you want to be an inspector?" she had asked.

His bark of a laugh confirmed that this was an irrelevant consideration; to Chris, it also implied that she was a daft female even to pose the question. So she worked on her application, smouldering with resentment but glad to be in control.

OK, so there were only two women heads out of 48 secondary schools in the county, but that could also be an argument in her favour. The local authority were trying to present themselves as progressive; what better way to do that than to appoint a female head ?

The knock on the door was not welcome.

"Come in."

Sylvia March. Biologically a sister, but not in any other sense.

"Miss Macdonald."

"Chris, please." The younger, more powerful woman gestured to the chair facing her desk. Sylvia hesitated, as if acceptance might weaken her case, but then sat down. She was holding a yellow sheet of paper.There was nothing hesitant about her tone.

"I understand from this note that you are requiring me to teach 11A3 about methods of contraception."

"Well, Sylvia – " and she could see her bridle, even at that – "it's not a personal request. This is part of our sex education policy, approved by the governors. I'm sure you can see the case for fully informing young people about methods of contraception."

"Oh yes. I can see the case. I just can't see why it has to be me that does the teaching."

"In our tutorial system, we do ask a lot of our tutors. We in the senior management team recognise that."

"And?" She was back again, with a focussed, hostile glare.

"I'm sorry. I'm not with you."

"Precisely. You are not with me. I am in the classroom, dangling sheaths in front of spotty adolescents who are probably more familiar with them than I am, while you are in your senior management office recognising that you are asking a lot of me."

Chris returned her stare. Stay calm, reasoned, neutral. "I realise that it must seem unfair."

"I'm glad you realise that. Because it is." She could feel her anger rising. What right had this girl to be so aloof, superior?

"Although I have found that such occasions can be a good way of getting to know members of the tutor-group. You know, I think we can learn from them as much as they can learn from us."

"I'm sure you're right."

"You are ?" Sylvia March, a convert ? For a couple of notches, Chris let herself relax.

"Oh yes. Should I wish to learn about glue-sniffing, stealing cars or sexually transmitted diseases, I have no doubt that members of 11A3 would be delighted to enlighten me. However, since I was employed here to teach foreign languages, I should be grateful if you could find someone else to carry out this particular task."

"If you like, I'll do it myself."

Sylvia stood, and straightened the chair. "An excellent solution, if I may say so."

Chris looked up, anxious to keep control, finish the job. "Perhaps you'd like to sit in…join in, perhaps, if you feel like it? " Keep the questions going, offers open, don't let her close it down. "Or just observe?"

"No, thank you. I have every confidence in you, Miss Macdonald. I'm sure you'll do it very well." And, for the first time in their encounter, Sylvia March smiled.

"Is it any good?"

Not many teachers managed reading in the staffroom, let alone a serious novel. Jill put it down, but kept her finger in the place.

"Yeah, it's OK. Not brilliant."

"What do you reckon to Terry, then?" There was a glint in Jackie's eye. Something going on.

"He's OK, too. Also not brilliant."

"Go on."

"All right. Enthusiastic, good with the kids, bit slap happy on timing, and his record-keeping's hazy – but then he is a bloke."

Jackie laughed. "Just an impression mark. It doesn't have to be an inspection report."

"Well, you asked."

"Fair enough. But -" she paused, teasing "I didn't just mean the teaching."

A slow, rising stare.

"Do I fancy him? Is that it?"

"Not necessarily.But, well, yeah."

"Just because you and Steve are locked into marital bliss doesn't mean we all have to do the same, right? Besides, if he's looking at anyone it's Marion Harper."

"He's got more taste than that. Hasn't he, Jill?"

But she was back in her book.

Parnaby confronted the morning post. Mountains of verbiage, from the government, the local authority, and a jungle of acronyms anxious to assist him in his role. But their idea of help was based on the assumption of his incompetence: "Have you an overview of the curriculum ? Are your assessments properly recorded ?   Are you on top of your financial position ?" The answer to all such questions was a resounding "No", and the accumulating "No"s swelled to a mocking chorus as he sliced through the envelopes.

Joyce looked on in pity. "I can do them if you like."

Colin would liked nothing more than to hand the whole lot over. But he felt guilty that she, who was paid so much less than him, was less qualified, less experienced, should have to relieve him of this burden. Could she do it, really ? As calmly as she suggested ? And if so, why couldn't he ? Beyond that was the fear of what would happen if the others knew. Other heads prided themselves on sifting the post; this was where the power was, knowing what to keep back and what to pass on, having a map of who knew what. What would these demonic calculators make of a head who delegated such power to his secretary ?

"All right," he said.

And while he was at it, get her to sort dilemma number two.

"What do I do about Rod and Chris?"

"You've put up with them so far. Why should today be any different?"

"They've both applied for Priory Hall. I've got to do references."

"So long as it's not for your job I don't mind."

"Don't start that again."

Joyce wagged a reproving finger. He might have been a first year boy.

"You said, last September, it was going to be your last year."

"Yes, I know."

"And then, in the spring you said 'Well, if Martin Walters can manage another year, I suppose I can.' "

"That's not fair, Joyce."

"It's true."

"I know it's true. That's why it's not fair. Maybe I should have gone for early retirement, but I didn't, and you're stuck with getting me through another year."

She had made her point, and it was time to let him off. But she allowed herself an indulgent grimace. "Rather you than those two, anyway."

"Now, Joyce. They're both capable professionals." The boy was back again, being the Head. "The point is, what do I do?"

"You write what capable professionals they are. Tell lies for them like you do for everyone else. There are days, I can tell you, when my word-processor chokes on your references."

"But if one gets an interview and the other doesn't, they'll blame me."

"What are they, eight year olds? No, don't answer that." She slowed down, as if explaining the operation of the petrol engine to an excitable grandchild. "Look, they're getting thirty thousand pounds a year. If it bothers you that much you could write the same for both of them."

There was a sudden gleam in his eye. His gaze shot to the ceiling of his office, as if deciphering a message from the gods. Incredulous, she watched his depression lift.

"But that's brilliant."

"No. It's rather cowardly, but if it solves the problem, do it." She scooped up the post. " Do you want some coffee?" She was moving to the door, when there was a perfunctory knock and it opened.

"Sorry." Rod Spencer brushed past her, unapologetic. "Colin, you must see this." He brandished a large, glossy pamphlet, eerily similar to the reading which Parnaby had just bequeathed to Joyce. She stared at the head, willing him to reprove his deputy's mode of entry, but he succumbed to its urgency.

"What is it?"

"King Edward's publicity campaign. They're using the OFSTED report."

Joyce was unimpressed. "Why? Was it good?"

"Statistically, they're a superior operation. In league table terms, they're well ahead. I really do think the time has come to act."

"Mmm." Parnaby looked like a man baffled by jargon. "What do you suggest?"

"This must top the agenda of our next management meeting."

"But we were going to look at exam results – "

"That can wait. Last year's pupils are history. It's next year's that count."

Rod had an appointment with destiny which Colin didn't want to keep."Yes. Interesting. Er..I'll think on that one, thank you. Could you...um...leave it with me?"

Terry and Jackie sat side by side in the staffroom, working. Across from them, Sylvia March flicked disdainfully though the "Shellworth Journal."

"So the marking matters, then?" At King Edward's they thought marking was a chore, like cleaning toilets, and here was Jackie elevating it into an art form.

"That's where Brian is brilliant." Brilliant? A sleepy layabout with leather patches on his elbows? Her Christian charity must be soggy at the edges. Her bright eyes pierced his defences, read his thoughts. "He's a genius. Get a look at his kids' books some time. I mean it. You'll learn something."

The notion of looking through another teacher's books – and, by logical extension, of another teacher looking through his books – was distinctly unnerving. The doodles, the torn corners, the casual accumulation of obscene messages…Were these standard, or unique to him alone? And if he never saw anyone else's books, how would he know?

Jackie had these files, which told her everything she might ever want to know about the kids she taught – their attendance, the work they had done, books they had read, punctuation they found hard to do. It was more like a library than a teaching aid, and there was no way he could manage that. Like Van the man, he would do his own thing.

Sylvia was rocking quietly. "I am sorry, Jackie. I can see you're busy. But I really have to share this with somebody."

"What is it?"

"You know Mick's invention, the burglar alarm?"

"I've heard him go on about it, yes. But I don't understand how it works."

"Nor, from the sound of it, does he." Sylvia exploded into a helpless giggle, and passed the paper across. Terry looked over her shoulder as Jackie read the story:

" 'SCHOOLBOYS SOUND ALARM. Two Shellworth teenagers, Dale Adams, 16, and Muptaz Singh, 15, have invented a burglar alarm which they hope to launch on the open market.' And it doesn't even mention the school. Rod will be upset."

"What about Mick?"

"Not even a footnote in history. Still, serve the blighter right. Fancy trying to pinch the kids' idea. Thanks, Sylvia." She handed

49

it back, chirpy, positive but businesslike. "Now, where we we?"

"You were telling me about marking."

"I shall swing for that bastard." Jill strode past them to the pigeonholes, found nothing, and stood, seething. Jackie looked up.

"What's wrong?"

"There's nothing wrong with me. Nothing that a quick execution wouldn't fix. Rod bloody Spencer, that's what's wrong."

Terry was riveted. He had never seen Jill angry, and he marvelled at Jackie's calm, and that Jill was not more angered by her calm. Women, truly, were a mystery.

Like a chat show host, Jackie probed the wound.

"So what's he done now?"

"First of all he misses Valerie's poem out of his sodding magazine, and then when I stick it up on the wall with a cool display to make it up to her, he tries to cover it up with this sodding Careers poster."

Terry tried to lighten things. "Sorry, but should you be using that adjective twice?"

A mistake.

"And what the hell has that got to do with you?"

Levelly, she stared through his skull, and out the other side. In an irrelevant corner of his brain, he noted that here was another brown-eyed girl. Her and Lavinia both. He withdrew, panicked, grovelled.

"Sorry. Er, you're quite right. Don't mind me."

Sylvia rescued him. "They're sent to try us, dear. Deputy heads. A bit like mosquitoes. Nobody loves them, but somewhere in God's great design they have a place. My dogs have fleas, and I can't see what possible purpose they serve. Ours not to reason why. But this'll cheer you up." She passed the Journal across, and within the triangle of female concern Jill's equilibrium was restored.

Terry's confidence was less easily repaired. That evening, in the chilly solitude of his flat he reproached himself again. It was the same old problem: feeling at home, the well-oiled tongue, trying to charm the girls. He had had a couple of conversations with the dishy Marion Harper, who turned out to be very decorative but had little to say. And now a clumsy shot at a joke had messed him up with the two teachers who could help him most. He should have learnt by now. Focus on the work, stay off the bloody charm. Lavinia was more than enough.

He reached for another pile of marking, and opened the ring binder file he had christened earlier in the day. T. O'MARA - ENGLISH : PUPIL RECORD. He wouldn't get into archives, but he would make an effort. Grimly, he attacked the next pile.

He was still at it half an hour later, when the knock came at the door.

"Terry - you're marking."

Rick McManus, looking for a drink. Rick was Terry's one link with King Edward's, a drinking partner still in his twenties, but several steps ahead. Rick had sussed the education business, because he knew that's what it was, and business was where his talents lay. A sharp lad, Rick, always smooth, lively with the chat and more than ready to pay his round. But he wasn't keen on marking.

It would be good to send him away. It would establish Terry's independence, and save his purse, not to mention a disturbed night's sleep and subsequent hangover. Ten minutes later, they were nursing pints of Guinness in The White Horse.

"So, how's it going, Tes?"

"Mustn't grumble. I'm getting paid."

Rick, in his designer tracksuit, which had replaced one of his six working suits, skimmed over Terry's tatty pullover and jeans, and measured the squalor of his life.

"That bad, eh? And you're doing marking. There's two things wrong with teaching, the marking and the kids."

"Is that right?"

"And most of the staff. What are yours like?"

"Usual mixture."

"Don't tell me." Rick put on his Oscar Wilde pose, left hand on hip, right hand flourishing in mid air. "There are three types of teacher – those that have resigned, those that are resigned and those that should resign."

Terry went on. "The English people are OK. Looking after me, you know?"

"So, talent there, right?"

"Give us a break. I told you, I'm not into that. for now."

A foxy, suspicious look. "Oh yeah. Your Lobelia."

"Lavinia. That's over. And, like I say, I'm celibate."

"Sure. Till the weekend, anyway."

"How's Cheryl?"

"Magic. Absolute magic. Cheers." A wink, as Rick swigged the last of his pint and offered Terry another. He was half a glass behind already, trying to slow the pace to what he could afford. He counted his money as Rick went to get the drinks.

"So, how's it with you, then?"

Rick took a huge initial gulp out of the fresh pint, and licked his lips. "Champion. I'm at the start of the goldrush – and I've got a day and a half off timetable."

"So how is it you've managed that?"

"I am a fixer, my son. It's as simple as that. They recognise my skills. Well, the head does. We work well together, as they say." He crossed his fingers. Stock gestures, corny phrases, a familiar routine were all revitalised when Rick was on a roll. Terry the actor was reluctantly impressed. "So he gives me what I want. Some of the other staff aren't so keen."

"I can imagine." And he thought of Jackie, Jill.

"But I'm boosting revenue, raising the profile, getting the customers in. So I think they'll be happy to let me get on with it."

"There's a guy does that in our place. Deputy, called Spencer."

McManus spluttered at least thirty penceworth of Guinness across the table.

"Sorry about that. Waste of good drink. But Hot Rod Spencer, really? Do me a favour. Rod is in a different league."

"You don't rate him, then?"

"How can I put this? Spencer is to school marketing what Tweetie Pie is to nuclear physics."

"He's very serious about it."

"Oh, sure he's serious. He's just no good. He thinks perform-ance indicators are something to do with stage lighting."

Terry, who knew about stage lighting but not about perform-ance indicators, said nothing. Maybe the marking would have been a good idea.

"Well, cheer up, Tes."

"I need a job, a permanent job. Then I'll be as chirpy as you like."

"Come on, drink up. We can squeeze another in before we go."

Terry gazed into the depths of his Guinness, looking for an-swers. Job, job satisfaction, woman, cash; Rick had them all, and the one thing Terry could be sure of was a hangover.

"Good morning, Joyce. Is the head in?"

"Sorry, Miss Macdonald. He'll be out all day, at County Hall."

"Well, he might have said. You know about tomorrow?"

"It's Friday, isn't it?"

She'd have killed a kid for that. Since it was Joyce, she said nothing, but logged it in her brain. She was good at keeping accounts.

"Rev. Hapgood? AIDS? Year Ten?"

"Pass." And Joyce, whom Colin had also driven to despair, felt a brief, unspoken pang of sympathy.

"Oh, it's hopeless. Sorry, I know it's not your fault."

Joyce waited, watchful.

"Tomorrow, we have Rev. Hapgood coming in to talk to Year Ten about the AIDS hospice that he runs. I gave Colin the details last term."

A familiar line, and probably accurate. Joyce tried to look loy-ally non-committal. "Well, I'm sorry, but he hasn't passed them on to me. This isn't anything to do with Mrs. Chalmers?"

"The chair of governors?"

"She rang to say she'd like to come in tomorrow. Nothing urgent, she said, just carry on as usual. It sounded rather omi-nous."

"No, that's fine. I'll be happy to take her round. Thank you,

Joyce, you've made my day." The full Macdonald smile was a rarity these days, so she found the decency to smile back.

Outside Spencer's office, Muptaz looked at his watch. Dale, shifting uneasily, was less composed.

"I told you we shouldn't have done it."

"No you didn't. We agreed. We couldn't let Wally walk all over us."

"So why are we getting done?"

"Who says we're getting done?"

"Muptaz, use your brain. Did you ever know Spencer talk to anyone unless they were getting done? He's programmed into bollocking, that's all he does."

Muptaz had a fleeting vision of the Spencers, like the Simpsons, a loop of continuous family chaos, running all the time. "You reckon he's like that at home? Calls his wife into the dining-room to explain why his tea was overcooked?"

"Don't ask me. Further maths I can cope with, but the home life of teachers...well."

Spencer's door opened, and for the first time ever the public relations smile was beamed towards two pupils.

"Ah, lads. Won't you come in?"

They were invited to sit down, and outline their invention. Spencer listened carefully, throwing in odd exclamations of approval.

"Well, I must say, I am most impressed." Not a bollocking at all. Or at least, not so far. "And you got a good write-up in the paper. Although I was sorry to see that the school wasn't named."

"We told them. They just didn't print it." Muptaz reassured him, radiating innocence. Spencer was impressed. So was Dale, who knew he was lying.

"I'm glad to hear it. Because I think we can put that right. Develop the idea, and promote the school. How does that sound?"

Dale looked at Muptaz, who offered a cautious "All right."

"Good. I knew you'd be keen. I need to talk to the governors, and some other contacts, but I'm sure we'll get a good deal."

"You mean money, sir?" Dale looked across in admiration at his friend. Muptaz was doing his best, but he was out of his depth. Spencer was chuckling happily to himself.

"Business always means money, Singh. But it's also ideas, enterprise, pushing the corporate image. I think we can go a long way on this one. I'll send your parents the details when they're finalised, but your contribution will be recognised. So, um, you can leave this one with me. OK?" And the clincher, as he shook their hands.

Dazed, cheated and helpless, Muptaz and Dale walked out into the corridor as if hypnotised. Rod watched them go, and then sauntered, whistling, in the opposite direction. Time to look in on Joyce, as he was deputising for Parnaby, and could indulge himself in the illusion that the head's secretary was answerable to him. He wasn't actually sure he'd want Joyce Davies breathing down his neck all day, but the occasional contact was fine. He might as well get used to it.

"Still hooked on Mozart? You're an addict."

"He's lasted two hundred years, and should see me through the week." She carried on typing.

"I just looked in to see if everything was all right."

"I think we're coping, thank you."

"What's this, in the diary? Mrs. Chalmers, with Year Ten tutorial?"

"Miss Macdonald arranged that."

"What? A Tory councillor coming in to find kids being told about AIDS? She must be out of her mind."

"I'm sure I couldn't say." She continued to type, but a sharper observer, with or without Rod's glasses, would have detected an undercurrent of glee. He straightened up and adjusted his tie, reassembling the professional role.

"I know Chris has done good work in this area, but politically she has a lot to learn. Does Mr. Parnaby know about this?"

"She only rang this morning. He's been out all day."

"We'll have to put her off." He breathed in, fired by crisis, flooding his lungs with the oxygen of power. "I'll take full responsibility."

"I'm sure you will. I'm happy to pass on any message, but

perhaps you should speak with Miss Macdonald first."

"Yes, naturally. That would be best. I'll be in Mr. Parnaby's office, if you could let her know – "

His body language said, go and fetch her. Hers said, do it yourself. But the tone of her voice was utterly reasonable, laced with sweet regret.

"I'm afraid she's teaching. All afternoon."

"Right. Thank you, Joyce. I'll take care of this one."

The seventh Friday of term. Nearly halfway through the first term, which might be one of ninety. Nobody blew any trumpets, but as he came into school Terry thought he was doing OK. He knew about the buzz of performing – standing in front of the class, lively explanations and challenging questions, reading a story well while the kids hung on every word. But there was another, quieter, buzz, as he walked around the back of the classroom, watching them work on a good idea he'd prepared. There were no riots, no dust-ups with other staff; he'd kept his mouth shut, kept his hands to himself, and almost kept up to date with his marking.

Mick, at least, had noticed. "So you made it, kid."

"It looks that way."

"What're you doing next week, then? Back to the land of Guinness?"

"No. I'll be staying round here."

"Not chasing after Maid Marion, are you?"

"I don't know what you mean." But it was hard to hide a smile.

"You'd be wasting your time. Take it from one who knows. Jill Williams, that's your best bet." Mick gave his irresistible imitation of the friendly bookie, passing on a tip he should suppress. Nudge nudge, wink wink.

"You're not serious?"

"Don't you fancy her? I fancy her."

"You're married. You're not supposed to go round talking like that."

"Maybe, but you want some fun before you go. Go on, ask her."

"Thanks. I'll bear it in mind."

This time he didn't even bother to knock. Chris Macdonald was in with Parnaby when Rod Spencer burst into his office.

"Oh, hello, Rod."

"I'm sorry, but I do think this visit poses problems."

"Which visit would that be?"

"Hasn't she told you? Chris has asked Mrs. Chalmers into school, when she's got this lefty London vicar talking about AIDS."

Chris was a sheet of ice.

"Correction. Mrs. Chalmers asked herself in."

Finally, Colin caught up. "Oh yes. She rang this morning to confirm. It seems she got the idea from you, Rod."

"From me?"

"Don't you remember? Governors are always welcome to take an interest in the work of the school, no standing on ceremony, please drop in…"

His discomfiture was heightened by the rare sight of Chris Macdonald fully at ease, enjoying the sport.

"Yes, well…but you said it was a good idea."

"I did. It was, and it is. Excellent. We're all agreed." In desperation Rod watched Colin beam his happy smile between the warring deputies.

"But this is different."

"How do you mean?"

"Well, AIDS is a sensitive issue –"

"Which the government requires us to tackle." Chris was not going to let this advantage slip without a fight.

"Yes, but this lefty curate – "

"You know nothing about his politics."

"If he runs an AIDS hospice in East London then he's hardly likely to vote Conservative."

Oblivious, Parnaby chuckled. "These days, nothing would surprise me."

"And you know what the Tories are like about homosexuals."

Chris sat upright, her jaw rigid, closing for the kill. "I'm not sure I'm hearing this. Are you assuming he's homosexual, as well as left wing?"

"All I'm saying is, that's how they'll see it. These councillors, they don't see the subtleties. They think AIDS equals homosexuals, so we must be corrupting the kids."

"That's pathetic, even from you."

At last Parnaby saw the danger. "All right, now –"

"What do you mean, 'even from me'?"

"That's enough." Parnaby looked in turn at each of them. It was easier with kids. "It's too late to put Mrs. Chalmers off."

"She could go to Maths."

"She might want to go to AIDS. It's just possible that she doesn't conform to your bigoted stereotype."

"I'd rather not take the risk."

"Any risk-taking will be done by me." Parnaby felt tired. Just imagine, leaving all this. Walking out of the door, down the drive, and never coming back. It would be heaven. They sat, waiting for his verdict.

"I'll see Mrs. Chalmers when she comes in."

"So she won't be visiting tutorial?"

"I didn't say that."

"I can't urge too strongly, Colin, that I do think – "

"We know what you think. The question is, what does he think?"

"Thank you, Chris. Thank you both. I shall decide…when I have spoken to her."

In disbelief, they stared at him.

"Thank God it's Friday."

The weekly thanksgiving, of thirsty teachers greeting the weekend. But this time, not just the weekend. Half-term, a week of freedom. The staffroom coffee, water and limescale in equal parts, tasted like nectar.

"You're before me, for sure."

Sylvia smiled at Terry. "Thank you, young man. You are, despite appearances, a gentleman. You do have a comb?"

"Right, it's war!" Jill, brandishing a glossy poster in her hand, was angry again, and angrier still. Terry rushed back, where Jackie did not fear to tread.

"Not Rod again?"

"I don't believe it. He's been sent to haunt me. My life was OK, and suddenly, he's everywhere."

"Now that does sound like a nightmare." Mick was all heart. "He's in the ladies', is he?"

"You are so insensitive. Go on, Jill, what happened?"

"Valerie's poem ? My display ? The boring Careers poster that he stuck up and I took down."

"He put it up again?"

"Right. Didn't ask me, didn't tell me, he just put it up again. So I have taken it down, and it's not going to go back up." Each syllable was accentuated, a tough, deliberate emphasis, as she slowly tore the poster into strips and stuffed them in the bin.

"Tt tt. Ecologically wasteful, I'd say." And Mick got away with it, as Terry watched in disbelief. No, there was no justice.

"And now," drawled Sylvia, "an intellectual challenge. Can I finish the half-term by persuading Dennis Waite to grunt in French as eloquently as he grunts in English?"

"No problem." Again, Mick had the answer. "Tell him he's breaking into a Renault."

"That boy," Marion Harper observed, "is a toe rag of the first order." She was definite, and negative, again. Terry watched and listened, and re-arranged his plans. Maybe Mick was wiser than he showed.

"'Scuse me, Terry." Jackie pushed past. "Come on, Jill."

"I've got to drink this coffee. He's cost me enough as it is."

"See you, then."

As the staffroom emptied, Terry saw his chance.

"Jill?"

"Yes?"

He couldn't. She was just staring at him, those tough, wise eyes wondering what he meant. There was no way she'd say yes.

"Um…Tomorrow night. Saturday."

"Yes?"

"There's this mime group on. They're supposed to be good."

"Yeah, I know. I've got a ticket."

"Oh, fine. I just…well, you know."

"See you, Terry. Have a good half-term."

When Joyce returned from the ladies' Rod Spencer was there, hovering.

"Is the head in?"

"He's with Mrs. Chalmers. And she's asked for Miss Macdonald."

"I'll bet she has. Still, I tried. I had my doubts about this Hapgood chap, right from the start." He was a spotty adolescent, wanting approval, or a friend. But her kids had all left home.

"Do you want to go in?"

"No." A lethal, superior smile. "The damage is done now." But as he turned to go, one consolation occured. A Chris Macdonald fiasco wouldn't do his chances at Priory Hall any harm at all. Just so long as he could distance himself…

"Ah, Rod, I thought I heard you. Won't you join us?"

Parnaby, grinning like a fool, waved him into the office.

"Mrs. Chalmers, I think you've met my other deputy, Mr. Rod Spencer." Other? Why didn't he say first deputy? Or at least senior.

"Yes, of course." Mrs. Chalmers, potently scented, shook his hand. "Thank you so much for the magazine. There's a lot of good work."

"We like to think so."

"Though you're too modest about some of it."

Parnaby was intrigued. "How do you mean?"

"One of your English teachers showed me a poem."

It couldn't be. He'd covered it up, twice.

"About a drug addict. Very powerful. Our social committee's running an awareness campaign. It's just the kind of thing they're looking for. A shame it couldn't be in the magazine."

"Yes. Well…did you have a good day?"

"First-rate. I have to confess an ulterior motive. My son-in-law is a curate in Stepney. He's on this speakers' list, and when he said he was coming here, I couldn't resist it."

"Your son-in-law - Rev. Hapgood? Really ? I didn't know."

"It was most impressive. The maturity with which your youngsters are prepared to tackle serious issues is most commendable. You may find this hard to believe, Mr. Spencer, but there are schools who are frightened of tackling the issue at all."

"Well, that hardly seems possible, does it?" A satanic gleam from Chris Macdonald.

"So, thank you again for the invitation."

"You're very welcome. Here, let me see you out." Parnaby nodded, smiled warmly, and escorted her down the corridor.

"Well done."

"Thank you, Rod. It seems to have gone well."

He fiddled with his ring, looked at the carpet, and his shoes. "I'm not sure if this is the time, but...er..there's something you should know."

"Yes?" She was back in neutral, no edge to her voice. A polite, enquiring look, which he still dare not face.

"I've got an interview. For Priory Hall. After half-term."

"Me too."

Shaken, he conquered his nerves and looked at her. "I'm sorry?"

"I'm quite pleased, actually. Maybe I'll see you there."

He gaped towards her, like a fish on a line."You've got an interview?"

"Yes. Priory Hall. A week on Tuesday."

"I see. Well...er...may the best man win. Sorry. Um, you know what I mean."

"Yes, Rod. I know exactly what you mean. You too."

Terry loaded the marking into his sports bag, and emptied his pigeonhole. The staffroom, often occupied at four o'clock, was empty now. He turned to go, narrowly missing Pete Wrench as he bounded through the door.

"Hi, Terry. So we made it, eh?"

"Yeah. Doing anything special?"

"Recovering, mainly. Lying in, bit of running, catch up on some videos." He cleared his pigeonhole, and picked up a huge sports bag, ready to leave.

"You don't fancy a night out, do you? Tomorrow?"

"Sorry, already booked." Pete headed for the door, and then turned. The neat, clean, healthy hero. Part of Terry wanted to dislike him, but he was too decent, too straight for that. "Why, what are you planning?"

"There's this mime group, Amashlu. Thought they might be worth a look."

"They're great. Well worth it. That's where we're going. Might see you there, eh?"

"You're going anyway?"

"Yeah. Me and Jill. See you, Terry."

He drove home alone. Van shared his misery, with the desperate pleading of "Baby, Please Don't Go", which didn't help at first. But then it did. For this wonderful man, who could sing, compose, play anything, who could hear all these instruments in his head, still knew how it felt to be gloomy and alone. Holidays had to be good news: no lessons to be planned for a week, and the chance to catch up on films and lie in. He had noone special to see or think about, and a shabby little flat to himself, but the tapes would see him through.

CHAPTER THREE:

NOVEMBER

By the Tuesday, Terry was bored. Not from guilt, but from lack of alternatives, he did his homework. He got his marking up to date, skimmed the reader his second years would be tackling, and scribbled some lesson notes for the next half-term. And to himself, he confessed he enjoyed it. Jackie was right: each piece of work his kids did threw up new ideas, things they could work on, different ways of writing.

In their books he met missing full stops, characters pinched from soaps, tiny paragraphs or no paragraphs, stories with corny endings – and each of these could be a future lesson. At this rate he could muddle through till Christmas.

The card from Lavinia didn't help. Cheery as ever, as if she'd had her tonsils out. "I'm past the worst now. Got a teaching job in Derrry – dishy head of department. Come on over and see me sometime – love, Mae (Lavinia) West."

He couldn't go back. She was tougher than he was, yet again. She was over it and friendly. Not bitter, not angry, not reserved – still a friend, but a friend across the water. While he was a tangled mess of memories, spiced with frustration and seasoned with guilt.

It was her hair he missed. Lavinia had the longest, smoothest hair he'd ever seen, in silky chestnut waves. She spent hours brushing it, and he could watch her, hungrily, for hours. He'd run his hands through it, like stroking a cat, but not any more. Others would drool about tits and bums and legs, but what turned Terry on was hair.

And maybe that was what got him looking at Marion Harper, the long, blonde clone of Meryl Streep. Because, if he was honest, there wasn't much else. Pleasant enough, and in the first two weeks she seemed interested in him, but only in a distant way. No energy, no bite. Whereas Jackie had this rich auburn bob, bright and short, functional but charged. Jill was something else again. He'd never been out with a black girl. Never been out with anyone taller than him. And to go from stroking Lavinia's hair to Jill's would be moving from an Afghan to a brillo pad. Though he wasn't sure that Jill Williams was the sort who would want you to stroke her hair.

Not that she was available. Terry had gone to the mime group, and at the interval he'd seen Jill and Pete, chatting by the bar. He could easily have joined them, but he stayed on the fringes, nursing an ice cream, and moped.

Action. Get doing, be busy, and for Terry that meant a play. Get on a stage, and the frustration seeped away. It had worked before, at college, but that was "The Crucible", and he was John Proctor, torn by lust for Abigail. Which was how he met Lavinia.

As Terry the teacher he'd be the overall director, above such things. Use the kids, use the hall, give them something to remember. At King Edward's they did a Gilbert and Sullivan every Christmas. To his relief Terry had come at Easter and missed it, but the photographs and posters still adorned the foyer walls. Painstaking, popular and safe; Rab Butler would be different – please?

The angel arrived at 8.30 on the Thursday evening of half-term, beamed via Channel 4. He was watching the box, reckoning that an obscure documentary was preferable to a flat sitcom or hysterical gameshow. And there was this Brazilian union leader, hunted down by the cattle barons, preaching resistance under threat. The subtitles said that they got him in the end, but that was OK – all the best plays killed off martyrs – "The Crucible", "A Man for all Seasons." Tragic heroes weren't meant to stay alive.

So it would be traditional, as well as topical, original, even ecological; Terry couldn't get worked up about packaging, but there were plenty of kids that did. The more he thought about it, the surer he became. "The Life of Chico Mendez" could end up as a hit.

Rod Spencer wss also busy. He worked in his own study, attacking a word-processor in a centrally heated detached house with four bedrooms, but the comfort of his surroundings did not dilute his efforts. In his brain he was a man possessed, a dedicated monk.

King Edward's had launched their promotion early, using quotes from their inspection report. Rod thought that this might be illegal, but was not contemplating a challenge in the courts. (Temperamentally, nothing would suit him better, but there wasn't the time, let alone the cash.)

His dream was the campaign, the promotion of Rab Butler that would enable it to pull in more pupils than King Edward's. History was against him: more kids, brighter kids, had always gone into the town. Colin Parnaby was known to be soft, pleasant and dozy, while Higham was a pompous, arrogant swine. Parents therefore sent their kids in droves.

Rod relished a challenge. If willpower, effort and cunning could boost the Butler intake, that would be a victory against the odds. It might also help his future chances, in the unlikely event that Priory Hall decided not to choose him as its head. So Rod spent the half-term devising an unstoppable recruitment campaign.

Happy New Year. First day back. Tina strolled round the staff car park, with Dennis in tow.

"It's easy. A quick flick with a screwdriver, and they're off."

"Then what?"

"Then you give them to me, and I sell them."

He paused, and waited for her to turn to face him. "Who to?"

"Never you mind." Gently, she took his arm and nudged him into movement again. "I'm the brains of the operation, Dennis, and you're the muscle. All right?"

Dennis didn't argue. Nobody had ever put his name and brains in the same sentence. He wasn't going to push it.

"You get a good time. And half the profits. You stay with me, Dennis, and we'll hit the headlines. Together." She squeezed his hand, winked and smiled. Deep inside Dennis's skull, something was flushing his brain.

Tina Clark and Waite, holding hands? That couldn't be right. Teenage sex had always worried Rod; his memories of grammar school were crowded with model planes, cricket and mock exams, so he found it hard to see how pimply adolescents could get so worked up about girls. But when it came to a bright exam candidate like Tina Clark, voluntarily spending time with a year 9 oaf like Dennis Waite, a deeper outrage was involved. Like an Afrikaner farmer watching his daughter dance with kaffirs, Spencer plotted revenge.

He steered his Rover out of the car park, and on to the by-pass. He soon left the council estates behind. Familiar territory, they were, a well-known seam worked to extinction. Rod was off towards a new frontier, to stake an original claim.

"OK, then?"

"Yes thanks. I don't know where half-term went, but I'm fine." Terry looked round his room, at the scraps of litter on the floor, and his irregular mounds of marking. Somehow it looked worse when the kids were gone, and he saw the mess through Linda Jones' eyes, but at least the chairs were up. "Your lad all right, is he ?"

"Lee? All right? Nobody else seems to think so." But she laughed. Being Lee Jones' mum wasn't, apparently, as great a penance as staffroom gossip might suggest.

Idly he picked up one of the scraps of paper, and started to read it.

"What does it say?"

Mercifully, he skimmed through before reading it aloud. The class he'd had were Year Eight, aged 12 – 13, boisterous but not evil. Almost innocent, he'd have said. But the message he was reading was worse than the lavatory walls back home.

"Oh, nothing." And he casually ripped it into pieces, before throwing it in the bin.

Jackie poked her head round the door. "Time for your seminar, Mr. O'Mara. Hi, Linda. Everything all right?"

"Fine thanks, Mrs. Grabowska. And yourself?"

"Yes, thanks. Come on, Terry."

He grinned, sheepishly. "She's showing me how to be a teacher. You won't tell Lee?"

"If you're teaching him, love, you need all the help you can get."

He burrowed through the printed sheets, the marking and the text books to dig up the ring-binder which rested at the deepest of these layers. Then he followed Jackie down the corridor into the staffroom, and opened it on the table. Jill was not impressed.

"National Curriculum, in the staffroom? Must you ?"

"He's got to know, Jill."

"Really?" There was a tense pause between them."OK, if you say so." And Jill returned to her book. Did she never lighten up?

"OK, assessment." Though it was one-to-one, Jackie helping Terry, it felt like a lesson. "There's two kinds, teacher assessment and tests. The tests are there to check that the teacher assessment has got it right."

A derisive snort from Jill, but her eyes stayed on the book. Jackie' s eyes, encouraging but watchful, stayed on him. "So at the end of year nine, your kids do these tests, just like an exam. There's some old papers in there."

He went through the folder. Essays, letters, comprehension, just like the old days. And Shakespeare, but reading not acting. Answering questions about a printed scene. It was as though he'd never been away.

"Yeah. Got it. We did stuff like this, right?"

"Yes, Terry. So did the politicians, years ago. It makes them feel at home. There's your own assessment, where you come up with different levels, and that page, there " (flicking confidently through the folder) "is what tells you how to turn lots of different levels into one. Have you got that?"

Her tone said that this was basic, but the writing on the page was gobbledegook. Lots of words, lots of numbers, a million miles away from the kids he taught.

"You're sure this isn't the maths?"

She laughed, but wasn't going to be sidetracked. "Oh, no. Though I think that's just as bad. They're still going on about vulgar fractions. Do you know what a vulgar fraction is?"

It was lovely, the mechanical click when a joke fell into place.

"Oi tink it's a turd. Boom boom."

"Oh, very good. The old ones are the best." But the sparkle in her eyes said she liked it, and even Jill looked up from her book.

He risked it. "So what about you, Jill, what do you think of all this?"

"What do I think of the folder? The National Curriculum assessment of English?" Everything – her ominous tone, Jackie's apprehensive look, his own gut feeling – said this was a bad move.

She was very deliberate, trying to be fair. "We need a system that makes sense, that people can trust. Teachers can make mistakes, and not all of them are good at assessing."

"Me, for instance. I mean God, what do I know?" He was trying to make it easy, lighten it, help things along. She looked at him as if he was a slug.

"But we can do that. We're professional, serious, hardworking. Given time and money, we can have a system that works. What we don't need is Daily Mail thinking that says all the kids in the country are on a ladder, and this quick little test will tell you which rung your kid is on. That's what I think."

An ominous, familiar tone, the accent of commitment. The constant background of his childhood, shriller at school, deafening at college. Part of the price of Lavinia, that he'd been prepared – grudgingly – to pay. He really didn't want to get back into that, again. She was still looking at him, eyes like shotgun barrels.

"I also think that this is planned, expensive lunacy, decreed by one government as a rightwing coup and taken over by another which hasn't got the nerve to ditch it. But I don't need to teach you about politics."

No indeed. You could come from Belfast and not be politically involved. Most of his life Terry had fought for the sacred right to apathy, and he had his answer ready:

"So far as I'm concerned, a commitment is a member of a band."

He'd used the line before. He still liked it, and there was nothing wrong with the delivery, but Jackie wasn't laughing and Jill was picking up her stuff.

"Was it something I said?" he asked, but by then he was talking to himself.

Colin Parnaby picked mournfully at the bulky document on his desk. "It's bad news, Joyce."

"But you were expecting it, surely?"

"Oh yes. We never claimed to be high fliers. It's just that when it's spelt out like this, fifty different tables, and we're in the bottom half of all of them...Well, it hurts."

"Exams aren't everything."

"I know." Slowly, sadly, he nodded. "Are the kids happy? Do they get an interesting time? Do staff get a decent deal? Those are the things I care about, and nobody ever produced league tables for them."

She moved briskly towards his desk, beaming optimism. "So, stick to what you believe in, and put that lot in the bin." She peered into his coffee cup. Only half drunk, as usual.

"If only I could." He read through the pages again, as if hoping to find a league table for common decency that might place them above King Edward's. "There are thousands of copies of this. Dozens in the libraries, each of the junior schools, parents can get them on demand. It wouldn't surprise me if they were delivered free with the evening paper."

"Come on, drink your coffee."

He seemed not to have heard. "Perhaps they'll feed them into

Eastenders. Your local league tables, serialised in soundbites. 'And now, over to Albert Square, where parents are considering their choice of secondary school'…"

"My word, you're bitter."

"Yes. Yes, I'm afraid that's spot on. Bitter is the word, exactly." Finally he picked up his saucer in his left hand, raised the cup with his right, and took a token sip.

"What are you going to do about it?"

"There's not a lot I can do, is there?" Gently he replaced the cup and saucer. "I've finished, thanks."

She stared at him, challenging the platitude.

"Well, not before July." She took the cup and saucer, but did not move away.

"You could make a decision. And stick to it,"

"Fair enough. I will, I promise."

"And in the meantime?"

"In the meantime, Rod has a few ideas."

"I'm sure he has." She moved towards the door.

"Don't scoff, Joyce. That's more than I do. I might as well give him his head."

"Because nobody else will, you mean?"

He shook his head. He understood her resentment, but would not echo it. "Well, partly. He was very cut up about Priory Hall. Chris didn't say much, but she wanted it, too. Funny, both of them desperate to get this job, and I'd happily give it up tomorrow."

The lay-by was more like a tip. Muddy and strewn with rubbish, with trailers parked the entire length of it. Rod carefully locked his car and walked towards them, feeling like a pioneer. One thing was for sure: King Edward's wouldn't have beaten him to this particular patch.

A couple of grubby kids were chasing each other round the bushes. Like Amazonian Indians, they paused to regard the advance of the suited stranger. Did he bring beads, Christianity, or running water?

"Hello?" Rod coughed, smiled and held up a pamphlet. "Are

your mum or dad at home ?"

Mick got to his pigeonhole and cursed. A green slip, signed by Rod Spencer: "Please cover Phil's break duty - sorry, I'm out of school." There was a time when Mick had thought he might end up that way – wearing a suit, office of his own, go out for a drive if you're bored.

But it all got serious. Weekend courses, dreary reading, chatting up the right advisers. Then along came the National Curriculum, and unless you had a doctorate in bullshit you didn't stand a chance. So he'd settled for the Technology racket, and having some time at the weekends. He moved across the busy staffroom to the crash door and barged through it, ignoring the protests of colleagues suddenly exposed to the winter air. He might only be a stand-in, but for Mick duties were there to be done.

"Dennis, come here!"

"Me, sir?"

"You sir. Your name's Dennis, yes?"

"Yes sir."

Keep it simple. Multiple choice.

"So, I'm talking to you. What are you doing?"

Sulkily, the youngster shuffled to approximate attention. "Looking at the cars, sir."

"That's what I was afraid of. Do us a favour and leave them alone. Right?"

"Sir." Face down, voice almost inaudible, innermost thoughts God knows. Dumb insolence. He ambled off, peacably enough.

Sylvia March strolled towards him, hunching her shoulders to tighten the thick fur coat in which she huddled.

"God, it's cold. Got any cigarettes?"

"Are you on duty?"

"You don't seriously think I'd be here of my own free will? " She was imperious, on duty, but definitely planning to smoke. He was impressed. He kept hunting through his pockets.

"Sorry. Just asking. Here." He offered her the packet, but did not take one himself. Not worth the risk of a bollocking. He got out his lighter, and lit hers.

"Thanks."

"I'll keep a look-out. How's the dogs?"

"Fine, thanks. Verlaine had a bit of a cough, but Rimbaud's OK."

"Good." Like a searchlight he raked the grounds; no riots, no escape. "I still don't get it, though."

"Don't get what?"

"Why you gave one of them a French name. I mean, If I'd got a Rambo, the other one would be Rocky. Stands to reason."

"Rimbaud – as in 'Les Illuminations'? "

No lights went on.

"My apologies. Different wavelengths."

He looked around, again. It was a familiar sensation, the blast of air as an intellectual reference hurtled past. He wasn't going to lose sleep over this one. His gaze panned the playground, and then went back to the staffroom.

"No sign of the management."

"Don't worry. Miss Macdonald is safely ensconced with the Equal Opportunities adviser, Mr. Spencer's cruising round the neighbourhood in his car, and Mr. Parnaby couldn't give a damn."

So he could have had a fag after all. But starting now would brand him as a chicken. He would suffer, somehow last until lunchtime.

She inhaled deeply, an addict rescued by her fix. "Thank you, Mick, from the bottom of my lungs." A wicked little smile. "So, how's the alarm business? "

"You are joking?"

"No, promise. It sounded very hopeful."

She looked earnest, genuine, but you could never tell with Sylvia.

"I thought it was all over the staffroom. Two fifth year lads took it to the local paper, and now Rod Spencer's pinched it as a marketing ploy for the school. I'll get bugger all."

"Oh, what a shame. And it was your idea?"

She watched, pitiless, as Mick's pride wrestled with his shame. "Well, I'd sort of worked it out...with the lads. Given them a hand, you know. They don't miss much, Dale and Muptaz."

She nodded sympathetically, and drew on the cigarette. "You've opted in, then, for the duration? "

He stamped briefly, wished once more that he'd joined her in a fag, and blew on his empty hands.

"Looks like it. But I'll win the lottery, or think of something else." This was no casual comment, but a solemn oath, an Arthurian knight's commitment to pursuit of the Holy Grail. "There's no way I'm patrolling freezing playgrounds till I'm sixty-five."

"Yes, I do know what you mean."

"How about you? Got your French job fixed? Sorted the transfer fee?"

"Not yet. But we do have the exchange next term. Let's say I'm reasonably hopeful," and her eyes turned away from the school, past the tights factory and beyond the fields, to a distant horizon of hope and freedom, just as the bell called them back. Another lesson.

He had to get a life. If a friend at college had told Terry his whole life would revolve round school he'd have got a laugh or a punch, depending on his mood. Yet now, it was almost true.

Nobody'd planned it that way, but as the momentum of work accelerated it was hard to do much about it. At King Edward's he'd had nights out with Rick at Nottingham or even Birmingham, heading into the smoke for a drink, a laugh, a pull. But chatting up girls with Rick was not much fun. He had the jokes, the patter, the car and the cash, so he defined the tone, and usually got first pick. Or the girls picked him. Terry had kept finding himself in his wake, getting second choice, killing time on his own. Until Rick met Cheryl, and the need to pull had passed.

Terry didn't mind. He wanted something calmer, cheaper, more in his control, but how did you get that in Shellworth? A small, boring little Midlands town, crawling with kids he taught.

Who else was he going to meet, except teachers from the school? And getting involved with them, quite apart from the limited options, hardly amounted to getting a life.

Hobbies, interests, doing something else. It was years since he'd done any sport, and he was too lazy to start that now. He got books out of the library, borrowed the occasional video, so he could graduate into a better class of couch potato, but that didn't amount to an alternative.

Which left drama. Sure, "Chico Mendez" was busy, demanding and draining, but it could still be good to get involved again, just act, do a part, be a piece in the jigsaw without having to think of it all. He could mix with a group of adults, no kids around, and maybe even meet someone. At home, and in college, there were more girls than boys doing plays, and lots of them were tasty, and there was no reason why this should be any different. It was at least worth a try. He'd picked up a leaflet in the library which said the Shellworth Players were holding a play-reading in the backroom of a local pub, so Terry combed his hair and went along.

It was a long night. Lousy play, very dull, would-be funny but laboriously read. Nice, middle-aged people, with happy memories of plays when they were young. He was right about the women. Seven of them, three blokes, and they were desperate for more. "How nice to have a man" they joked, endlessly, as Terry smiled and looked at his watch.

"Sorry. This isn't what you were looking for, is it?" He could only place her in that limbo between 25 and 40 which a couple of years ago had looked like middle age. She was stylish, with an amused look which said I have not given up, I am not getting old, I still have energy and life. Impeccable fair hair, a purr of a voice, and knowing, watchful eyes. Certainly, marks for trying.

"It's fine."

"I'm Sheila Thorpe." She offered her hand. "We'd love you to come again, but I guess you won't."

Was it that obvious? He feigned uncertainty. "I don't know. I'll have to see. Got a new job – may not have the time. Just dropping in, giving it a try." Feebly, he waved the leaflet, as if to prove his credentials, reassure her that he was not just messing them around. From the look of it, they needed him much more than they needed him .

"That's OK. You're new here, yes? Where are you working?" And he told her, and her kids were there, and he was just so relieved to know in advance that the most interesting, maybe only possible, prospect might be the mother of one of his pupils. In acting terms, there was nothing for him here, no challenge to make it worth giving up a night a week. Every other instinct clamoured to him to get the hell out. Whatever else he might get here, it wouldn't be a life.

Chris Macdonald sifted briskly through the pile of papers.

"Joyce, do you have my materials?"

She didn't look up. "Which materials would they be?"

"PSE. Contraception. With the diagrams."

"Oh yes. Those materials. I'm afraid there's a problem." And still, Chris noted, the older woman would not look her in the eye.

"What kind of a problem, precisely?"

"We are very busy, as I'm sure you'll be aware." She looked absent-mindedly around her area, as if looking for evidence. She was tired. "Actually, if it was left to me, which it isn't, I'm not sure that this is the kind of thing – "

"I will not have this. Your role here is to produce materials, not to censor their content."

Joyce knew it was a mistake, and her mistake, but she would hide it if she could. "I beg your pardon – "

"It is quite insufferable that as a deputy head I – "

"Can I help? " Parnaby, the peacemaker, beamed in the doorway.

"Miss Macdonald thinks I have censored her material. I was just trying to explain that Mr. Spencer's leaflets had priority."

Like a witch, Chris MacDonald froze in rage. "What? I have to wait for his publicity junk to be finished before I can have materials for teaching? And what kind of lunacy is that, if public relations take precedence over lessons?"

The current kind, thought Parnaby, but he kept it to himself. He flapped in the direction of his office. "You'd better come in."

Rehearsals of "Chico Mendez" were going well. Green freaks liked the rainforest angle, while there was enough cops and robbers, family and love interest, to attract traditional tastes. For a time he toyed with the idea of having Emma Sheargold as Chico. She would have been great, but there was a promising lad as well, and there were problems in making him Chico's wife. Emma was fine, very understanding and frighteningly keen. She dived into the role, and then embarked on some background research which was encouraging, if a little scary.

He thought he knew about plays. He did know a lot, and everything he'd ever done came in handy, but it was a new, unsettling feeling to be the boss. Always before, there'd been directors, lecturers, expert stage managers, people who knew what they were doing and enabled him to do his part. For the first time ever, it all came back to him. At any hour of the day a kid might appear, bringing the latest demand from a nightmare quiz – How do I switch this on? Where does the scenery go? What colour is the knife and how long should it be ?

For now it was preparatory work. Mimes and exercises on rubber tapping, the details of Brazilian life and labour. There were political angles that might prove tricky later, but Terry was an optimist.

"This looks most promising." Rod Spencer eyed Terry's cast, engrossed in their after school rehearsal. What was he after – canvassers? "I take it this is for public consumption?"

"Well…" the stage Irishman's shrug, act vague and non-committal. If he looked stupid enough, Spencer might just walk away.

"Don't be modest. A real opportunity, this. Establish ourselves in the local community, bring people in, a chance of coverage in the paper."

Kids were starting to look up, mutter questions about what was going on. Terry ushered him away, trying to look earnest. "It is, it's great, but I wouldn't be so confident about the publicity side."

"No, we're too modest." Rod turned, facing the kids more directly, and turned up the volume. "We don't sell ourselves enough. Now, you were at King Edward's."

"Only for a term."

"Their Gilbert and Sullivans sell out for a week, make over a thousand. Employers can't stop talking about them."

Oh God, please. Not that. "This isn't Gilbert and Sullivan."

"Never mind. Don't play 'em on their own ground. Do something different. Pantomimes are very popular."

The kids had stopped completely. Terry looked at them, and then back at Spencer, who would not be put off. Bright and businesslike, whatever the facts. Hadn't he seen the damage he'd done ? Did the glasses actually stop him from seeing what went on?

"I'll have to go. But it isn't a pantomime, truly it isn't."

"Not to worry. We'll push it anyway. Might be able to do something on sponsorship, if you need something for sets and costumes. How about that ?"

"OK, you lot, don't go. I'll be with you in a minute. It's very good of you, but it won't be an ambitious production. Very simple, minimum lighting."

He remembered Rick's crack about performance indicators, and failed to suppress a smile.

"I'll leave the budgeting to you. But you have got finance?"

"Er, well, not at the moment. But maybe the ticket money..."

"That's it, then. I can see my role clearly. You take care of the artistic side, and I'll get the backing. Keep up the good work." And as his heels drummed across the hall and down the corridor, the good work could finally go on.

Mick surveyed the promised land. It was a dusty, foetid cupboard, with a door he'd had to force, but that's what made it special. Nobody had been here for years, nobody claimed at as theirs, it was his for Mick to fashion as his own. With love he pocketed his massive bunch of keys, and started to explore.

It was a graveyard for equipment. A banda machine, an epidiascope, even a Betamax recorder. All these toys which had once been greeted with awe, consigned to a dusty oblivion behind the caretaker's room. And then he saw the treasure.

"Video camera" now means a small, light plastic box that you can balance on one hand. Video camera then, back in the dark ages, was two heavy black boxes, a camera, and a mile and a half of connecting leads. Useless. But in Mick's fertile brain it set off an idea positively sparking with potential.

It would be hard to argue that a new video camera was essential for the teaching of technology. On the other hand, a school promotion video, provided free to feeder schools and offered on loan to parents, might be a starter. Rod Spencer was known to favour such ideas, and he could provide the finance. Mick would offer the labour, to take on responsibility for producing copies.

For that though, he'd need a couple of video machines, linked together, and an editing suite in which to work. Mick looked around at the gathering dust. It took a creative eye to see it, but for not much work, not much money, this could be a cosy little den, with background music, tapes whirring, and Mick with a cup of coffee and his feet up, watching production roll. The scenario was lodged, in detail, in his head, as Mick walked quietly out of the door, closed it and locked it, with the only available key. More than twenty shopping days to Christmas, but one big chunky present was almost in the bag.

Parnaby scratched his chin. He had got used to Rod and Chris, their energy, their ambition, their fierce mutual hate. On good days he felt above it, grateful for the work they did but detached from their constant feuding.

This was a bad day. They were sat in an uneasy triangle by the window of his office, with nothing between them but a low coffee table and a sense of impending doom. Discontent over Rod's promotion campaign spread far wider than Chris, and there was that general, dangerous feeling that SOMETHING SHOULD BE DONE. What, exactly? Once more, Colin looked at life's questionnaire and could not fill in the box. He couldn't sack Rod Spencer.

He couldn't ask him not to promote the school. Cut-throat competition was government policy now, and supported by the LEA, the same body which five years ago had promoted co-operation and the rational allocation of pupils to schools. It was hard to keep up,

Chris was furious. "It's intolerable. Capitation has been frozen, I'm unable to invite speakers in from the Family Planning association, and now I find that Mick Wall has been granted six hundred pounds to buy a camera."

Rod opened his hands in imitation of a reasonable man. "It's an investment. Look on the noticeboard. Every week there are competitions for schools with video cameras. If we play our cards right, we could recoup the cost in a term."

"We're a school, not a game show." Parnaby had to admire her firm, dull clarity. She was so quick, so sure of what she thought. " We're not here to win prizes. Our job is to ensure that kids get a decent education."

"And if we don't get the numbers through the door we shan't be here. This is a commercial imperative. It's time you realised, our jobs are on the line."

"Oh, please." Chris' gaze swept upwards, greeting the refrain with a satirical contempt Colin shared but dared not voice.

"Look, we shan't get anywhere by simply shouting at each other." He smiled wanly, and looked from one to the other. They were implacable, and also, he saw now, united in one other respect. Both had a strengthening conviction of his own irrelevance. He knew, because he shared it too. "We have to find a way round this, a way of working together."

"You're in charge. You tell us."

"Yes, Chris, thank you. This video camera –"

"It's paid for." Rod was in, a quiz show competitor, finger on the buzzer. "We've got it. That's the bottom line."

"Why do you keep talking like an American accountant?"

"There are spin-offs for the curriculum."

"But that wasn't why you bought it."

Parnaby glanced from side to side, Wimbledon at speed.

"Mick Wall came to me with a promising scheme for promoting

the school in the community."

An instant, scything laugh. "Mick Wall's main motivation is in lining Mick Wall's pocket."

"That's not a professional assessment."

"Maybe not, but it's true. I should know."

"All right, that's enough." Colin realised he had, finally, been able to get a word in, made himself heard. "Now listen. We're not rolling in money. We can't match everything King Edward's do."

"Have you seen the chip van?" Rod's outrage was genuine, a moral appeal for support, and quite oblivious to anything that Parnaby had said. As was Chris.

"A free hamburger for every child you send?"

"No, it's one of their parents. He parks outside the junior schools, handing our leaflets. 'It's not too late to change your mind.' I tell you, it's a jungle out there."

"That doesn't mean we have to get all the wild animals. I registered two kids from that caravan site that bordered on the psychotic."

"I thought travellers were one of the sacred victims?" He treated her to a dangerous, sarcastic smile, but she kept her cool.

"Those kids are not a good idea."

"In our position, any kids are a good idea."

"Stop! Stop this at once." Parnaby was on his feet. "The way you two are talking, you'd think we were on the verge of extinction." Could be, but nobody must say it. To keep their attention, think of what came next, Parnaby stayed on his feet, paced away from them to the desk, and turned. "We are still a school, and we are still open, and I will not have you talking as if we are about to close. Rab Butler is in the business of educating children, and will stay that way while I am head." They were listening. He returned to them, and stood by the window.

"From now, all expenditure over a hundred pounds must be approved by me in person. This meeting is closed."

Joyce watched in disbelief as Rod and Chris filed, silent and crestfallen, out of Colin's office. Better late than never. The worm had turned, and Parnaby was in charge of his school again. Pray God he didn't get a taste for it.

CHAPTER FOUR:

DECEMBER

Chris Macdonald sat at her desk, facing a list of telephone numbers, none of which she wanted to call. She was young, talented and successful; nobody got the first headship they applied for. There was an art to applications, and an intelligent candidate used the experience of being interviewed, profited from the pain. That, at least, was the theory.

It was meagre consolation. She was used to winning, and it was disconcerting to have education professionals look at her, question her, listen to her answers – and then turn her down. All the case studies said that this would be the price of getting a headship, but it still came very steep.

The staff didn't help. She could swear there was amusement, almost satisfaction, as the news had spread – not Rod, not Chris. Didn't they want her to succeed? Before, when she'd got the head of department job, the deputy job, they'd been pleased for her. But now, as a deputy, she had somehow forfeited the normal human rights – to sympathy, condolence, support. Other teachers returning unsuccessfully from interview were cossetted and consoled, but in her case it seemed to be a joke. Couldn't they see the vulnerable human being, the heart behind the suit?

She looked round at her tidy office, the packed filing cabinets, the lines of wallet files, the flowcharts on the wall. Was all that thinking, effort, time – all that for nothing?

It could have been worse. Rod might have got it. She had never, seriously, imagined that he would, but in the Top Ten chart of her fantasies that was Nightmare Number One. It hadn't even been a man, which was good, probably....although if it had been a man, then there was a good reason why Chris herself had not got the job. This way, they preferred another woman to her, and although the magazine articles suggested that all women were united by a sisterly bond of mutual affection and support, there was no sign of that at the interview.

Simon had been gruffly sympathetic. It was a bad time, but it wasn't their fault, and they were stuck in it together. The old dream, of advancing education from different ends, looked like a sick joke now. But Simon's rage had mellowed, with the recognition that this was not simply a personal vendetta with fate, but that his frustration was the common lot of professionals, a national disease. Just as Chris was one of a thousand deputies, hawking themselves as potential heads, so he was one more adviser with a poisoned role.

Fewer creative courses, visits to schools, chances of development work; more meetings with councillors, analysis of official documents, and clerking of governors' meetings. Simon sat, pen in hand, as local dignitaries discussed precisely whose dogs had been fouling the junior school's football pitch, and wondered where he had gone wrong. And, looming large on the horizon, the certainty that to stay employed he would have to train as an inspector.

Though Chris was fed up, Simon could offer no wise advice or relevant experience. He was down to rock bottom. All he had to share was the sympathy of a fellow victim, and this was a powerful bond. Together, they shared their impotent despair.

So, back to work. Work, in this case, was a list of local employers. Rod Spencer, in the ceaseless hunt for sponsorship, had been greasing his way into local boardrooms, but Chris had purer motives. Livelier lessons, better learning, as the outside world is brought into the classroom, through the presence of speakers for

Careers. She would sidestep the obvious people, already sullied by Spencer, and secure a whole new range of contacts, conquering her personal disappointment by finding fresh satisfaction in her work. Besides, it would look good on her CV.

Terry stood in the playground, trying to mimic Mick's nonchalant control.

It was hard to be that solid without the extra five stone, but as this powerful black lad approached Terry worked to appear relaxed.

"Sir?"

"Yes. What can I do for you?"

"Can I go home, sir?" Huge round eyes, pleading.

"What, now?"

"Yes, sir. It's me gran. She's well ill, sir."

The English teacher in Terry chickened out of this particular challenge. This was about power, not parts of speech. Delay, stay neutral, engage bureaucratic mode.

"Are you school dinners?"

"Yes, sir."

"Well, shouldn't you find your tutor?"

"I've tried, sir. Can't find her, sir." Terry paused, and looked away, looked around, hoping the kid would give up. He didn't.

"Oh, all right, then."

Terry watched him go, a lumbering hulk in Year Nine. Dennis something. A lot of the staff had it in for him, but he seemed harmless enough.

"Excuse me, sir?" Tina was one of his. A mature girl, year 10 going on eighteen, that his Aunt Teresa would describe as buxom. She flicked her hair back with a toss of her head, and treated him to the five star treatment – generous smile, energetic eyes. "Sorry to bother you, sir, but would it be OK if I nipped to the shops? I'll be back for registration."

"What is it, Tina?"

"I've got to get a present for my auntie. Her birthday. I shan't miss lessons."

He hesitated, and looked around again. No support, no witnesses. Why couldn't they leave him alone ?

"And you are my tutor." Big blue eyes, but she didn't push it. Just stood there, waiting, knowing he would fold. Sod it.

"OK, then. But make sure you're back in time."

"I will, sir. Thanks."

A little wave, and a smile that warmed like whisky. He watched her walk down the drive, as Mick Wall came across.

"Ey up, youth, you can get arrested for thoughts like that."

"It is OK, is it, Mick? Them going out of school at lunchtime."

"Not really. Depends on the reason."

"Oh, great. Still she did ask nicely."

"Oh, she would. Tina usually gets what she wants, but she does know how to ask." A connoisseur, Mick watched her sway into the distance. South Pacific got it right – nothing walks like a dame. He turned back to Terry.

"No, you can usually tell the dodgy ones."

"How's that, then?"

"They always have these daft excuses."

"Like what?"

"Oh, you know. Their grandma's ill, or they've got to buy a present for their auntie. Still, you're not thick enough to fall for those."

Rod strode through the staffroom. This was deliberate, to show the staff that he was purposeful, that being turned down for Priory Hall had not diluted his zeal. He was still a competent, hard-working deputy.

Not that anyone cared. The snatches of staffroom conversation that he overheard hovered around the usual irrelevant topics – children, television, cars, holidays - and nobody seized on his entry as the occasion for educational debate.

He looked into the former staff workroom, to check that the wallcharts were still in place, the ring-binders sitting on the shelves. Nothing was changed: the National Curriculum office, power hub of the school's pedagogical engine, was immaculate, untouched.

Except, he noticed with some satisfaction, the suggestions box. This was his one concession to Chris Macdonald, who seemed determined to introduce a note of trendy democracy into his scheme. Quite why it was important to ask teachers to comment on an operation which had largely been defined without them he could not fathom, but as a gentleman he had graciously conceded. Which made it all the better that there was now a legend, inscribed in large capitals above the welcoming box. The invitation still stood – "Any suggestions?" But now it bore a response, in clumsy, felt-tip capitals : "GET KNOTTED."

They weren't going to crucify him. He preferred Drama to English, mornings to afternoons, and younger classes were usually easier. There were times his kids could be silly, and days he was less prepared than he should be, but basically he reckoned he would cope.

Twice a day was registration with 10A4, but as the chores ticked by so he got to know his group better, separate in his mind the ones who in September had seemed identical, and learn a little more about what made them tick.

So as he sauntered in after lunch on Thursday, three minutes late, he wasn't expecting trouble. They were a bit boisterous, a few exclamations of "Phew !" as overacting boys sniffed the air and looked around, but Terry was halfway through the register before he caught up with the smell.

It was quite pleasant. When he was a kid it would be stink bombs, but now it was deodorant – not nasty, just twenty times the required strength. But an improvement nonetheless.

"OK folks, it's nice to be hygienic, but that's a tad too much. Kim, open the window will you, please ?"

"It's cold, sir."

"What's the matter, sir?"

"I don't know what he's talking about."

"Why do you want the window open, sir?"

It was trivial. Why did they make so much of it ? And why did he feel himself getting mad?

"Do we have to?"

"Yes. It smells like a bordello in here."

"A what?"

"What did he say?"

"Bore something."

This was supposed to be a bright class, fourteen, fifteen years old. There were some pleasant kids, but en masse they could be a pain. Silly, loud and very wearing.

"OK, thank you." The actor's voice, clear and firm. He stood, apart from the desk, stock still, weight balanced evenly between his feet. Eventually, as he watched , waited, nodded to the recalcitrant few, they listened. Except for Johnny Navarro, a bright computer freak with a mental age of nine and a half.

"What's a bordello, sir?"

"It doesn't matter."

"Go on, sir, I don't know what it is, honest."

"I bet he doesn't know."

"I thought teachers were supposed to explain things..."

"What is a bordello, sir?" Tina, charming and legal, back on time, had taken up the refrain and was not going to let go. A whiff of talc, and it ended up as this. Did he really plan to spend thirty more years of his life on childish arguments? Calling the register twice a day for ninety terms? This time, at least, he managed it.

"Right. This is ludicrous. Get your stuff together and go to your next lesson."

"What's a bordello, sir?"

"It's a whorehouse. Now –"

Like a cold shower, silence.

"What did he say?"

"Is he calling me a whore?"

"He's not allowed to say that."

"I'll have my dad up."

"Now, get to your lessons. NOW !" Olivier would have been proud.

After school, Dale and Muptaz walked slowly past the tennis

courts, occasionally looking at the football game. Further, following the straggling procession home, past the clump of trees, to the outer field, and privacy. Dale, short, thin and bitter, set the pace.

"Face it, Muptaz. He's stuffed us."

"It's not our fault."

"OK, so he's a teacher. But it was our idea, and we should be making money out of this. Spencer's wrecking it."

"Not entirely." Muptaz was anxious to be fair, as well as to catch up. "He's got some contacts, guys who'd never talk to us."

"Yeah, but they're never going to pay us, neither. They buy alarms, then the money's going to school fund, right?"

"Right."

But it wasn't. It was a crime, and they wanted justice. Muptaz gazed vacantly away from the school, to the red brick square of the tights factory, where many of their peers would work. Assembly line, mass production. He turned back to his friend. "You know those boxes ?"

"The bright red ones? I should do. I've made enough of them. I designed them, didn't I?" He was almost crying with rage.

Muptaz went on, soothing, scheming: "So you could make a few more, right?"

"Are we talking independent production here?"

"Could be."

"But we can't afford the parts. That's where Spencer's got us - we can't invest."

"We don't need parts – to make boxes."

"Just the boxes? You mean, no alarm inside?"

"You've got it. There's lots of broken tables behind the bikesheds, and Wally won't know how much of his red paint has gone for a walk. We could be back in business." That was the thing about Muptaz. Don't get mad, get even. Dale watched the warm, slow smile spread across his face, as though he knew he was bound to win.

"But who's going to buy a red box?"

"You're in charge of production, right? Leave the marketing to me."

Jackie had told him that teaching English would get easier, and it did. In the English office were files with teaching ideas, mostly from Jackie or Jill. And each of them had their own teaching folders, complicated and time-consuming to maintain, but increasingly looking like a good idea. How else could you hang on to all the stuff that was buzzing through the brain ? Every chance he got Terry looked across, skimmed pages, tried to remember headings, and later jotted them down.

As he taught, Terry found the ideas breeding off each other. He spent more time on his marking, and even enjoyed some of it. Maybe dozy Brian Summers was on to something. Rick would have disowned him, but as the weeks went by Rick became increasingly distant from what Terry wanted to do. And a closer look at the words, the ideas, the mistakes, gave him the chance to do more drama.

Parnaby had made him go on the course, but he wished he hadn't. Rowley was full of himself and short on ideas, so that Terry gave up early on. Even so, it wasn't tactful to prolong the "dreaming on the beach" sequence for a full minute after the others had stood up.

But it was Rowley's fault. He was daft enough to ask Terry what he thought, so Terry told him. As a response, it was concise, honest, direct. Dramatically, it achieved a kind of catharsis, certainly for Terry and, to judge from the giggles, for at least a couple of the customers. But Philip Rowley, adviser for English, was not amused.

Terry didn't need a course. He had plenty of ideas. Adverbs, for instance. Kids wrote stories, poems and plays with a freedom he'd never done, but they didn't know the parts of speech, the crayon colours that had dominated his early years – red nouns, blue verbs and yellow prepositions. So, it couldn't hurt to show, to dramatise, how different kinds of words might work in different ways.

Loudly, angrily, shyly, sweetly – different ways of talking. Or walks - quickly, slowly, pompously, casually. A neat idea, that. Kids could pick their own, write them down and act them out for the others to guess. He could collect lists on the board, a communal expansion of vocabulary. It was a breeze.

"Sir, sir, sir!"

"All right, Lee." Not one of life's volunteers. A tall, skinny kid, with no talent for English, or much else, so far as Terry could see. Until now. Linda would be proud.

Lee Jones stood, and looked around him, to check the audience. His shirt was hanging out and he had the posture of a slob, but the same natural grin and wavy hair as his mum. He walked to the front of the room, rolling his hips. Yes, well…the kids were giggling now, but Lee was high on performance, helplessly in control. He blew Terry a kiss, and they shrieked; then he turned towards the blackboard, with his back to all of them. In the shared, awed silence, Terry watched in fascination as the hands appeared, caressing Lee's ribs, his hips, his buttocks. Belatedly, he looked out to check the audience, and saw Mr. Spencer at the door.

"Jones. My office. Now."

He was transformed. The lovesick girl was a shambling oaf, and Terry was back where he started. Responsible.

The shame was still with him at the end of the lesson. He released them, but there was no sign of Jones or Spencer, and he didn't know whether to go and ask, or to wait for the worst. Jill came in, and paused inside the door.

"Terry, could you do us a favour?"

"Sure."

"Some drama with my Year Eights, Friday 4. I'll take whoever you've got."

Friday 4? His fifth year drop-outs? She must be mad.

"Be glad to, but you do drama with them, don't you?"

"Yeah, but I'm not trained. You know what you're doing."

He looked round at the mess, the disordered chairs, the bits of paper on the floor. He replayed the mental tape of Lee Jones' performance. The prosecution rests. Jill had picked up something from the debris, one of the kids' slips of paper.

"Mmm. Sexilly. Sounds interesting, but it's only got one L."

"Lee Jones. Linda's lad. A memorable performance."

"Adverbs, right?"

"How did you know?"

"I do it, too. But I don't let them choose their own. I've got a set of little cards, ready made, covered in film. Still, you do what suits you. OK for Friday, then?"

"Sure. No worries." And she went, and left him thinking. So you fixed the words, had them ready before you started. You didn't get the kids' ideas, but they couldn't mess you about. And that way, you could make them think about new words, different words. Less chance, more control. That was Jill all over – no easy laughs, no unnecessary risks. Get it all covered. Maybe it was duller, but it saved time – and would have saved Lee Jones, not to mention Terry. How much freedom was the freedom to make crude jokes? This business wasn't as simple as it looked.

It was easy to find a space, but most of the food had gone. Going into lunch late was the price of a social conscience, if teachers insisted on holding meetings in the first half of lunch rather than the second. Sharon would rather eat first and then talk, if anyone had asked her, but they hadn't.

"So what was that all about?"

"You know Ms. Macdonald. We're the young women for the future, and she's got to get us mobilised." Valerie motored through a pile of baked beans, en route for her hot dog.

"So it's another piece of work?"

"It's quite interesting. Looking at books and lessons, seeing if they're biased."

"Against girls, you mean?"

"Have you ever seen a text book biased in favour of girls?"

Sharon thought hard, trying to be fair, although she feared she was wasting her time. "Mmm. See what you mean. Though Kevin said something the other day, made me think."

"Kevin Stone? You're making it up."

"No, really. That's why I remember it." She watched with distaste as Valerie spooned up the last few dollops of gravy.

"Go on, then. What did he say?"

"If there's supposed to be equal rights, why do we do a longer cross country course?"

"And that's it?" She put down the spoon, pushed her plate away, and reached for a chocolate biscuit.

"I thought that was pretty good. For Kevin."

Valerie ripped off the wrapper. She was not impressed.

"Have you finished that story for English?"

"We haven't got her on Friday." Sharon straightened her things, for the second time. She'd spent a large part of her life waiting for Valerie to finish lunch. "We've got the new one, Mr. O'Mara."

"The one with the straggly hair and the leather jacket?"

"I think he's nice. In a sixties kind of way."

"Yeah. Bob Dylan crossed with James Dean. Why have we got him?"

"Miss said. He's meant to be good at drama."

Colin Parnaby finished stirring his coffee, and looked up. "I think it's going to be all right."

Joyce stopped sorting his files. "You mean the summer. Early retirement?"

"No. Here. Rod and Chris have got over Priory Hall, and I must say I like the look of Terry O'Mara."

She snorted. "I should have said that the look of him was the last thing you would like."

"All right, so he could smarten himself up. But he is very good with the kids."

"So he'll stay?"

"I don't know. Depends on the budget." Each year, they shared in the national suspense: how much cash would the government let them have ?

She spared him, for a moment of reflection.

"You have put in for retirement?"

"Well, I've put out some feelers."

"I don't mean matey chats. A real, signed application."

He looked around, helpless, innocent, threatened. Then picked up a pen, as if demonstrating his urgency. "I'll get on with it right away."

A sharp knock at the door, and Rod was in. "I'm so sorry – "

"If the door's shut, Rod, then you know I'm busy."

"Yes, but – "

"And if you don't wait for me to answer your knock, you can't possibly know who it is."

"I realise that, but –" He stood, hovering, one arm forward, raising a point of order. The clear message was that what he had to say was so important that any incidental rudeness could be forgotten, let alone excused.

"So please, next time, if you would be so kind, don't come in until you hear me call. Understood?"

He suspected that Parnaby would never have managed such firmness on his own, and Joyce's wintry smile made him sure. She left them to it.

"Do sit down, Rod. Now, what's the problem?"

He sat, perched on the front edge of the seat. "These outside speakers, for Careers."

"Yes?"

"Are we sure that they're appropriate?"

Parnaby waited until each of his finger tips had made contact with its opposite.

"Who's we?"

"I know Chris invited them –"

"But you think she made a mistake?"

He recoiled, embarrassed by the crudity of the charge. Parnaby recognised with relish a way to damp him down. Show Rod his reflection in a mirror, and he'd run a mile.

"Well, come on then, what are you saying?"

"Well..er..do we know who they are?"

"She's not just pullling them in off the street, surely?"

"No, I'm not suggesting…but I just thought…"

"Yes. What did you think?"

It was quite fun, this. He wants to load the bullets, make him pull the trigger.

"Oh well, if you're happy, that's fine. I'll um..be getting along."

And as the door closed Colin savoured the peace, the relief, that he didn't always have to feel guilty, to react. Sometimes the answer to a Spencer question could come from Spencer, rather than himself.

Sod's law said that just when you were busting a gut, the nasty things would happen. "Chico Mendez" was going well, and Terry was showing all the symptoms of a successful producer – sleepless nights, occasional amnesia, frequent explosions, and imminent collapse. Then disaster hit him, twice.

Most of his teaching took a back seat; kids were occupied, but his real thinking was devoted to rehearsals, at lunchtime and after school. For Jill's class, though, he made an exception. He wanted them going back, raving, about this wonderful foray into the world of drama expertise.

So the lesson he planned was full of stimulus and suprise, different activities, subtle changes of mood. He'd forgotten that another part of his brain had encouraged the set crew to get on with painting on every legal occasion, and quite a few that weren't. So as he triumphantly led Jill's class into the empty hall, the sight of five huge scenery flats, resting on newspaper, dripping with paint, was not exactly what he'd planned.

Outside, the heavens exploded in symbolic frenzy, worthy of "King Lear." This may or may not have been an omen, but its practical effect was to bring in a horde of shivering footballers, accompanied by an apologetic Pete Wrench. Yes, Pete did owe him a favour, but it was not going to be repaid today; in fact, he was going to ask another. At which point Joyce Davies arrived with a message asking Terry to speak to the police, who were investigating the theft of an elderly Morris Minor from the school car park.

"Brilliant," Terry observed. "Shall I come, or just cut my throat?"

When the police had gone, and he'd reclaimed Jill's class from the room where Pete had parked them and the bell had finally proclaimed the end to this misery, it was a relief to get to the lunchtime rehearsal, and a meeting about the play.

He had shown the kids a video of Chico Mendez, and he had

outlines of the scenes on paper. If possible, he didn't want a script, but some of the kids were scared that they'd forget.

"I'll do them one if you want. Just for their scenes." Jackie, as ever, was eager for work. Never look a gifthorse angel in the mouth.

"Are you sure?"

"I've seen them rehearse. Just take a few notes, knock out something. It won't be Shakespeare, mind."

Terry mimed a cigar. "I don't want it good, I want it Tuesday."

"Right you are, Mr. Goldwyn. I heard about your car. Sorry."

It had been found, five miles away, parked on a roundabout, and set alight. Not that unusual, but it wrecked his routine. The insurance wouldn't get him another car, so it was buses and lifts from now on.

"OK, that's fine, folks. Pick up your stuff."

He gathered his own piles of paper, as Jackie finished her notes, and made sure kids straightened the furniture before they left.

"It's OK, Terry. It's going to be good."

"God, I hope so. No, you're right. It'll be fantastic, really it will. Maybe." He winked.

"It's just what these kids need."

"You wouldn't like to tell Rod Spencer that?"

"What's he got to do with anything?"

"I think he'd rather we were doing Gilbert and Sullivan."

"So?" She stared, challenging. How lovely it must be to know that you're right.

"Fine, Jackie. But just tell him, eh?" His face was looked, his voice subdued.

"You're doing great, Terry. Uncle Colin rates you, and you're good with kids. I reckon you could be here some time – if that's what you want?"

He smiled to himself, then looked back at her, but said nothing.

"Sorry, am I being nosey?"

"No. I just don't know. I'm here for a year. Temporary contract. The man with no name, who breezed into town and might just breeze on out again." She watched him closely, as he slipped away, rescued by the comic routine.

"So where will you breeze to, O'Mara?"

He picked up his bag and looked at her, bleak and lost.

"God knows, Jackie. I wish I knew."

For once, the staffroom was animated with a single conversation, gripping every teacher in the room.

"How do they know they were ours?"

"Come on, think about it. Attractive girl with wavy blonde hair, 16-ish. Plus, a black lad about 14, well-built but not very bright. Recognise anyone?"

"Tina and Dennis – our very own Bonnie and Clyde."

"It's not funny. They could have been killed."

Terry came in as Marion Harper was speaking.

"With luck, they'll lock them up and throw away the key."

"What about the car?"

"It was only a Porsche."

"You don't think it was them that took Terry's?"

"No chance. Pinching a battered moggy would ruin Dennis' street cred."

"Listen to him. The proud owner of an M reg Lada – only a Porsche, he says."

"So I'm jealous. How does Dennis get to drive a Porsche?"

"He has talents. Not many of them show in the classroom, but he knows his way around cars."

"And into them, from the sound of it."

"What about Tina?"

"Do you want to rephrase that?"

"But where does she come into it? Why is she knocking around with Dennis?"

"The heart has its reasons."

"It's obvious. It's got to be race." Silence. The buzz of chatter stops and Terry, who offers the comment as one of a lively dozen, finds himself alone, on a tall, isolated podium. The staffroom, the world, waits.

"She's white, he's black. Curiosity. God, it's natural, isn't it?"

95

The embarrassment is palpable. They are inhibited English, he is extravert Irish; they share agreed jokes, recognise known limits, he is in a whirling, sucking void of his own creation. And Jill Williams carefully puts down her book, smiles perfunctorily and asks "You know about this, then, Terry?"

All he wants is to die.

As her heels clack down the corridor to Parnaby's office Chris rehearses the arguments. It's got to be Spencer. Anything about the Careers speakers must have come from him, and if it's come from him it's got to be a complaint. He's jealous, because she hasn't used his precious contacts, because she's had the energy to get off her backside and create some links between the school and the outside world which will actually benefit kids, rather than boost the budget and redound to the greater glory of Rod Spencer. She is sad but not surpised that Parnaby is prepared to play along, but she will not go down without a fight.

"Chris. Come in.Cup of coffee?" He looks older than he did. Chris nods, and tries to smile at Joyce, who makes no attempt to respond. Surely she can't survive here for long; if Parnaby finally does retire, how could his successor tolerate her genteel impudence?

Colin waits until they both have coffee, and Joyce has left.

"I wanted a word, about the speakers for Careers."

She settled in the easy chair, looked out at the familiar view, and prepared for the familiar row. She switched on her earnest listening look.

He writhed, as usual. "I'm not sure it's a serious problem, but...er...I did think we ought to talk about it."

He fidgetted with a sheaf of papers. When she was a head, she'd bollock people properly, and not pretend to be making a minor adjustment to the curtains.

"It's this." He handed over the papers. A neat, word-processed report, four A4 pages clipped together, headed "The Equal Opportunities Awareness Group."

"I thought this was about Careers ."

"It is. Have a look, there, page 3."

In disbelief, with a growing surge of rage, Chris read the report. This group, *her* group, of intelligent, critical young women were analysing "Bias in the Curriculum" :

"…at least two of the outside speakers were sexist. One commented on the appearance of girls in the group, and assumed that managers would be male. Another was racist in his description of foreign competitors, and the comments on trade unions were ignorant and hostile."

"What do you think?" Parnaby was smiling at her, ludicrously enthusiastic. How could Spencer have got to them so fast ?

"Um…er…I hadn't seen this."

"No. I asked them for it. Emma was talking about what they were doing, and I said I'd like to have a look. They said it was just a draft. I'm most impressed."

"I'm sorry, I don't quite – "

"You should be proud of them. Independent thinking, critical judgement. I know it hurts when they come out with something we don't like – " the jolly smile, offered as a sop, plunged like a knife – "but it's good for the soul. Don't you think?"

The procession moved solemnly, to the amplified chant of the "Missa Criolla." Reds, yellows, greens, Latin american, straight faces, slow movement, reverent tone. Slow, keep it slow, Terry muttered, but only in his head. Nobody dare speak.

Lovingly, agonisingly, the director had to admit he'd got it right. They'd got it right. Like a spectator at a Grand Prix, you lived in dread of the giant crash, but so far it hadn't happened. At last, maybe for the first time, they all knew what it meant, had wiped the grins, were keeping the rhythm slow.

The placards said "Chico Mendez lives" in English, for the peasants in the audience. Except Emma's. " Viva Chico Mendez!" she had painted, in bold, immaculate red capitals, and she carried it aloft like a cross. Reports suggested that Chico's real-life widow was not so saintly but hell, this was a play. For the work, the nail-biting, the sleepless nights, the arguments and the strain, in the end you get the reward. And fifty kids have a memory that will last them all their lives.

The audience liked it too. A bit radical for some tastes, and not a sell-out, because this was not King Edward's, and the show was not by Gilbert and Sullivan. But on stage the kids had done great, and their parents were pleased.

Even after the applause dies down, there is a lasting glow, a rosy confidence that good will triumph. Eventually, shame and pressure make the government act, proceed against the killers, and against the odds an honest, dedicated hero like Mendez can survive his killing, live past his martyrdom, triumph beyond the grave. Terry, who read the papers and knew that Mendez' killers had wriggled off the hook, was saying nothing.

Mark Hutchings, vice-chair of governors, was saying plenty.

"That was great, Tony."

"Terry."

"Terrific stuff. And that girl – she's something special, isn't she?" He whistled extravagantly. Terry's opinion of Emma Sheargold was similarly high, but it felt cheapened in this company.

"I'm sorry. He may be leader of the Labour group, but he's still an unreconstructed chauvinist."

Terry felt a hand on his arm, as a familiar purring voice carried him away, in a cloud of exotic scent.

"Sheila Thorpe. We met at the Players, remember?" He took in the shining fair hair, the attractive, made up face, and the expensive clothes. You saw women like this all the time – on telly. "I'm Mark's partner. And a big fan of your work." There was a quaver in the voice, as though it were carrying significance beyond the actual words.

"Thanks. It's very much a team effort. Jackie and – "

"You don't have to tell me." She patted his arm. "I know the work involved in something like this. But a team needs a leader, Terry – it is Terry, isn't it ?" Serious, searching eyes.

"Yes." He nodded, dumbly.

"And you're certainly that. It's nice to see a man who can work with women."

He looked round for distraction, allies, escape, but Jackie was sorting costumes and Jill was at the far end of the hall, talking to Pete Wrench. He tried to project silent distress signals but although the flags were fluttering she waved and wandered off.

"So, what's the next step?" She was smiling at him, encouraging, disconcertingly close. "You're not going to stop there?"

"I honestly couldn't tell you. Christmas holidays – that's my next step. After that – who knows?" He opened his hands and shrugged, a mime cliché of indecision.

"And what are you doing for Christmas?" She was concerned and friendly. Attractive, too, but working just a bit too hard. Which made him hesitant and dumb.

"Well, I'm not too sure..."

"You must come round for a drink. We'd love to see you, wouldn't we, Mark?"

Mark acknowledged the increase in volume, turned for a second to nod vacant agreement, and then resumed his conversation.

"You see? That's as much of his attention as I ever get. Still, if he's out at a meeting you could come anyway. Say, the 22nd, about seven?"

"I don't know. That's very good of you, Mrs. Hutch...I mean, Ms Thorpe."

"Sheila, please."

"If you'll excuse me, I've some tidying up to do."

"Of course. I'll be in touch."

Her smile lasted longer than his, as he fled to the dressing rooms. Costumes on the floor, stray knives and guns, programmes and parts of abanadoned scripts. A mess, and a relief. He was still sorting them five minutes later when the door opened.

"It's OK, she's gone." A beam from Jill, white teeth, pink mouth, black face. Neapolitan delight. He'd never seen her so relaxed.

"Who?"

"You're not fooling anyone, O' Mara. When Sheila's got your number, you are one dead man. But the play was great. Well done." One more brief, friendly grin, a flicker of warm love from a brown-eyed girl, and she was gone.

"If you don't apply, I'll do it for you." He had never seen Joyce like this – erect, tight-lipped and stern.

"You can't do that."

"Just watch me. It wouldn't be the first time I'd forged your signature."

"Maybe, but I knew about the others."

"All of them?" She was still standing there, implacable, but a trace of mischief flashed in her eyes. Parnaby held her stare briefly, and then looked at the floor. He was completely in her power.

She moved towards him, the pantomime witch backstage. "It's all right, I'm on your side." A softer, more familiar tone. "Our side. Just don't forget Martin Walters." She put a hand on his shoulder, and he looked up, forgiven, but still there was a shadow on his face.

"You saw the letter?"

"I do the post, remember?"

"OFSTED. They're coming here."

"Yes, but not till February."

"Did you see that list of the paperwork they need?"

"Rod will love it. Keep him happy for weeks."

He looked plaintively at her. "Don't mock, Joyce. We'll need to pull together, to get through this."

She bustled, picked up papers, straightened ornaments, signalled optimism. "King Edward's survived, didn't they?"

Parnaby was still mournful, oblivious to her efforts, boxed in his gloom. "What they found at King Edward's will be very different from what they find here ."

"Really?" She swung suddenly, in case the view from his window offered hope. "I'm not so sure about that. And besides, by July we'll be finished with it." She paused, as the witch returned. "Won't we?"

By the time the end came, Terry was almost sad. He'd got used to his teaching, knew all his classes, and "Chico Mendez" was a hit. Now he faced a lonely week at home, and the necessary meeting with Lavinia. He was the only teacher at the disco who fancied another week of term. Pete Wrench, for one, couldn't wait.

"Ten days in the Cairngorms – magic."

"Never took to wind-surfing, myself."

"You mad Paddy. Ski-ing, climbing, walking – I'll come back a new man."

"I was wondering about them." Jackie chuckled as she passed. "They talk about them in the magazines, but I never get to see one. At least" she looked round at the crowded, hectic pub " not on this staff." She moved to pick up her coat.

Pete grinned, as he watched her move off. "A good 'un, eh?"

"Yeah. One of the best." To Terry, it was all so simple. All she had to do was ditch Steve, and come and live with him. His problems would be solved.

It had been a good night, but now, for the older, the settled, the married staff, it was time to go home. So, seize the time.

"What do you make of Jill, then?"

Pete was a decent guy, but he wasn't good at bluffing. "Jill ? Mmm. She's different, very different. No question. Nice, though. Still, got be off. Take care, Terry, and go easy on the Guinness, eh?"

Pete moved off, and Terry wandered aimlessly, chatting a bit to the hardened few who remained, drinking a bit more. Then Jill emerged from the Ladies, heading for the coats.

"Can I get you a drink?"

"No thanks, I've had enough."

"Me too, but I need the company."

"You'll get that when you're breathalysed – oops, sorry. Tactless."

She put her hand to her mouth, acting friendly, but still was ready to go. There wasn't anything to say. But he said it anyway.

"You going away?"

"Go home, see the folks."

"Where's home?"

"Leicester. Lots of excitement in Leicester." Her grimace said different. "Then I'm off for New Year. Scotland. See you. " And she grinned, and went for her coat, the way she'd meant to before, back on track again.

Well, of course. Pete Wrench, non-committal about Jill, going to Scotland. Jill going to Scotland. He was a fool even to ask. The monastic vow was the clever move. Keep to that and it would all be fine. But could he, could anyone, do that? Just work, and call that a life? It sounded sad. And yet, compared with August, he was doing fine. Back to the good, the boring resolutions: play it a day at a time. Don't get laid, get paid. See Lavinia. And then, maybe, a happy new year.

CHAPTER FIVE:

JANUARY

He had seen Lavinia.

Like a fool, he tried to get back to the operation, but that was long since gone.

"You've had your appendix out, Terry, have you?" And she gave him one of those teasing, inviting smiles, the ones that did the damage in the first place. "Well, it's worse than that."

She wouldn't say more. She kept him at arm's length, knowing – as he knew – that the only way to go on was to finish. This was the full stop, the last verse in the ballad of Terry and Lavinia. Yet again, she was in charge, and yet again he went along with it, feeling limp.

She looked terrific. The old convent purity, the sparkling brown eyes. The long chestnut waves were cut short, but she survived such sacrilege. It made her older, tougher maybe, but it moved the focus on to the warm, mischievous energy in her face. As they sat in the station café, he saw blokes stare at her, just as they always had. And he got the old jealous looks – "You lucky bugger, why don't you give me some of that?" – and he could have cried.

She was well into the new job, on top of the kids and bossing the teachers around. And yes, the sensitive, middle-aged head of department was impressed by her talents. He was also separated and looking for someone to understand him, but she thought she could handle that. She was enjoying the work, and it was going well. Not exactly a victim, Lavinia. Any school would be glad to have her, and a lot of kids in Derry were heading for a cracking time.

They hugged, she saw him on to his train, and gave him one last searing kiss. A Christmas peck, lightly on his cheek, that turned his guts to water. 'Bye, Lavinia. Take care.

"I'm sorry, Colin, but this is vital."

Chris Macdonald stood implacably in front of Parnaby's desk, as he shifted uneasily in his chair. Round nine of the heavyweight eliminator , Spencer v. Macdonald. If he retired, he'd evade them both.

"So, what seems to be the problem?"

What does he mean, 'seems'? It is a problem, that's why she's bringing it. Why do they think she's living in a fantasy world? Resolute as ever, Chris made herself focus on the agenda, one thing at a time. Keep it simple.

"The new kids we've taken in. The Jacksons, O'Donnells and McGraws."

"They sound a bit of a mixture." He chuckled, and then stifled it as he saw her flinch. So many pitfalls, now.

"It's not a laughing matter. I expect the staffroom clowns to titter at the fact that I'm worried about these kids, when my concern for travelling people is a matter of record, but from you I had expected a more mature response."

He marvelled, at the steady gaze, the fluent tone, the cropped head still and aimed, like a cannon. She was purpose personified.

"You're right. I'm sorry, Chris. Carry on."

"They've been trouble ever since they've been here. Karen Jackson's hardly been in school, Billy McGraw has been in four fights that we know of, and probably a dozen more. The girls in his brother's tutor group have made complaints, and every time Steve O'Donnell has PE something goes missing from the changing rooms."

"I see."

She checked the note in her hand, but needn't have bothered. She knew it off by heart. "Please don't tell me that many travelling kids are decent, that they get a rough deal from other kids, and that they're innocent until proved guilty. I know all that, and I'm not prejudiced. But I am certain that it was a bad idea to recruit these kids en bloc."

And that was the key. Rod's recruitment campaign. Parnaby wondered, idly, if Chris Macdonald would still be worried about these kids if he offered to sack Rod Spencer. Just a thought.

"It's tricky. We're not actually full."

"I know that. King Edward's is full, so they can turn kids like this away, and then miraculously find a space if a bright kid comes along - "

"I didn't say that."

"You don't need to. We all know what happens."

"The point is, these particular kids. We can't just throw them out. Any suspensions would have to follow detailed enquiries, and then be processed through the governors..." He glanced down at his diary, already packed and groaning. She waited for him to finish, but she didn't wait long.

"I'm not pretending that there are simple solutions. I just thought I ought to bring the problem to your attention. Obviously, it's for you to decide how best to proceed."

Obviously. A polite, submissive smile, as she moved towards the door. The more he asserted his authority, the more she left things to him. Dropped them in his lap, with little labels attached which read "For Immediate Attention", and meekly walked away. He hankered for the old days, of spineless indolence.

In December, Terry had been full of good intentions. Catch up on the marking, plan ahead, sort out the plastic bags and boxes of loose papers which had accumulated during the previous term. He'd just nip across the Irish Sea, sort things with Lavinia, and be ready for the start of term.

It didn't work out that way. Christmas, Lavinia, New Year; lots of reasons to drink, not much opportunity to work. Not much inclination, either. His brain was busy enough, hosting a series of video clips, fantasies and flashbacks, but none of it could be called productive in teaching terms.

Teaching terms applied from the first Monday in January, like a cold shower. It was a mild, distant consolation that the rest of the staff seemed similarly shocked, although he couldn't share their concern about the imminent inspection. He'd felt on vulnerable view ever since teaching practice. Besides, Spencer had witnessed Lee Jones' erotic performance and Terry was still employed, so there couldn't be worse to come. So he changed the tape, from "Astral Weeks" to "Moondance" and back again, and Van Morrison got him through the week.

He missed Lavinia. He missed his car. Sure, it had cost him plenty, and if he had been an idealist he'd have said that not having a car brought him closer to the kids. Terry wasn't an idealist. He was cold and wet, and fed up with waiting for buses. He used his walkman, when the batteries worked, but he missed the tape-deck, humming along at the wheel with "Gloria" or "Brown-Eyed Girl." What he needed was money, security, a set of wheels. It didn't seem much to ask.

And now there was extra work. On top of the English, and a test his third year kids would have to take, the PSE programme had moved round another notch. Chris Macdonald's yellow sheet for January informed him that in tutorial sessions this term 10A4 would be tackling ATTITUDES TO GENDER. There was an appetising menu underneath – Discrimination at Work, Rape, Sexual Harassment and Domestic Violence. And a helpful little hand-written note: "Sorry if this looks a bit formidable - do check with Jill Williams if you're stuck."

"What exactly did Chris say?"

Rod sat in one of Colin's comfy chairs, covering his back. He had expected Chris Macdonald to be jealous of his strike-rate, but he didn't think she'd have the nerve to go to Parnaby. Who was, yet again, playing with his finger tips, watching them touch, and move away again, as if somebody else were pulling the strings.

"It's not just Chris. These kids are causing problems for other staff."

"Teething difficulties. Just settling in. I'd have expected more tolerance, from her…"

"That's not fair. Chris is not opposed to travellers, any more than you, or me." Parnaby broke up the bits with pauses, daring him to challenge. Well, is Chris prejudiced? Are you? Am I? No more fidgeting; he knew where he was going. "It's wear and tear in the school, pressure on staff and kids. Sometimes the gains of picking up new kids are outweighed by the cost of absorbing them."

Rod rearranged his long legs, crossing them the other way round, but he still seemed uneasy with the result. "It all depends, Colin, on what you mean by 'cost'. And besides, even if we wished to, we couldn't simply turn them away."

"It's not a question of turning away. You drove round, asking them to come in."

Spencer bit his lip, with all the passion of a keen young acolyte whose faith is held in doubt. "It's true that I've put some effort into our recruitment. I thought that was my duty."

"It is, and we appreciate it."

Sulkily, he rose from the chair. "Anyway, they're on the roll, and we need them for form 7. If you're going to chuck any of them out, at least wait until we've put in the returns."

The counsel of the devil. The budget rules all, get in kids to keep the numbers up, get the money for the numbers, and then ditch them if you must. Maybe Rod Spencer was headship material after all.

The area behind the workshops was sordid, but deserted. Muptaz looked around, and then faced his friend. "So, give us a look."

Dale opened a cupboard, and took out a bright red box. "It's just like the others."

"That's it. You get a box on the side of your house, that looks as if you've got a burglar alarm. Are the burglars going to climb up and check?" He looked eagerly, intensely, for his enthusiasm to be returned, or at least acknowledged.

"You're not going to charge the same? "

"Course not. The posh end, where Spencer's selling, they pay top whack. We leave them alone. We go round the estates, flogging these – what , ten quid a time?"

Once bitten, Dale remained sceptical. "It's not the same as sixty."

"But it is all ours. Tax free. So, how many have you done?"

"Twenty-six, so far. I'm waiting for the wood. You don't want to go back in and break the legs off a few tables, do you?"

After school. Jill was sitting alone in the staffroom, reading as usual. She looked up as Terry sat next to her.

"Sorry to interrupt."

"That's OK." She closed her book, but her finger marked the place.

"Chris Macdonald said to ask if I was stuck. And...well, I'm stuck."

"Fine, but I've got to go at four." She put in a bookmark, and put the book down. "So, what is it?"

"Rape and sexual harassment – shouldn't take long."

"Can't you be serious?"

Can't you be funny? He wanted to say. But didn't.

"Yeah, course. Don't mind me, the Irish clown who can't resist a laugh."

"So this is just a wind-up?" She was reaching for her book.

"No, sorry. I'm serious. It's just hard to get the tone right, do you see?"

"Do I?"

And as she looked him steadily, eyes twinkling, he was shocked to consider that she might now be winding him up. He couldn't work out what lay beyond this air of cool solemnity, of seeming to know all the answers. Did she really not know that this was how she looked ? And if she looked like that to him and didn't know it, what on earth did he look like to her?

"OK. What have you got so far?"

He handed her the yellow sheet. "There's these headings Chris gave me, and there's a section in the book - but to my mind it's a tad traditional."

"Stone Age is the word. Right, what are you after?"

"Me?"

She grinned at his startled response, and relaxed into teacher mode, on safe, professional ground. "Don't get scared. You. As a teacher. Are you trying to tell these kids something, get them to think, question their opinions, or what?"

"I'm not that sure. This wasn't my idea, you know."

"Maybe. But you're responsible."

The slow, rhythmic way she said it didn't make the unfamiliar word any more attractive.

"You're getting paid, right?"

This was the bit he recognised. He nodded.

"So, you're in charge. Not talking all the time, but it's you that decides what happens. That's what teachers do."

What was this, Education for Beginners? He said nothing.

"Right. Now I'd say – but this is me, right? You don't have to go along with it – I'd say I want these kids to think about how men and women treat each other. Not preach at them, not say everything's hunky-dory, but think. OK so far?"

"It's fine. Brilliant, in fact." He was floating along. She could do anything she wanted.

"So, what problems will you have?"

"Oh, that's easy. I don't know anything. I'm not an expert, the boys are different from the girls, there's a hell of a mixture in the group. Johnny Navarro is just out of short trousers, and Tina Clark's forgotten more than I'll ever know."

"Don't be so sure. Tina's got a good act, but a lot of it's bluff. Just like the lads."

"I'll take your word for it."

"You'd better, believe me." She grinned again. "But you're right. It's not easy. If you like, we could split them for a couple of weeks. Your group and mine. You take the boys, I take the girls."

"Or the other way round, eh?" He smiled, easily, but her face stayed the same, Friendly, but serious. Just the job.

"Maybe later. This way to start."

"It's OK. I was joking."

"But I wasn't. What do you think?"

"I'm not sure I know enough."

"Forget the expert bit. This isn't about you. If you were getting ready to tell them the story of your life – "

Terry fended off the nightmare, but she ignored him.

"This is about them. What they know, what they think. All you're there for is to help them get that clear. So, go through Chris' headings, and assume you're running two sessions with boys. What are you going to give them? What will you ask them to do? And have something ready in case they can't handle the discussion. You know how it is – with men?"

And now there definitely was a warm, roguish smile, as she reached for her book and put it in her bag.

"You really know what you're doing, don't you?"

"I hope so. I'm getting paid too much to be dumb. Right, I've a meeting to go to, and a ton of marking to take home." She rose, and it was natural to walk with her to the door. He didn't offer to carry a bag, but with both her hands full there surely couldn't be an objection to opening the staffroom door.

"Marking's a big deal here, right?"

"In English, yes. It's Brian's speciality. When he interviewed me, we each got five photocopied pieces of work and we had to write a comment. That's how I got the job. Yes, it's a big deal. Good night."

As he watched her walk across the tarmac to her car Terry realised how dodgy his own appointment must seem to teachers who had arrived by the approved, competitive route. For him, it was a relief to have been smuggled in at the last minute, through the back door, with no serious interview, no other candidates. But to his colleagues that would not be a recommendation; rather, a source of suspicion or doubt, which only time and his efforts could allay.

After netball practice, Valerie waited for Sharon, and watched the teachers go by. "There you are. I told you."

"Told me what?"

"Ms Williams and Mr. O'Mara." They started walking home.

"Not that again. Just because they're talking doesn't mean they're going out." Sharon, who was tall and thin and had always been attractive, was sometimes surprised by Valerie's remorseless interest in other people's affairs. Perhaps it was compensation.

"But if they were having an affair, they'd talk, wouldn't they?"

"Teachers talk all the time. That's how they get to be teachers. But there's nothing going on with those two."

Valerie chewed thoughtfully. "What about Mr. Wrench?"

"Mr. O'Mara and Mr. Wrench? Could be..."

"Sharon, I'm serious. Mr. Wrench and Ms. Williams. He's quite dishy, in a trad sort of way."

"Tall, you mean?"

"And modern. Well, for a teacher."

"More than Mr. O'Mara?"

As she stopped to cross the road, Sharon was forced, finally to think about it. "No, that didn't look to me like a tete a tete. More like her sorting him out for mucking up our drama last term."

"He didn't muck it up."

"Yes, he did." Back on the pavement, it was easier to think. "We were supposed to be in the hall, and then Mr. Wrench came in. He put us in that classroom."

"He's bigger than Mr. O'Mara. And I bet he's stronger."

"So?"

"Maybe they had a fight."

"What, over the drama hall?"

"Or Ms. Williams. Have you done your history yet?"

"No. Do you want to come back and talk about it?" And they moved off together, as the lovelife of Rab Butler teachers gave way to chocolate hobnobs and the structure of the medieval village.

Rod Spencer had reached point no. 5 of today's tasks, as listed in his personal organiser.

"Joyce, have you got those extra brochures?"

"Mm. " A bitter January day, so her glance out of the window was more perfunctory than usual. She still didn't like what she saw.

"I'm sorry, but this is urgent. I'm due at a meeting of local employers in twenty minutes and there is a good chance that they will require copies of the brochure. I'm also taking six of the alarms."

"There's only five here. That van out there..."

"What do you mean, only five? I said I'd need six for this meeting. There were six on Monday."

The wilder he became, the more deliberate and calm was her reply. "I'm not talking about Monday. All I'm saying is, we've only got five here today." She looked out of the window again. "Maybe a burglar's helped himself."

"I don't think that's very funny." Stiffly, he gathered the alarms, and tried to balance the brochures on top.

"Here." He was like a kid, really. Joyce stifled the impulse to let him drop them all on his own, and straightened the pile for him. "There is a van loading up in the car park, which I don't recognise."

"I'm afraid I have a prior engagement. " He spoke formally, an actor in a film, trapped in the private fantasy of his executive appointment. "Perhaps you could tell Ms. Macdonald."

"But she's out of school."

"Goodbye."

After he had gone, she watched a teenager and a burly man load two more large boxes into the van. There was something not quite right. As she looked, they turned to face her, and waved cheerily. She ducked down out of sight.

Rick McManus was coining it. From a young teacher of business studies whose job had seemed to be at risk, he had moved into a position of entrepreneurial power. And this lunchtime, he was celebrating; the elite group of sixthformers he had trained had just won a national competition, demolishing teams from prestigious public schools. King Edward's were in the national papers, and

Mr. Higham had hinted that the governors might be particularly grateful. So Terry let him buy the first round.

"Closed circuit video, that's the thing."

"You're getting cameras?"

"We've got 'em. You wouldn't believe the difference it makes."

"Cuts down vandalism, does it?"

"Who knows? Who cares? No, it's free periods. Stuff your marking, nip on down to the viewing room. Kids fagging it, teachers nipping out to the bank, the occasional torrid affair – it beats "Eastenders" every time."

Terry sipped the Guinness slowly, the bitter taste of Rick's success.

"Can anyone watch, then?"

"Oh no. Very top level, this is. One of the deputies does very little else. But he can't work the hardware, so I have to be there to help him out." He gave a predatory grin. "If I ever wanted to retire I could blackmail my way out in weeks." He sipped his drink, and turned, at last, to Terry. "Anyway, how about you?"

"No, I'm not retiring. I'm trying to get a proper job."

"At Rab Butler?"

"Why not?"

"Dodgy future, I'd say. Still, that's your problem. Any chance?"

"I dunno. The head's a decent enough feller..."

"Parnaby? Bit dozy, I heard."

"Yeah, fair enough. But nice with it. I don't know about computers, either."

Rick's expression hardened, as his memory clicked on the Gossip file. "Isn't he knocking off his secretary?"

Terry shrugged. "Who knows? A job, that's all I want. He can be sleeping with every cleaner and dinner lady, if only he'll make me permanent."

"You sound keen. There must be a woman."

"Rick, you've a one-track mind."

"No, you've a one-track mind. Do you ever hear from Lobelia?"

"Lavinia. That's gone. Went back at Christmas. Finished, really."

Rick rubbed his hands. "So who is it now?"

"Don't even ask. You want another?" Terry stood, half reaching for the glass, hoping he'd decide against. No rush, no cash flow problems. All Rick had to calculate was his bladder capacity, roughly the size of Wembley. Terry's fingers counted the pound coins in his pocket.

"Go on. Why not?"

Terry took the glass."I just want to get this inspection over with, and collapse at half-term. That'll do me." He moved to the bar and ordered.

"Which team have you got?"

"Couldn't say."

"We had Mary Prendergast. She is a character, I'm telling you. Looks like a little old lady, but if Prendergast inspects you you've been properly inspected. Ta." He acknowledged the fresh pint, and swigged.

"But there's more than her?"

"Oh yeah. You get the works, the whole team. They put our lot through the wringer."

"But you got a rave write-up?"

"Sure. All part of the deal. Make it look tough. It's all show."

Terry sipped, saving money, taking time. "That's not how it looks to Rod Spencer. He's taking it very seriously."

This time Rick was ready. He put down his glass before the giggle took control.

"No really, he spends a lot of time at it. He's flogging this burglar alarm -"

He tried a sip, but the Guinness trail ran down his suit jacket, as he flourished a handkerchief to wipe his cheek.

"I'm sorry, Terry. He's wasting his time."

"But you don't know that."

"We bought the first one. We took it apart, we know how it works, and we know how to stop it working."

He looked carefully, for signs of bluff. But if Rick was bluffing, there wouldn't be any signs. Tight thin lips, cold blue eyes, nothing given away. That's how he got on.

114

"Anyone who's bought a Rab Butler burglar alarm can still get burgled. It isn't what you'd call a market leader."

"And these competitions, like this thing you won. He does those. He's got a bid in for the computer money, the Japanese outfit, you know?"

"Sayonara systems ? He can forget that."

It seemed so unfair. "But he puts a lot of time in."

"Even so. He can forget it. What's his handicap?"

"You've lost me."

"Golf. That's the key." Rick was riding high, a winner who could see it clear. "The finance director at Sayonara plays golf, and the school which gets the Sayonara money will be represented by a good golfer who's a member of the right club and knows when not to try too hard."

He stood, a trim, neat figure who looked good and knew it. He did a slow, vain mime of a golfer's drive, following his imaginary ball into the distance, way past the bar and the ladies' toilets. "Whenever I'm going out of school, I say I'm on a course. And sometimes it's true."

"I don't believe it."

"No, I don't think you do. But then – " Rick moved towards the door, smiling, confident of his knowledge, his control " – I don't believe in leprechauns. I'll see you, Tes." A wink, a wave, and he was gone. Terry thought he was going to be sick.

Colin stood in his office doorway, lost in admiration, while at her desk Joyce disposed of form 7. The annual interrogation, where schools told the government exactly how many pupils they had, in each class, in each year, at 11.00 am on Thursday, January 22nd. It had to be done, but it was a relief that it could be done by Joyce.

"We're down on last year."

"Yes, I know. Still, it gives us a bit more room."

"Fewer kids, less money, less staff. If it wasn't for Rod's recruits we'd be in trouble."

"We may be in trouble anyway. I don't think Rod's extras are going down that well with the staff."

"Maybe, but the numbers are down." The glasses always made her look stern, but the figures on the paper seemed to add an extra layer of steel. "You'll be sacking someone before the end of the year. Have you checked the part-timers?"

He shifted, and looked away. "I hope it doesn't come to that."

"You'll have to do more than hope."

"Perhaps I could sack myself ? I could save the school forty thousand, just like that. It's an idea…"

Chris Macdonald swept purposefully towards him, clutching a grubby note.

"Colin, this is urgent. The computers have gone."

"I haven't had them.."

She ignored his defensive, illogical reaction with all the contempt it deserved. "Nor has anybody else. On the staff."

And the heavy emphasis of those last three words made him feel distinctly queasy. "Have you asked Rod?"

"The computer room is his territory. Why would he take them out?" Why indeed ? The two management members stared at each other in vacant deadlock, as Joyce made her tentative, decisive move.

"I think I can throw some light on this."

"They've taken the computers!" Rod Spencer stormed towards them, outraged. " The bastards!"

"I'm sorry, Rod. I don't know what you're talking about."

"I do." Chris Macdonald flourished the paper in her hand, with a grim, triumphant smile. "The Jacksons, the O'Donnells and the McGraws."

"You don't know that."

"I do, Rod, and so do you. They've been in the school a few weeks, sussed out where the goodies are, loaded them into the van, and made off."

As if obeying a director, Rod straightened his back, assumed an expression of moral disgust, and summoned his most formal tone. "From someone who claims to be unprejudiced, that's a scandalous accusation."

She returned his outraged glare with a calm, wicked smile.

"Maybe. Unfortunately, it's true."

"Are you sure of this, Chris?" Parnaby, two moves behind, struggled to catch up.

"Yes. Some of the kids saw them go."

Joyce took advantage of the pause. "I did see a van loading up some boxes, last Tuesday."

"Well, why didn't you say anything?" Rod stared angrily down at her, with an effort restraining himself from adding a final, damning 'woman' to the charge.

"I did. I tried to tell you. You were meeting some employers."

Chris tried to hide the smile, but not that hard.

"Still – " Parnaby looked around his divided team, desperate for some way to turn this rout into a tactical retreat. "At least we can include them on form 7."

"I'm afraid not." Now that her triumph was complete, Chris made sure her face was straight. She offered him the grubby piece of paper. "They left a note to say they're leaving. They've even dated it, today. There were a couple of text books with it, and £1.15 dinner money they'd borrowed, but unfortunately" – a consoling, devastating glance at Rod – "no computers."

Mick Wall skimmed the staffroom noticeboard with the usual casual glance and then was held, transfixed.

"I don't believe it."

"What's up, Mick?"

"This OFSTED team."

"What's the shock? Is there a teacher there?"

"Yeah. Philip West. My old mate Westy."

Jackie was incredulous. "Don't tell me, Mick. You haven't got friends in high places?"

"It wasn't high places then. Hills Lane Secondary, 1978. I was wood, he was metal." Chris Macdonald came in, saw the teachers gathered round the notice, and Mick in full flow. By reflex, she played it cool, looking for a neutral contact.

"You see, Sylvia, we've got Mary Prendergast."

"Really?" Not a good choice. Sylvia stared at her. " Which year is she in?"

"She's not a pupil, she's HMI. Well, OFSTED now. She's heading our inspection team." She aimed an enthusiastic smile at her colleague, but it ricochetted unnoticed into a pile of abandoned PE kit.

"I'm sorry, but I really cannot muster any enthusiasm for the prospect of being told how to do my job by a combination of well-meaning amateurs and failed headteachers."

She had started; she would finish. "Mary's different. She's one of us."

"Not a teacher?"

"Well, she used to be. And she's very hot on equal opportunities and pastoral care."

Sylvia treated her to an unnerving sneer. "But not the imperfect tense."

"I'm sorry?"

"Don't mention it. I teach languages. I expect that the pupils will not understand a single word I say, but I used to have some expectations of the staff. Ah well." 15- love, was the unspoken commentary as Sylvia swept away, and Chris wondered who to speak to next.

Mick, tactful despite his bluff exterior, resumed the chair and rescued her. "Hey…and there's more, folks. Pete Wrigley. He was a drinking mate of Westy's. I only met him in the pub. Right nutter he was - nine foot three and thick as two short planks. I think he played rugby for Cornwall, before the beer got him."

"It can't be the same one." Against all the evidence, Jackie liked to believe in a rational, benevolent world.

Terry was disappointed. "Pity. He sounds worth a look."

"Oh no. If you can miss a visit from Pete Wrigley, you definitely should." Mick looked round, relishing a character of epic scale. "I've seen some mayhem in my time, but if Pete Wrigley hits town, lock up your wives and daughters."

Jill strolled in slowly, catching the tail end, and sat down. "I despair of you, Mick, really. I only go out for a breather, and as soon as I'm back you're into stereotypes."

He grinned back. "Pete Wrigley is a one-off. OFSTED only, the lay inspector who lays everything in sight."

"So what do you expect me to do?"

Later, Terry found it hard to sort out. At the time there was just this puppyish urge to keep the joke going, be in the crowd, keeping OFSTED at bay, but also be matey with Jill.

"From the sound of it, you could do us all a favour."

Mick whistled, the chatter died. Jill was staring at him.

"What sort of favour, precisely?"

Precise was the one thing Terry didn't want to be.

"Well, from what Mick says –"

"Come on, kid, we've got a stock cupboard to sort." Jackie was standing, urging Jill into action, away from danger.

"No, wait a minute. What is this? What favour, Terry?"

"Forget it. Just messing about. You do the stock cupboard – better class of company altogether."

Jill allowed Jackie to shoo her out, just, as Mick Wall watched them go. He dropped a heavy, powerful hand on Terry's shoulder. "Don't let it get to you, mate. She loves you really."

Out in the car park, Rod Spencer harangued a group of mystified contractors. The rain was slanting down, their hands were cold, but nothing could diminish the man's enthusiasm. Joyce looked out of the window of Parnaby's office, watching with dismay.

"Colin?"

"Mmm?" He continued to read through another glossy account of the government's latest triumph in education policy. It was hard going.

"What exactly is Rod doing out there?"

"Something to do with security, he said."

"It's not video cameras, is it? King Edward's have them now, and he's very jealous." Her voice had a bit more edge, as she waited for him to look up. Eventually, he succumbed.

"I know they have. I also know that they cost more than a hundred pounds, and I haven't approved their purchase."

"I just wondered." She tried to make it sound airy, hypothetical.

"You don't trust me, do you? You think I'll give in."

"All I know is, he's been sending off for brochures from security companies left, right and centre. And he's got a gleam in his eye. Which in my book spells trouble."

In his, too, although he wasn't going to admit it. "Rod always has a gleam in his eye," he observed, rather sadly, as it occurred to him that it was a long time since anyone had said that about him. Maybe the first time Joyce had joined him for coffee…was it three, four years now? It seemed so long ago.

He was sat in his empty classroom, clearing the debris of the day, when she walked past.

"Jill?" She came back, and looked questioningly through the doorway. "Can I talk to you about tutorial? Blokes?"

"Sure." She came in, put down her bag, and sat opposite him, across the teacher's desk, ready for work. "So, what have you got?"

He handed over a pile of cuttings, and the notes he'd made for the lessons. Some ideas for role play, a list of questions for small groups, and a writing task entitled "How to Handle the Girls."

"I'm not sure I like the 'handle' bit."

"You should have seen the rejects – "Rules for Pulling", "Getting Off in Ten Easy Lessons", "How to Score with a Skirt." "

"You're really on a roll, aren't you?"

"That's why I'm asking for help, miss. 'Cos it's hard." And he gave her a cheeky grin, which also said, I'm serious.

"OK." She paused, and read on, more carefully.

"You see, to my mind it's got to be a bit jokey –"

"Why?"

"Because they're scared. It's hard for them to take things seriously."

"But why should they be any less serious than the girls?"

'"Search me. But they are. I mean, look at your class. Are you telling me the boys are as mature as the girls, as capable of discussion?"

"No, Terry. You're right. But why is it like that?" And she looked at him with anguish, a seeker after truth.

"If I knew that I'd be rich. I'm the beginner here, right? I just reckon it has to be light, jokey, to start with. Otherwise they'll get embarrassed."

She thought about it, nodding, recognising a teaching strategy different from her own, but which could work. "So long as it doesn't stay that way. There's no point in just making jokes. Especially not those jokes." She looked at him, and neither of them needed examples.

"Right, fine. And, er...I'm sorry about the inspection feller. Wrigley."

"That's OK. From what Jackie says, he is a bit strange. But this is good, Terry. I like the cuttings. Didn't know you read "Just Seventeen." "

"They're from a couple of girls in my tutor group. Said they'd break me in gently, what with my deprived childhood. Being Irish, and male, and that."

"Yeah, I can see it's a problem."

"How about you?" She was still looking at the paperwork, and he tried to make it casual, just slotted in. She didn't look up.

"No, I'm not Irish. Not male either, worse luck. Still, you can't have everything."

"I didn't mean that. You're from Leicester, yeah?"

"What did you think ? Deepest Harlem, with Motown singin' in ma ears?"

"It crossed my mind."

She sat back, moved away from the desk, crossed her arms and smiled.

"It was Johnny Cash, actually. And Loretta Lyn."

"You're kidding?"

"Nope. My dad was a country fan. On the buses."

"What about your mum?"

"Teacher."

"So that's where you get it from."

"Mmm..maybe. OK, Mr. O'Mara, tonight's tutorial is done. I've got to get something for my tea. I'd say this is coming along fine."

"Well, thanks."

"For a new teacher. And an Irishman. And a male."

And he thought, he hoped, she was grinning, as she swung her bag onto her shoulder and strode out of his classroom. Maybe he was doing OK.

CHAPTER Six:

FEBRUARY

Cometh the hour, cometh the man. The inspection was imminent, and Rod Spencer was raring to go. Mary Prendergast was a feminist virago well past her sell-by date, but Dr. Wrigley was a gift from heaven. Peter Wrigley, author of "Managing or Getting By?", the prophet of management for education. No-nonsense, cut the crap, go for the jugular – Wrigley had what it takes.

It did not occur to Rod that he personally might not have what it takes, so far as Wrigley was concerned. The man's presence on the site was enough to confirm victory, so long as Parnaby could be kicked into action. Rod had the floor of his office, and at least some of his attention, but it was still hard going.

"As I see it, the strategy's simple."

"It is?"

"Wrigley's a market man, he knows what sells, and we have to convince him that we know the selling business." He paced anxiously, desperate to kindle some enthusiasm. "Recruiting, promotion, local publicity and test results."

"You've done nothing else for the past year. We're not bad."

"Not bad is not good enough." He grimaced. "You know the testing plan I gave you last term?" He swivelled and returned to the desk, an American attorney in a black and white film.

"Yes, I've got it somewhere…" Joyce would immediately have

twigged that the paper was lost. Less alert to his leader's signals, Spencer allowed himself to believe that this flurrying mime through a pile of papers might come up with the goods. It did not.

"We need it. We need it now."

"But it hasn't been discussed by heads of department "

"In an ideal world I'd agree, but what we have here is a crisis." He sat down, next to the desk, and leaned forward. "You have read it?"

Parnaby bluffed. "Oh..er..yes. Naturally."

"Well, if we can get it under way, we might just overhaul King Edward's." He loomed over the desk, ever closer. "They've had their inspection, and they didn't have this scheme in place, but any week now..."

"Do you think so?" Were all schools teeming with little Rod Spencers, cloning such blueprints in their sweaty little hands?

"Sure of it. Carpe diem." Adrenalin rush at this opportunity to use one of the three Latin phrases of whose meaning he felt confident.

"But if there are snags?"

"That's the point of appendix F. Spot the trouble before it happens."

"And you really think you've done that?"

As he weakened, Colin knew it was a mistake. Was this how seduction felt, this easing, slipping into an accelerating slide ? He felt the surge of speed, the failure of restraint, the abdication of control.

Spencer played humble. " I'm biased. It's for you to judge. You call the shots, you carry the can..." An innocent shrug, as his wide eyes and open palms promised infinite devotion - and laid the blame. "All I'm saying is, if you want me to do the donkey work, I can have it up and running before Wrigley arrives. We'll blow King Edward's away." He rose, invigorated by the whiff of cordite.

"But we're in the same business."

"Yes, and it's all-out war. I smashed them on the computer deal; now we'll grind them into the dirt."

"The computers?"

"Yes, well, OK. We lost some of them. But if we get more now there's a chance to upgrade our mainframe, and build in some state of the art software. It's actually a blessing in disguise."

"If you say so. How much will this cost?"

"It's a bargain. A real investment. Computerwise, this will put Rab Butler on the map."

"But how much? More than a hundred?"

Sylvia March, languid in purple, stretched her legs and purred into the staffroom phone. "Yes, Miss Thorpe...no, I understand, really...I'm sure you were very good at French at school. So was I, actually....no....no....that's not relevant in the least. Look, I don't wish to be rude, but the simple fact of the matter is that I am Craig's teacher and I have marked his work as worthy of a D, which is what it would get in a public examination. Whether you saw it, checked it, or wrote it all yourself, even if you were professor of French at the University of Oxford, would make not one iota of difference. Good day." She hung up.

"You're too soft," Mick admonished. "Give it to her straight."

"Stupid woman. Just because she does her son's homework for him she thinks he'll get better grades. Her tenses are all wrong, and she's hopeless with accents."

"Parents today – I blame the kids, myself."

"Nice one, Terry." Mick nodded, as at a promising apprentice. "I think we'll let you stay." He drained his coffee mug, and shoved it into his overall pocket. "Right, I'm off to the testing bay."

"Vehicle maintenance?"

"No such luck. Invigilation, in the hall."

"But it can't be exams, in February?"

"Naughty, Sylvia. You haven't been reading Rod's messages of love."

"Hang on, Mick. I'm in the hall next. Year nine drama."

"Not any more, son. The testing times are upon us. Welcome to the OFSTED world."

Angry and confused, Terry rushed to collect his class, and start the long, harassed search for a space. The hall was transformed. Examination desks stood in regular rows, like stamps on an album page. Cursing, a caretaker was completing the pattern by the stage, while Terry's class ran up and down the aisles. How was he going to survive, let alone impress the inspectors, if he didn't have a room ?

Joyce liked her central, open space, the combination of power and freedom, but as the pressure mounted it increasingly exposed her to the strains of others. She sensed Rod hovering at her elbow, but refused to look up.

"Joyce ? My test papers?"

"Wait a minute, please."

His fingers drummed on the desk. "It is urgent."

"I'm sure it is. But the head wants more brochures, and I have some diagrams to print for Miss Macdonald."

Curious, Rod picked up the sheet, and abruptly replaced it. "Is she serious?"

"Perhaps you'd like to ask her?" A sweet, lethal smile.

"No, no, that's fine. The test papers?"

She shuffled through the neat piles, and grunted with satisfaction. Everything was exactly as it should be. There is no way she would have laid herself open to so obvious an attack.

"They're not due for another fortnight."

"Originally, no. But now they are. Mr. Parnaby's agreed that the programme should be brought forward, so it's in place before the inspection."

"Has he ?" Pause, internal memo. Some backbone stiffening to be done. "If that's the case, then I'll see what I can do."

"So long as they're ready by 1.15."

"1.15 today?"

"Of course. That's when they're sitting the test." He smiled, more to himself than to her, and moved away down the corridor.

Monday morning. A Rover purred into the school drive. What had once been an open expanse of tarmac was now segregated. A padlocked iron gate cut off the area nearest to the school, with the forbidding sign "CAR PARK FOR SITE EMPLOYEES ONLY."

The Rover turned obediently into one of the parking bays marked out beyond the gate. The car stopped. From the driver's seat a small, middle-aged man emerged, and walked round to open the passenger's door. A wispy little lady with grey hair got out. Then, from the back door, a huge figure emerged, with a black executive case. They ignored the arrows which directed them to RECEPTION and started to walk, slowly, observantly, round the perimeter of the school.

Mick watched them from the hall. Not a religious man, he said a brief prayer for Rab Butler and all who taught in her, but particularly for himself. Even the knowledge that one of these was his mate Westy could not dispel the ingrained teacher impulse, unease at the advent of a suit.

Dennis Waite sat in the back row, bored. Dennis was often bored in lessons, but this was a different sort of lesson. No video, no talking, no moving around. Just sit still and say nothing for an hour. There was some reading and writing to be done, for those that liked that sort of thing, but reading and writing were not among Dennis' strengths.

There was no mate near enough to chat to, no Tina to lead him into town. Dennis was bored. Slowly, idly, he started to tear little strips off his exam paper. The little strips were chewed, one at a time, until they became soggy pellets, lined up at the front of the desk. With a controlled detachment he fired them, at one-minute intervals, timed by the examination clock.

Each one hit a different neck, and it was only after a startled yelp from his fourth victim that Dennis felt Mr.Wall seize him by the left ear, raise him to his feet, and escort him out of the hall. As he went, he noticed a little old woman, watching and taking notes.

Phil West leaned back in an easy chair by the window and surveyed Parnaby's office. They'd agreed Mary would snoop round while he softened up the head, and after years as a teaching peasant he still got a buzz from bossing around the boss. Wrigley would have what football managers liked to describe as a roving role.

"I don't want you to get the wrong idea about us."

A hamster in an occupied cage, Parnaby looked as if he was incapable of getting an idea of any kind.

"We are not Her Majesty's Inspectors, but our scrutiny will be no less rigorous. OFSTED has an element of lay inspection, and some of your staff may as a result see us as amateurs ."

"Surely not."

"But that would be unwise." West rose to his feet, and scanned the wall. Kids' work, quite nice but nothing special. No computer on the desk, no management texts on the shelves, another harmless dodo. From his pocket he took a newspaper cutting, with the headline "QUALITY AT KING EDWARD'S", and handed it across.

"We can make your school, or we can break it."

"Quite so."

"And which it's going to be will partly depend on you."

"It will ? Well…er….we're anxious to co-operate in any way possible. It's a good opportunity for us, to see ourselves as others see us…and, um…well…we look forward to hearing what you have to say."

"Bullshit." Or at least, that's what he thought he heard.

"I beg your pardon?"

West flourished a handkerchief, as though he had simply sneezed, and smiled pleasantly. "A word of warning. Some of your colleagues may find Dr. Wrigley's approach somewhat unconventional. As I am sure you are aware, he is the author of a best-selling guide to management techniques. He is also used to getting his own way. My informal advice would be to avoid obstructing him in any fashion whatsoever."

"Am I to take that as a threat?"

"You're in charge here, Mr. Parnaby. You must decide that for yourself."

Out in the car park, it was cold. Mick Wall led Dennis past the staff cars, round a new metal gate, and then he stopped, by an old maroon Rover.

"That's the one, Dennis. I want it spotless by lunchtime, and I don't want any badges missing. Got it?"

"Sir."

Dennis slipped into dumb insolence, and put the bucket down.

"Come on, then. Let's see you."

The water was warm and soapy, as he swirled the sponge around. Maybe this wouldn't be so bad. In any case, it was better than the testing bay.

Sylvia sat in the staffroom, cherishing a free period, marking a set of books. The staffroom door slammed, and Terry rushed through, into the workroom, and crouched down. Only belatedly did he see that she was there. He emerged, and stood, sheepish. "Sorry."

"Don't mind me. Is this some kind of simulation?"

"No. This is the real thing. Terror."

"It must be interesting, being a drama teacher." Her eyes stayed fixed on the books, as her red pen pecked away.

"That's what I used to think . Could you do me a favour?"

She looked up. "I'm no good at drama. I look terrible in black."

"Could you look outside the staffroom? A tall bloke, inspector."

"Oh, the gorilla." She put her pen down, and closed the book. "You mustn't mind him."

"I do. I mind him a lot. I'm in the biology lab, doing a lesson on fear. This man suddenly gets up, and says 'I'm not convinced.' I'm telling you, you could hear a pin drop. And the bastard doesn't even teach.

So I asked if he'd like to take over, and he says no, he just wants the kids to get the smell of fear. Then he picks up this scalpel, and asks if I'd like to sing as a counter-tenor...well, that's when I came out."

Retold, it was pathetic. He had fallen for a simple bluff, and failed. They'd screw him, get him thrown out. Sylvia rose gracefully, sauntered to the door, and looked out. She looked both ways, shut it and came back. He had never heard her sound so warm.

"Don't worry. Safely back in his cage. He tried to muck up my lesson but I soon put him straight. He thought he'd be witty and sing "La Plume de ma Tante" with a string of onions round his neck."

She got up and retrieved two sheets of paper from her pigeon-hole. She skimmed the pink one quickly. "Not today, thank you. Luckily I did a year at the Sorbonne, so I've a fluent line in French insults. I don't think it's anatomically possible, but it seemed to shut him up." Then she came to the green one.

"Blast! I'm covering Mr. Harwood next. Again. More boring Geography. 'Work in pigeonhole', it says." She shrugged dismissively, as her hand moved across the pigeonholes. From Harwood's it retrieved an aging sandwich. "I'm not sure that this doesn't constitute a health hazard." She dropped the sandwich in the bin, and returned to the pigeonhole, to find a videotape and worksheet. "Ah – the wonders of technology."

Jill Williams hurried in, and collapsed, exhausted. "Hi, Sylvia. Are you free?"

"No longer, alas. I'm covering. Here, have a cheerful little message from Chris Macdonald on the effects of solvent abuse." She dropped the pink sheet on to the chair next to Jill.

She read aloud "Drowsiness, bad temper, inability to respond to stimulus."

Sylvia moved to the door. "That seems to be most of year eleven accounted for. Enjoy your free, it may be your last."

Jill waved an acknowledgement as Sylvia left, and then noticed Terry.

"Aren't you teaching?"

"Oh, sod it. Er..yeah. Yeah, so I am. Fancy you knowing that. I'm not really myself, today…" Dazed, uncertain, defeated, Terry staggered off in search of fresh humiliation. Sadly, she returned to the pink sheet; the symptoms seemed to fit.

Joyce looked out at the gloom and drizzle as Spencer used her phone.

"Yes, Mr. Carter, and I'm grateful. I'll get the paperwork done, but it was vital to have the new machines in this week. Believe me, if there's ever anything …No, not at all. There's no problem with payment. We do have these inspectors in. I don't know if it would be possible for you to drop in Friday morning, have a word with them …? The computer room, eleven o'clock. I'll lay on coffee. That's great. Thanks, Mr. Carter, till Friday at eleven, then." He hummed cheerfully, as he put the phone down.

"Mr. Spencer?"

"Sorry, but Mr. Carter is a co-opted governor of the school and our future is at stake. Must dash." His long legs strode down the corridor as he hummed away, content at having made the decisive move in his chessboard clash with fate.

Next to the phone was Chris Macdonald, also breathless, also self-important. "Hello, Lorna? Hi. Chris here. We've got Mary Prendergast in school, and I thought you might come in, show her some of the stuff we did on homosexuality. Our computer room's free at the moment –"

Joyce waved frantically, in vision, but beneath her notice. "Yes, poor Rod's had his hardware pinched. It does sound nasty, doesn't it – such an intimate violation." She chuckled. "So we should be able to put up a display. How about Friday? Say, eleven?"

Joyce tried again, but she was wasting her time.

"That's great. I'll look forward to seeing you. Bye." She put down the receiver, and stared down, her bullet head focussed on the seated secretary. "I have to say, Joyce, that life would be a lot simpler if you left me to manage the content of the pastoral curriculum, and you looked after the filing."

The inspection made a difference. A squad of suited spies, lurking in playgrounds and classrooms throughout the day, clipboards in hand, could not go unnoticed. The kids were excited, nosy, generally pleasant. The teachers were in school, on time, and perpetually on edge. And even some of the governors were around.

"Mrs. Grabowska!" An anxious, shrill demand.

"Hello, Sheila. Sorry, I'm in a rush – OFSTED, you know."

"I shan't keep you. I want to get hold of Mr. O'Mara."

"Well, don't we all?" Jackie flashed a smile, and put down the plastic bags she was carrying, to get a better grip.

"I'm sorry?" Sheila was puzzled, a non-teacher in a foreign land.

"Just kidding." She picked up the bags again, and moved off. "Have you tried the hall?"

And she was gone. Sheila watched her bounce off down the corridor, loaded with marking and confidence. He couldn't be in the hall, because the tests were there. Surely she would know that. Were they trying to tell her something ?

In The White Horse, Thursday lunchtime, Mick Wall and Phil West held their reunion. Mick bought the first round, while Phil performed.

"I'll tell you one thing. It beats teaching."

"Yeah?"

"The training was tough, mind. You pay your own travel and subsistence. Living in the mobile home, baked beans on the camping stove – they don't show that in the adverts."

Mick looked at his former colleague. He was a small man, but he'd looked after himself. He had hardly any paunch, the remains of a tan, an expensive silk tie and the heavy tweed coat he had carefully hung up. He wasn't exactly struggling.

"Sounds like they're doing it on the cheap."

"Now, Michael, showing your age. Market opportunity is the phrase you're looking for."

"I don't get you."

"Once you're in, you're coining it. Thirty thou a time for a week's work – not bad, eh?" He chuckled, and gave Mick a matey nudge, just like the old days. But they were on different planets now.

"You get thirty thousand, for this?"

"Not me. The team. Plus three thousand for the software and the paperwork. Mary gets the most, of course. But she's worth it."

"She looks like my gran."

"Right. She wears a suit, and she can talk bullshit with the best. But she knows more dirty jokes than you've forgotten, and when she's on vodka she can be really mean. That's between you and me, mind. But Mary's what gets us the contracts. She makes us respectable."

Mick Wall looked increasingly puzzled, facing a crossword where he couldn't understand the clues. "And what about Doctor Thingy?"

"Wrigley? A little taste of spearmint in the night?" He laughed, a sinister little giggle. "No, Pete doesn't make us respectable."

"So how did he get into it?"

"When this started, that was the rule. You had to have at least one inspector who didn't know anything."

Mick nodded. "So he's ignorant?"

"Correction. Was ignorant. A quick learner, is our Pete. He's sussed it all - management, finance, business systems."

"But lessons, kids? He doesn't know anything about them?"

And now Phil West was confused. "So?"

"Doesn't that matter?"

"No. They soon pick it up." He sipped his beer. "There's this course, for beginners."

"So how long's that?"

"Five days."

Mick had always played safe with the risks, stuck with alchohol and nicotine. If he'd ever tangled with ecstasy or LSD, surely it would feel a bit like this, heady but adrift. "You're making this up."

"No. All you need is a bit of nerve and a letter heading."

"But you do have to write the reports?"

"Not really. Pete's got 'em all on the computer. You just knock in the codes, and out comes the report. I'd guess your place was a 4G 3E 9X, but I could be wrong. It's up to Mary."

Mick gazed, befuddled, at his former mate, an expert on Mars. "So you don't need to be here at all?"

"No. The governors prefer it, but we could do it all over the phone. You have got a fax?"

"What if the press got hold of this?"

"They love it. It's standards, accountability, all the things we never had in the bad old days. We don't just do the reports, we write the hand-outs." He reached in his pocket for a cutting. "Here, that's the place down the road."

"King Edward's?"

"That's the one. That's a 5G 4E 10X." He handed it across the table, careful to avoid a puddle of beer. "Keep it. A reminder of quality. Fancy another?"

Mick looked at his watch. "No, better get back. We've got these inspectors in." A brief, nervous laugh. "So this is it, then, till you retire?"

Westy drained his glass. "Mm. Could be. We might go into preparation."

"What's that?"

"Going round schools, getting them ready to be inspected."

"And they pay you for that?"

"Sure. Big bucks. Some guys get more for that than they do for the real thing. They go in with a folder of policies – anything you haven't got, there it is. They do the training, but they never actually inspect a school at all." He beamed, relishing Mick's discomfiture. He was the first kid on the street to know the truth about Santas Claus.

"So the training's wasted, then?"

"Oh no. They're using it, flat out. Someone, somewhere along the line, may be wasting money, but it certainly isn't them." He licked his lips, the flavour of bitter, the relish of success. "Like I said, Mick. A market opportunity."

Mick, almost crushed, saw a flicker of hope. "I don't suppose you've got a vacancy?"

"Sorry, son. Hard, really, with you being wood and me metal. I could show you some samples, though. Friday night, when we're done, have a dekko at the merchandise. A bright lad could make a few quid that way."

As Terry entered the staffroom, he saw that Jill was alone. Sat in an armchair, hands holding the book as for a bible reading, her frizzy head bowed in concentration.

"Is it good?"

She looked up, disconcerted. "Sorry?"

"The book you're reading. Who is it? Any good?"

"Terry McMillan. Yeah, it's OK."

All she wanted was for him to go away. He didn't move away, he didn't sit down. He kept at it. "Who's your favourite author?"

She snapped, "What is this, a quiz show?" and then seemed to think better of it. After a moment's reflection she offered, " Now, it's probably Toni Morrison."

"Is that Van's kid brother?" She laughed, for about a nanosecond. Who the hell was Tony Morrison?" So you're not a Virago fanatic, then?"

"How do you mean, Terry?" Very calm, tensed.

"One of those feminists who can't read anything unless it's written by a woman."

She looked up at him, incredulous, and this time the laugh was unrestrained. What ever it was, it hit the spot.

"What's up?"

She shook her head. Slowly, the gravelly voice rolled out. "It's OK. It's nothing, really. Don't worry about it." But she was still having trouble controlling seismic spasms of laughter. What made her jokes so much better than his? And what was the joke, anyway?

"You're always busy, aren't you?"

"Here I'm busy. Though I sometimes read on the firm's time. I'm paid to work, Terry. Catch me on a holiday, and I can relax. Watch the Simpsons, go to movies, play some CDs. But they pay me here, so I might as well work. Yeah?"

He shifted uneasily. Given the situation, what is the actor's next best move ? "So, what do you do to relax?"

"I eat drama teachers." She smiled seraphically. "Why?"

"I just wondered if you were doing anything Friday, eh?"

"As it happens, I am. Sorry."

She turned back to her book, and Terry turned to go. At the staffroom door he was shunted gently to one side by Mick Wall, a concerned observer of his failed attempt. "Keep at it, lad. She'll soon be eating out of your hand."

"Yeah. That's what I'm scared of."

"How do you mean?"

"Will she stop when she gets to the bone?"

At half-past ten on Friday, Nemesis arrived. Joyce knew it was coming. To herself, but to no-one else, she admitted that she was looking forward to it. Both of them had it coming.

"Joyce, I've got Lorna Samuels coming in at eleven, and..."

"Chris, have you been in the computer room?"

They stood, like duellists, focussed at opposite ends of a corridor of hate. The line of it crossed her desk, but they were oblivious to that, and to her.

"It's not out of bounds, is it? I didn't think there was anything more of value to be stolen."

He vowed that her sarcasm must have no effect, so there was a brief pause, while the venom was absorbed. "I don't think that's very funny. As it happens, I'm expecting a new delivery of computers, and there's Gay Rights posters all over the wall."

She stood her ground, squarely facing him. "Are you worried that they'll affect the electricity supply?"

He tried to stand taller, talk formal, beat her down. "I have Mr. Carter coming in at eleven to speak to the inspectors –"

"But they'll be in the computer room."

"I know."

"– talking to Lorna Samuels."

"I don't think so." He turned, magisterially, to Joyce. "You were here when I arranged it." The line of fire became a triangle, as Chris also turned.

"Joyce clearly heard me fixing things with Lorna."

"There must be some mistake."

"Maybe, but I don't think it's mine."

"Perhaps we should ask Colin to resolve this – "

"If you really think that's necessary, then – "

"No." Her knowledge of the truth, and her concern to protect

Parnaby, made Joyce's intervention more definite than she'd planned. Both deputies, shocked out of their status, gaped at this rash ancillary who had stopped them in full flood. She had no choice.

"At eleven o'clock, the inspectors are finalising their report, as I tried to tell you both, earlier in the week. They are therefore unavailable to see either Mr. Carter or Miss Samuels, and I have taken the liberty of informing both to that effect. If you do wish me to make bookings on your behalf, I would be most grateful if you could say so explicitly. And now, if you'll excuse me, I have some urgent condoms to print."

Four o'clock Friday, the staffroom, and the sense of exhausted triumph. Look, we have come through !

Mick caressed a mug of tea, and winked at Terry.

"Well done, young 'un, you made it."

"Only just."

"There's tea in the pot."

Terry sank gratefully into a sagging chair. "No thanks. Just a week on a health farm."

"Get out there, kid. It's the weekend."

Sylvia was not impressed. "I suppose that means the usual recipe – sixteen pints, three nightclubs and a vindaloo curry?" She gathered her belongings together.

Terry turned to Mick. "I asked, Mick. She turned me down."

"Don't take no for an answer. The name of the game is pursuit."

"As in cycling, or trivial?" Sylvia, eavesdropping, loitered at the door.

"Don't discourage the lad. "She smiled, waved and left. "So, who's the competition?"

Terry shook his head in rhythmic gloom. "I don't know. Well, I've got an idea. But it's no use."

"It's no use sitting there. Get out, kid, see what you're up against. If you don't ask, you don't get."

"I'm asking, Mick, and I'm not getting. I might as well go home."

Chris Macdonald fretted with her organiser as she loitered for some news. For the third time since lessons had finished she came past Parnaby's door. Joyce, without looking up from her desk, gestured at a pile of orange papers. "Your condoms are over there."

"Thank you."

"The Inspector took one. Mrs. Prendergast."

"Really?" To Joyce, the excessive enthusiasm of her reaction looked pathetic. "What did she say?"

"She asked for a couple of glasses, and took a bottle of vodka into the head's office."

"You're joking." Joyce looked at her, firmly. "You're not joking. Sorry, Joyce, I should have known. Have they been in long?"

"Over an hour. He doesn't hold his drunk so well as he used to. I have a feeling this could be a long night."

She was thirty yards ahead, and in comfort. The tall tracksuited figure jogged easily along the pavement, skipping on and off when she met a road, avoiding kids and obstacles with mild sidesteps that never broke the rhythm of her run. Her back was straight, but without apparent strain, as if it was natural to move like that, fluid, in control. The queen of the slipstream, with Terry floundering in her wake.

He was in agony. His right shoe was leaking, each breath was harder to draw and there was a pain in his side slicing through him like a knife. He was a lifelong shambler, a shoulders-stooped sway-around mover, who could be a hilarious disco dancer or convincing soldier in a play, but left to his own devices he was a mess. Now he remembered why he gave up sport in the sixth form, watched football rather than played it, gave his last set of boots to Oxfam. He remembered now, when it was all too late.

He kept Jill in his sights, hanging back so she wouldn't see him, but determined not to let her go. One way or another he would find out tonight, the state of play, the other man, how bad his chances were. In the flat it had seemed like a good idea, some kind of resolution, but now, panting and slopping through the driving rain, he felt a total prat.

He should never have listened to Mick Wall. Mick would be at home, sitting in the warm with a glass of whisky, Tina Turner on the stereo and kids playing by the fire. He'd be going up to bed with Karen, maybe for the rest of his life, while Terry stupid O'Mara was flogging around the streets. And why? Because he'd been daft enough to listen to Mick Wall.

He'd settled into a breathless rhythm of stumbling self-pity, and almost lost her. He saw a glimpse, vanishing to the left down a narrow lane, off the main road, into the dark. Terry sprinted to catch her and then realised the noise of his feet would give him away. He tried to stop abruptly, but the soles of his trainers were worn and would not grip. Hopelessly off balance, depressed, defeated, he toppled on to the damp, cold asphalt, grazed his knee and elbow, and lay there in the rain.

It made no sense at all. She had turned into the Welbeck Road, heading towards school. His private video replay had worked through the possibilities – a solo run in the moonlight, a quick jog to a sordid flat, a Rolls purring to the kerbside to pick her up. Even a tryst in the park; he was ashamed of this one, but he was tired. But at ten to seven on a Friday night Jill Williams was definitely running to school. Terry knew he was mad.

In the staffroom, Phil West, lubricated with lager, was making the sales pitch he did best. Despite himself, Mick was impressed. Hills Lane Secondary was a long time ago.

"This is a good one. Computer programme for assessing new kids – scores on attendance, non-verbal IQ and behaviour. Push 'em through at 11, and this'll give you their scores at 14. It will even" he added a meaningful stare, to deter scepticism, "give you a reliable estimate of their performance in Shakespeare. The tests, that is."

"Three years later? You can't possibly say what will happen in those three years. Whatever happened to teaching?"

"What indeed? By then, lad, you are long gone. You have sold your programme and moved on. It's near enough accurate, and it's selling a bomb. If you know at 11 which kids are worth taking in and which aren't – well, you're halfway there."

Mick surveyed the staffroom floor. The large suitcase was opened out, to reveal racks of videos, shelves of computer programmes – "SUM QUALITY", "PUNCTUATION FOR PROFIT", "KARAOKE KING LEAR FOR SLOW LEARNERS."

"And all this is part of the job?"

"Good God, no. This is a sideline. But it fits very snugly, goes with the job. If your Inspector reports that your Maths is weak, and your kids don't know their tables, then it's ever so reassuring to be able to tell the governors that you have bought – from the very same inspector – a programme that will put that right. Neat, huh?"

"But what if it doesn't put it right?"

"Like I told you, Mick, you're long gone. Another customer, another school."

Joyce looked at her watch. Three hours they'd been there. He had his own toilet, which was a mercy, so long as he'd the sense to use it. She'd heard nothing, except occasional laughter, and more of that from the woman. Tough old bird, that, not to be underestimated. Back at four fifteen she'd left strict instructions that they weren't to be disturbed, and Joyce had a strong feeling that that ruled out the usual stratagems – urgent parents, family illness, phone-call from the chair of governors. If she was going to break it up she'd have to use the firebell, and that was very definitely a last resort. She looked again at the crossword, knowing she was wasting her time. There wasn't an unsolved clue there that she hadn't read ten times already.

Phil West, inspector-cum-entrepreneur, was moving into overdrive. Mick was caught, a fly in his web, but a fly with a finite wallet. How on earth was he going to pay for this stuff?

So Rod Spencer entered a silent room. On the staffroom floor was the range of QUALITAPES ("Learn at home to score at school") with Mick Wall appearing stunned, while Phil West looked on with a benevolent smile. Spencer's entry changed the rules. Mick was a mate, but this was a client with an order book.

"Mr. Spencer! Just the man. Sit down."

"They're still in there. What's going on?"

"Don't worry. Mary has it all in hand. Believe me, Mrs. Prendergast knows exactly what she's doing."

"Well, that's a relief, 'cos Uncle Colin hasn't a clue." Mick's observation was instinctive and demonstrably true, so he was unaffected by Rod's attempt at rebuttal.

"Mr. Wall, I must protest ."

"It's all right. You can talk freely, you're among friends." West pointed to the goodies on display. "What we have here is a strategy for cancelling King Edward's lead."

"You do?"

"It must be galling to keep taking second place to a potato."

"Well, it is."

"Why don't you join us? Mick's just nipping out to replenish the store of lager."

"I am?"

"You are. Oh, sorry, I seem to have left my wallet behind. You don't have a tenner, do you?"

Like a man in a trance, Rod paid up.

"Thank you. Now, we can send Mr. Wall on his way, while I show you how to grind King Edward's into the dirt."

The outline of the gym loomed ahead. Panting, gasping, Terry leaned against a tree and tried to throw up. He was past caring about exposure; just get home to a hot bath, and he'd renounce all thought of sex.

Ahead of him was Jill, jogging steadily, composed. How did she do it? The calm, the poise, the control. Was there nothing inside that tough, fit frame that mirrored his suffering, matched his insecurity?

She opened the gym door. Inside there would be Pete Wrench, lying on a mat, naked – or maybe hanging from the wallbars, offering endless gratification. He mustn't look. It would feed jealous nightmares for years. Weighed down with the guilt of his upbringing, the consciousness of sin, Terry staggered through the night towards the door.

"Hi. I'm Tracey – come on in. Beginners always welcome."

Jill had shed her tracksuit, and looked radiant in a green leotard. "Evening, Terry. You never said you were into aerobics."

There had never been a night like it. Colin was in charge of his head, his movements, his bladder – but only just. All three tottered on the brink of oblivion, but still there was a sense of peace. At some deep level he felt a tremor, a faith that the worst was over, nothing could wound him any more; also, paradoxically, that he had done quite well – that despite appearances, form, expectation, he was not the disaster that he had assumed.

Joyce was slumped on her desk, snoring gently. A Mozart tape was playing, softly, distant, and down the corridor he saw the dim figure of Mick Wall, negotiating a central pillar.

"Working late?"

"You could say that. How did we do?"

"Hard to tell by the end. I'm not that keen on vodka, and these people talk a language all their own."

"Yeah, I know. 5G 4E 10X."

"Good lord. That's exactly what she said. What does it mean?"

Mick reached in his coat pocket, and handed over a grubby cutting. In disbelief, Parnaby read the rave review of King Edward's. Were they really ? Could Rab Butler be reported in these terms?

"Well, that's a relief. Mick , if there's ever anything I can do…I can face her again. Joyce, wake up, dear."

"Um…er…I've got to do Mr. Spencer's tests."

"Mr. Spencer's fine." Mick chuckled. "The only test he'll need is a breathalyser."

"And his tests are a dead duck. Mary said –"

"Who's Mary?" Joyce was awake, alert, suspicious.

"Mrs. Prendergast. She said he's a pushy young jerk who ought to be kept in his place."

"But I've said that for years."

"I know. But now it's official. Come on, time to go home."

They limped out into the night, like refugees from Eastern Europe. In the car park they found Terry, soaking wet, trying to do press-ups. Through his brain ran a garbled mixture, Van Morrison, Motown, Johnny Cash. Untune that string and hark what discord follows, and he must be mad to think he could run...talk to Jill...try to be a teacher...

"What's up, young 'un?"

"She said I wasn't fit."

"She's right. Get up, you pillock, and get some kip. Mr. Parnaby, there was just one thing?"

"Yes? For you, tonight, anything. Just name it."

"If the tests are over, that will close the testing bay, right? Could Mr. O'Mara use the hall for drama again?"

Colin Parnaby racked his weary brain. There was something there, a flickering light of warning, but it was late and he felt love for all the world.

"Yes. Why not ? Excellent idea."

He ushered Joyce towards her car. He might not remember on Monday, but for now it seemed like victory.

Terry stumbled towards a mirage of coherence. "Mick , to my mind you're one in a million."

"I'll bet you say that to all the girls." Brutally, kindly, he yanked Terry to his feet. "Come on, young 'un, take a look at your very own teaching kingdom. Others make the headlines, rake in the cash, but here at Rab Butler we each have our own little nest, a place we can call our own."

They walked back together, inside the door, to look at the hall. In the dark they could see the lines of desks, soon to be removed, and in front of the stage – a blackboard. On it, the caretaker had written

"DECORATERS IN. ACCEPT FOR LUNCH, HALL IS OUT OF BOUNDS."

CHAPTER SEVEN:

MARCH

A week's holiday gave the staff a chance to recover from the inspection, and – as the earlier Terry would have said – for him to get a life. It wasn't that easy. He could get a drink with Rick McManus any time he wanted, but that was costly in more than money. Not only did he have to endure the triumphal refrain of Rick's scams and nifty deals, but they all, in the end, came back to school.

The drama group was out; he was low, but not that low. Before, the time had always filled itself happily enough without proper hobbies, and he wasn't going to cultivate an interest in archaeology, holiday Spanish or ice-skating just for human contact. But what else was there?

In the old days he'd have wandered in and out of pubs, clubs, discos, on the pleasant two-way gamble that he would meet someone he knew, or someone he didn't. But now there was an extra edge. Every place in town where a young person might want to socialise was sure to be teeming with pupils – aggressive manly shouts of recognition, giggling groups of girls daring each other to ask him to dance, and even if he behaved with the restraint of Francis of Assisi, the blatant certainty that every move, every word, every nervous tic, would be magnified and reported back to school. So he retreated, back to the flat, to music, TV, and a worrying sense of getting old.

He wouldn't have admitted it to a soul, but school came as a relief. The bustle, the noise, the company, the weak jokes, all reassured him that he was alive, part of the world, and not just a sad solitary marking time. More like running to keep up. Terry's teaching career had started in a chaotic, well-intentioned whirlwind, and back in September he had cheerily assured Jackie that he would be fine "when things settled down."

"What do you mean?" she had said. "This is as good as it gets." The whirlwind was standard, and the change had to come from him, rather than any alteration in the pressures and demands. But he coped. After "Chico Mendez" he'd got his lunchtimes and afternoons back, doubly precious for having been sacrificed before.

In his teaching the original excitement of survival through improvisation faded, giving way to a steadier competence, where he got better at the English, more confident with the drama, clearer about how to combine the two. As he explored, so he had ideas and materials to bring to department meetings, things to contribute as well as things to pinch. From sneaking a look at Jackie's teaching folder, he progressed to an official loan. He took it home, went through it, took notes and devised a simplified method of his own – not the 5 star de luxe special, but an economy version which was still light years ahead of what he had before.

Jackie was as enthusiastic as ever, chirpy but impressed with what he did. With Jill it was harder to tell. As always, she listened carefully, attentive and still, but it was hard for him to look at her without recalling the humiliation of the aerobics class. He wondered how he could have been so daft, and blamed Mick, and then blamed himself for listening to Mick. Physical pursuit was not his style, and he should have known that all along. If he was going to make a prat of himself, he'd do it his way.

Though there was one consolation. Pete Wrench had not been there. Whatever it was that had lured Jill out for exercise every Friday night, it wasn't the lure of Pete Wrench's body. Or his mind. Though his mind was, Terry had to admit, quite impressive. If your dominant image of PE teachers was the neanderthal Dermot Monaghan, then this witty, ironic intellectual who went to the theatre and read books was a pleasant kind of shock.

Pete was in the staffroom, looking at Sylvia's notice about the French exchange. She was going, and tons of kids were keen to go, but only if enough staff were willing to volunteer. Time was short and there were few takers, but he seemed to be taking it seriously. He turned to Marion Harper, who was browsing through a holiday brochure.

"Do you fancy Paris, Marion?"

"Oh, yes please." Her dull face perked up with more animation than Terry had yet seen.

"The trip, I mean."

"Oh, with kids." And the warmth was gone, like water in the sand. She hated kids, the job, the obligation to clock in every day. He couldn't have coped with that. Relieved for himself, Terry marvelled that he had once seen such potential in this embittered woman who now appeared so sad. There was, truly, no art to find the mind's construction in the face.

"How about you, Terry? Are you up for it?"

Bright, bushy enthusiasm, verging on commitment.

"I've got enough on. I'm thinking I'll play the apathy card on this one, sit back and let someone keen go."

"Like Jackie, you mean. Or Jill. Hey, did you know she was a country fan?"

Terry nodded, "She said something about her dad liking Johnny Cash – but that's not something I'd confess to a colleague."

"You're not kidding. He dropped into a deep, sensual hum "Der der der dum, I walk the line."

No question, he was good. "And I wouldn't have had you down as a closet cowboy." There was something , a tremor of unease, before Pete replied.

"It's the new stuff she likes."

"Right." New or old, it meant nothing to him. I say Motown, you say country, let's call the whole thing off. There was no way he was wearing a stetson, for anyone.

"So how about you, Terry? Who do you listen to?"

"There's only one. Van Morrison."

"Van the man, eh?"

"You're a fan, then?"

"A bit. I liked that thing he did with the Chieftains."

"Yeah. Though they say they haven't spoken since. Nothing to say a genius can't be a pain. I have an uncle in Derry who's a Chieftains fan. He lives there and it's the only Van Morrison he knows."

"So what else should I hear?"

"I'll lend you a tape. Maybe ten tapes. Do you realise he made "Astral Weeks" two years before I was born? Can you believe that?"

"Not till I've heard it. Lend me some, eh?"

And he clapped him on the back, lightly, affectionately, picked up his sports bag, and walked out of the staffroom. Not a trace of guile in his frame. The ineffable hulk.

Killing time. Sharon and Valerie sat in the front desk, next to the wall, waiting for Mr. Spencer to arrive. They were always on time, and he seldom was, but he had their books so there was nothing to do but observe the corridor and chat.

Sharon watched teachers coming from the staffroom. "There's something about him."

"Mr. Wrench?"

"No. Mr. O'Mara."

"Yeah. It's his hair. All over the place. Give me Mr. Wrench any time."

"I don't know, though. He looks sort of Celtic and unattainable." Sharon went into one of her dreamy moods, composing a fantasy which Valerie resented, because it left her out.

"You're only saying that because he's Irish. Having an accent doesn't make him any better."

"It does to me." She went coy, tossing back her hair, flaunting her advantages, savouring the dream.

"Well, I think he's weird. Hey, maybe they both are. Maybe

146

Wrench and O'Mara are…you know..an item."

"Valerie, don't be daft."

"It's not daft." And she was happy now, doggedly confident, on familiar, safer ground. "Ten percent, they say. That makes four of the staff. If I were a homosexual teacher I'd look around for another one."

"Here's Spencer – at last. Hey, you don't suppose…."

With Mick Wall's blank cheque of approval, Muptaz moved through the workshops like a member of staff. Technicians knew not to challenge him, as he passed through to find Dale, standing by a row of bright red boxes.

"How's it going?"

"I've nearly done." He stood back, and looked carefully at the last one from different angles, checking he'd missed nothing. "How about you?"

"There's some resistance, but I'm not sure why."

His eyes followed the brush. "Not Spencer?"

"No, we're underselling him, no problem." Muptaz eased himself up, till he was sitting on the one bench that wasn't covered with newspapers and boxes. "The market's dodgy. It's as though someone's been round and told them that these alarms don't work."

"Watch it." Dale put down the brush, and looked towards the doorway, which was now filled by Tina Clark and Dennis Waite.

He stared at them. "You got permission?"

Tina ignored him, and spoke to Muptaz . "We've got a proposition for you."

Dale replied. "Sorry, Tina. He's engaged. Does Wally know you're here ?"

Muptaz was more guarded. "Who's we?"

"Me and Dennis. And a few more. My brothers."

Muptaz put the brush in a jar of spirit. "Come on, Dale."

Dennis moved slowly to block him, but Tina was in charge. "It's OK. Nobody needs to get excited. Your little business, now."

"What little business is that?"

Tina looked at him, and then panned round, slowly, at ten red boxes, shiny and wet. Muptaz tidied the spirit away, put the lid on the paint and stored it in the cupboard. He took his time. "All right. What do you want?"

"A cut."

"And why should we give you a cut?"

"Because your sales are going to go up." She smiled, ever so reasonable.

"They are?"

Dale moved alongside Muptaz. "And what makes you so sure of that ?"

"When do people buy alarms?"

"They're not – "

"Shut up, Dale."

Tina smiled. "It's all right. I know they don't work. But even if they did, when would people buy them?"

"When they think they're going to get burgled."

"That's right, Muptaz. You're a bright boy. So, when do people think they're going to get burgled?"

"When next door gets burgled." There was a sudden burst of laughter from Dennis. And then it made sense. "Oh no, I get it."

Dale was puzzled, angry, threatened. Muptaz looked at his rat-like friend and couldn't help, despite himself, feeling sorry for him. On his own, with his mum, and that little bit slower on the uptake. "What's going on?"

"Think about it, lads. Business could boom. Come on, Dennis." Meekly, he followed her out, as they joined the masses deading for afternoon registration. Muptaz looked at his mate.

"It's quite simple. We give them a share, maybe make a bit more. But do you want a police record?"

After school, Terry passed Jill's classroom. It was bright, lively and tidy, and she was sitting marking. Enough to make you sick.

"Can I ask you something? Personal?"

She gave an unconvincing look of mock alarm, put down her red pen but left the book open. He only had limited time.

"How do you come to be listening to country music?"

"You mean, on account of it being all about blokes cheating on their wives and their wives letting their blokes walk all over them?"

Yup. He couldn't have put it better. "Something like that."

"I told you about my dad, and the Johnny Cash thing." She suddenly brightened. "Did I tell you he christened my brother Sue? Just to toughen him up?"

"You're joking ."

"Yes, Terry, I'm joking." She looked disappointed. "But there's good and bad, same as anything else. Just because the guitar's a bit twangy doesn't mean it's rubbish. There's some good lyrics in the new stuff." He could see her thinking, reading cover notes in her mind, as if it was a set text.

"Who, for instance?"

" Lucinda Williams, Mary Chapin Carpenter?"

He shook his head. They were just names, women's names.

She was high, a teacher on song. "They've still got the classic feeling, that you get in Patsy Cline, Loretta Lyn, but they're thinking, too, about themselves, about what's going on."

"You make it sound like poetry."

"It's poetry to me, Terry. Does that bother you?" Her lips broadened out into an expansive, enthusiastic beam, and in her head, he could tell, the tunes were playing. She shut the unmarked books, and piled them into her bag.

"So you didn't fancy the Paris trip?"

"Yes I did. I'm going." She checked the desk, gathered both bags, and stood up.

"I didn't know."

"I only decided yesterday. Sylvia was desperate, so I thought, why not?" she shrugged, and moved to the door. He reached to open it for her, hesitated, and then did it anyway.

"So who else is going? Staff, I mean."

She moved through, into the corridor. "Sylvia, Martin Evans, I think. Pete Wrench, and me."

"And that's it?" Like an eager puppy, he followed her down the corridor.

149

"I think so. Why, are you interested?"

And, suddenly, he was. Her, and Pete, could be fun. Could be he was missing out. "Me? No, not really."

"Don't be shy. Sylvia was asking. If you want to go, tell her." And now they had got to the front entrance, the heavy double doors.

"Can I ask you something?"

"Sure." But the way she stood, the way she looked, said don't take all day.

"What's the etiquette say, about opening doors?"

"Etiquette?" It was a derisive, outraged boom. "You're asking me about etiquette?"

"You know what I mean. Feminism. Treating women right. Are you insulted if a bloke opens a door for you?"

She laughed. So it wasn't serious. He was a fool to ask. But then she dropped into her calm, serious "I am a teacher" voice, the one she used with dim kids.

"It depends on how it's done. If it's a hint that I'm helpless, or the man is in charge, I don't like it. If I happen, like tonight, to be carrying two loads of marking and a bulky file, that's fine. Thanks." She nodded and moved past him, about to walk away, but then she turned. "Take it easy, Terry. It's really not that hard. So long as you ask, you'll get by. Goodnight."

Sharon, normally a bright, busy centre of energy, was a pale waif outside Colin Parnaby's door. Being a woman, though a great privilege, was not a deal of fun. She had to go home.

Chris Macdonald did not contest this, although she did think it was Spencer's turn to go. She had argued, many times, for a rota, but Colin thought that this sounded mechanical, so it was left to decency and common sense, which meant that any menstruation problems came to Chris.

"Anyone at home? Are they on the phone?" With Sharon being a nice, well-brought up middle class kid, the answer to both was Yes. Chris dreaded the double No's, the ones who had no phone, but were sure their mums would be in, and who then turned out not to be, after a three-mile drive. This at least would be straight-forward.

Or it was until they reached the gate. When this boring steel contraption had first been erected Chris had paid little attention. It didn't add to or detract from the facilities, and while it was ugly she couldn't honestly claim that there was significant damage to the quality of the environment. Now, however, it was locked. Her car, like all the staff cars on the inner car park, was denied access to the outside world, and Sharon could not get home.

Chris drove up to the gate, and got out to examine the padlock. New, chunky and definitely locked. There was a kind of wild pleasure mixed with the anger that surged through her, as she recognised the distinguishing marks of a Spencer cock-up. She tried the office, but Joyce knew nothing about a key for the padlock. She also knew that Rod was in conference with an influential employer and was not to be disturbed.

"Sod that" said Chris, and stormed off.

"...so it's an ambitious package that we're putting together, but when it's in place I'm sure you'll find it worth your while to – I'm sorry, Chris?"

"Yes. So am I. The key, please? To the padlock?"

She held her hand out as if demanding cigarettes from a twelve year old caught in the act of smoking, and her tone of voice was much the same. Mr. Rothwell, of FLATPAK, did not look in the least put out. He had always suspected that teachers were an arrogant, incompetent load of fools, and this morning's events did nothing to dispel the illusion.

"Ah yes, the key. The caretaker has one. I was hoping to discuss this at the management meeting tomorrow – "

"But I need it now. Please?" She held out her left hand as though her right were holding a revolver. He passed the key across.

Sharon was feeling sick. Businesslike, taut and silent, Chris opened the gate, hurled the key and padlock onto the back seat and drove off, crunching the gears and squealing down the drive.

"Left at the bottom, miss...er, sorry. Can you stop?"

Spring at last. To some it was birds and flowers, to some the mating season, but to Sylvia March it signalled the start of the Exchange. A coachload of kids to Orleans for ten days. A nightmare to organise, but once they were there another taste of life in France – she would be human again.

It got harder. Each year kids were dozier about bringing deposits, more choosy about what they ate, more neurotically subject to allergies about which their mothers fussed. When Sylvia retired she could have it all, the pleasures of going abroad without the penalty of taking kids. Meanwhile, it was worth the price. Just.

She went to Joyce to confirm the bookings, and the arrangements for French currency - thirty-five separate bags, each with the kid's name on, amount in English, amount in French, to be collected from the bank next Tuesday. They'd done it all before, so there shouldn't be a problem.

"I'll drop in for the cheque on Monday, then?"

Joyce was ferreting in a desk drawer, and did not look up. "Yes, I think so. Mr. Spencer said it should be fine by then."

Sylvia looked as though she had been deposited on a Martian film set. "I'm sorry, I don't follow."

Joyce shut the drawer. She put on her 'don't blame me I'm only following orders' voice. "It is complicated ."

"No, it's not. I've chased these kids for money, I've banked it with you, and I want to get it out again on Monday."

Joyce drew breath, and spoke slowly, understanding the other woman's outrage, because she shared it totally. "Yes, I do understand that."

"So where does Mr. Spencer come into it?"

"He's carrying out a transaction with Mr. Carter, I believe."

Sylvia leaned forward. "Mr. Carter the new governor ? Bytes and Pieces?"

"That's the one. Something about the replacement of the computers."

There was a specially malevolent sparkle in Sylvia March's eye as she delivered her ultimatum. "I warn you that if that man is speculating with my money –"

"It's not strictly yours, Miss March."

She put both hands on the desk. "Please don't create difficulties. It's more mine than his, and if it's not here on Monday I shall contact parents and possibly the press. I hope I make myself clear."

"Yes, perfectly." Inwardly, Joyce cheered, though nothing showed as she announced "I'll tell Mr. Parnaby."

"I'd be most grateful if you would."

Colin Parnaby was not in the mood for shocks. It took him weeks to get over his Friday night with Mary Prendergast, and only Joyce's efforts, backed by the reassurance of the report in the local paper, reassured him that all was well.

Once reassured, he began to consider the future. Joyce was appalled.

"We've been through all that. There's nothing to decide. You are stopping at the end of the year. I do not intend to work here as your wife, and time is not on your side." Heartless, she played her trump. "You've not forgotten Martin Walters, surely?"

"You're right. It's just that I'm used to this…it'll be a wrench."

"Not for me. Those two get worse every day, and I don't think you're the man to sort them out."

"Rod and Chris?" He feigned uncertainty, but neither of them were fooled. "What's happened now?"

She told him, about the car park gate, the money for the Exchange, the mounting agenda of grievance it would be his lot to resolve. Maybe he wouldn't be too sad to go, after all.

Tina Clark came out of the girls' toilets, carrying a hairbrush. Outside was standing the faithful, lumbering Dennis. It was quite sweet, really. Terry felt like confiding – "I know mate, life's a bitch when you're in love" – but he caught himself in time.

"Eyeing up the talent, young 'un?"

"Hi, Mick. No, just flying the flag. There's nothing happening."

"I'm not so sure." Mick watched, suspiciously, as Tina handed her hairbrush to Dennis.

"You middle-aged blokes, you're all the same. Just jealous of someone with a bit of spark."

"Dennis Waite – spark? I've seen more spark in a suet pudding. Hang on a minute…" No question. It was weird. Dennis was sucking the end of the hairbrush.

"Leave them alone, Mick. They're in love."

"I don't think so. Waite !"

It was a sergeant-major shout from a Carry On film. Dennis dropped the hairbrush and turned to Mr. Wall. Tina scooped it up and started to walk away, till the megaphone stopped her in her tracks.

"Tina!"

"Sir?"

"Come here. I want it."

Terry felt like a spare part, tried to signal detachment from the sordid scene. He couldn't help it, but Mick had an old-fashioned, autocratic streak, that got you down at times. The secondary modern inheritance.

Perhaps he was older than Terry had thought, past it all. Maybe he was jealous of Pete and Jill, living it up in France. Forgotten how to be young. It might get him in the end. It must be rotten to be so jealous you had to spoil their fun. And he wasn't at all sure Jill would approve, of this macho crushing of tenderness. But Mick was unmistakably in charge.

"The hairbrush, Tina?"

"Hairbrush, sir?"

"You heard me. Hand it over."

"But it's not mine, sir. It's my sister's." She flashed a look, half recognition, half appeal, but Terry dare not respond.

"Give it here."

Leave her alone, you great bully. But he couldn't say it. Mick, the casual joker of the staffroom, was suddenly a remorseless interrogator. He held out his bear-like paw, stared into Tina's eyes, and announced, with ominous calm:

"If that hairbrush isn't in my hand in five seconds you're going outside Mr. Parnaby's door and I'm ringing up your dad."

Sulkily, her hand reached in her bag. "I'm just looking after it. For my sister." She handed it over.

Mick held it to his nose, and sniffed. "Mmm.Thought so."

"What is it, Mick?"

"Vodka."

Colin did not look forward to the meeting. If he was honest, there were very few meetings which he positively welcomed, but meetings of the management team were especially repellent. It was partly the intimacy, that there was Rod and there was Chris, and only Colin himself left as a neutral human being, to dilute the hatred that they shared.

But it was also guilt. Beyond the sparring, he felt a common resentment flow from them, an expectation that a head, a proper Head, would take a lead, set a pattern, somehow draw a line. They might not like it, but that at least they could respect. Like a spectator, he saw the need, but he could no more supply it than perform a triple axel in the car park. He was the way he was, and they were stuck with him.

Maybe it simply meant that Joyce was right. He was past enjoying it, past being useful, and it was therefore time to go. Certainly he'd weep no tears for the blasted gate, which had been a nightmare from the start. Rod was so keen on it, so eager to be responsible, that it had seemed a painless enough concession, but now that Chris had got her teeth in the idea he wished it miles away.

They were sat, in an uneasy triangle, in the comfortable chairs in Parnaby's office, but comfort was the last thing on anybody's mind. Chris looked angular and hostile as she made the first move.

"I do have to say that I think this whole business of Rod's gate is unacceptable."

Nothing there to trouble Rod. He uncrossed his legs, swept back his already flattened hair, and flashed her an unnecessary, insulting smile.

"It's not my gate. It's the school's gate. It's a perfectly reasonable addition to our security."

"So why haven't I got a key?"

Parnaby, umpire and spectator, saw this as a chance to intervene.

"I'm sure you will have, Chris. All the staff will."

"Do you think that's wise?"

He was wrong. He had blundered. Rod was looking at him as if he were a year 7 pupil guilty of a mathematical blunder. And, like a year 7 pupil, he knew he had blundered, but didn't understand how. "Well, Rod, perhaps you should outline what you had in mind."

"That's an excellent idea. What a shame you weren't able to do it earlier – preferably before the bloody gate was built."

"Alright, Chris, thank you. Rod?"

"Yes, well, I'm sure there's no need for us to get heated about this." A quick glance at each of his hearers, to check that they were listening, and that they registered that he was above the fray. "We're not alone, after all. You've seen cases in the news. Other schools are working on their security. King Edward's even have a closed circuit video system."

"So that's the next move, is it?"

"No. Well, not necessarily. I'm just saying, this is a national problem, and we have to respond." His long legs were causing problems again, as he tried to rearrange them comfortably. His eyes flipped around the room, from floor to ceiling and back again, as he strove to return to the logical channels that had been so obvious and attractive before he opened his mouth. "Now, if we can cordon off a safe area, close to the school, then there is less chance of staff cars being stolen –"

" – and no chance of ambulances or deliveries getting to the door. Perhaps we should invest in stretchers for the most urgent cases, to carry them to the gate?"

She was cold, driving, remorseless. What must it be like, Colin wondered idly, to live with a woman like this?

"If I may finish? Outside visitors will need access, and therefore caretakers must have a key."

"But if the caretakers aren't there – "

156

"We might have a bell, to summon them, next to the gate."

"Oh, terrific. The kids will love that."

Spencer looked hurt. "I don't think you're being fair."

"Fair? Who's talking about fair? I don't think it's fair for me to be ferrying home a kid with period pains, when I can't even get my car out of the car park. And while we're on it, I also don't think it's fair that any kid with period pains magically becomes my responsibility, whatever I happen to be doing at the time."

"If we could just keep to the gate."

It was a meek, mild offering. He was a midget, trying to referee a violent heavyweight fight, and no-one was ringing the bell.

Rod rubbed his hands, keen to expound the plan. "Right. Now, each of us must have a key. And the caretaker. But it's risky to issue them to all staff."

"Risky? Are you scared they'll drive away in the middle of the day?"

"No, Chris, but they might well lose them. Staff do lose keys."

"Yes, they do." Colin nodded slowly. "Maybe if we left one with Joyce…" And as he said it, he could have shot himself. One more chore, no addition to the paypacket. He could hear it now. "Yes, and if I do that, what *don't* I do instead?" He didn't have to fill each awkward silence, he didn't have to stick his foot halfway up his mouth. It just turned out that way.

"So what happens? A girl gets period pains, a female teacher drives her home."

"There's no need to get hysterical."

"Just a hypothetical situation, bear with me. Maybe it's a boy with period pains, and a male teacher takes him home. Anyway, they get to the gate, and the teacher borrows Joyce's key. They open the gate, drive through it, then stop to get out and lock the gate again."

"Oh, surely not." He couldn't help it. The way they both looked at him confirmed that his foot was back in his mouth. Go on, their faces both said. Finish it off. Why not go all the way down? He carried on, tentative, doomed.

"Well, if they've borrowed the key, don't they just keep it till they come back?"

"Leaving the gate open, and the site no more secure than it was?" Chris spoke in her most innocent tone, with her brightest smile on display. There was no need for sarcasm. The case was proved.

"Oh no. The gate must be locked. That's the point of the exercise."

"I'm not sure exercise is the word. Assault course, maybe."

"Yes, well…er, there's clearly a few details which need working out. Perhaps you could put all this on paper, Rod, with copies to staff?"

"I'll be glad to."

"I'm sorry, Colin, but I don't think that's good enough."

The lightness had gone. She sat, demure and steady, her cropped head pointed steadily in his direction. Like a revolver.

"I'm not quite with you."

"I think we should have had this discussion before the gate was built. We are, after all, the management team. And I assume that you stand by what you said, that all expenditure over a hundred pounds has to be approved by you?"

Would she never let up? Colin, desperate, turned to Spencer for relief. He was beaming.

"Well, you should have said. I didn't realise you were worried about the money. All taken care of, didn't cost the school a cent. Mr. Rothwell and Mr. Carter have been most accommodating. I don't have the details with me, but we can go through them some time if you wish…"

And that was enough. Rod might be lying, or bluffing; he might have committed the school to a loan from Mephistophilis plc, but Parnaby didn't want to know. Chris might look suspicious and Rod mysteriously smug, but for him this was a sniff of freedom, and within minutes he had adjourned the meeting and was driving home.

The conveyor belt of Mick Wall enterprises (Video production) was starting to pick up speed. In the early stages he'd gone carefully, chatting up Rod Spencer and assuring him that the school's publicity video would be the priority. But before that everything would need to be in working order, and this would require that Mick was familiar with the editing equipment. A pushover.

The manual was impenetrable, but he wasn't proud. He brought in Dale and Muptaz, which also mended the bridges broken during the alarm dispute. Alarms of all kinds seemed to be selling well, following a spate of burglaries in the Burlham estate. He thought the boys might be bitter, since Rod Spencer had hijacked their design, but their reaction seemed remarkably detached.

Home-taping of sound was technically illegal and universally practised. Every Monday staff and pupils alike greeted their friends, to return CDs and tapes they had illicitly copied over the weekend. The pupil entrepreneurs who most closely resembled Mick made a tidy income through selling pirate tapes. Nothing startling there.

But an editing suite, two video recorders in tandem, would enable Mick to extend this trade into vision – without the competition. At bargain prices, he could provide staff, parents, maybe even kids with a copy of the video of their choice. Hire a film for twenty-four hours, make six copies for the price of the rental and blank tapes, and selling them at a fiver a time he still made a tidy profit. With Dale and Muptaz trained he could run it through the day, without lessons interfering with production. Soon he'd be able to put down an instalment on Westy's tapes, a step up the ladder, one square closer to WIN.

As usual, Terry was late. The staffroom had emptied, time for registration, and he knew that 10A4 would currently be arranging themselves tastefully along the walls, around the light sockets and under the workbenches, but first he had to find his lesson notes. He'd had them at break, when he was sitting over there…

The phone rang.

"Yeah. Staffroom."

"Mr. O'Mara?" A distant giggle.

"Yes, this is Mr. O'Mara. Who's that, please?"

"It's Emma, sir. In Paris. On a trip."

"You what?"

"I'm lost, sir. I couldn't find the loo."

"Emma?"

"I'm running out of money. What shall I do?"

"Where's Miss March, Ms. Williams?"

"I told you, sir, I'm lost...."

The French pips were little different from the English variety. "You have been cut off" was a blunt enough message, in any language. Terry, with a group to register and a class to teach, but without his lesson notes, left a garbled message with Joyce Davies, and ran.

Rod Spencer, dogged deputy, was humming. The creative juices were starting to flow - and maybe he had Chris Macdonald to thank. Her taunts had wounded him, but they also made him think. The gate was there, and the keys would soon be ready. He'd got the video equipment, and by Whit he'd have a publicity video finished, with copies out to parents by the end of term. Now for the cameras.

Even he knew he couldn't afford the real thing. But a security camera works in two ways. One, it films what's going on. Two, it's up there, threatening to film what goes on, and when you see it you don't know whether it's filming or not. The roads were teeming with police surveillance cameras, but how often were they loaded with film ? Did anyone look at the tapes?

So, why not a dummy camera? Why not a lot of them, fixed high up on the wall, as a deterrent to thieves or vandals ? They would also stand as a sign, that this was no sink comp, but a place to be reckoned with, even – why not? – a flagship school.

The adrenalin surged as he wheeled his chair across to the filing cabinet marked BUILDINGS, the drawer marked SECURITY, the catalogues filed under VIDEO. On a good day, like today, it was a tidy, friendly world.

Terry hung about the car park, trying to cadge a lift. There were queues of parental cars, waiting to reclaim their offspring as the coach rumbled in at the end of the French exchange. Off came a stream of chattering teenage trophy hunters, followed by some weary-looking staff.

"Good trip, Pete?"

"Tres bon, merci." This fluent sample of repartee was accompanied by a very obvious mime implying the consumption of vast quantities of wine.

"Pay no attention. It was great." Jill had enjoyed herself. "Don't forget, Pete, union meeting tonight."

"No thanks, miss. I've earned a night off." He waved, and trudged off.

"Terry, you interested?"

He had received more enticing invitations.

"I'm looking for a lift."

"Yeah, OK." She moved towards her car. " But how about the meeting?"

He hovered by the passenger door, haggling. "Can I have the lift anyway?"

"Don't be soft. Get in."

"Yeah, OK then. Give it a go."

He must have been mad. Later that evening he panned slowly round a thin audience in a draughty room – all earnest, all sincere, all dull. There were pompous blokes in glasses, fanatics clutching leaflets, women in dungarees who seemed miserable unless they were busy all the time. College politics all over again, and he'd rather be in Jill's flat, emptying a bottle of red while she dished the dirt. Or anywhere, come to that.

But this was where she wanted to be. And they certainly wanted her. He couldn't help seeing how much she was at home. She beamed smiles at friends and colleagues, knew what they were talking about, nodded enthusiastically as the details of possible future agitation were spelt out. Couldn't she see that this was a pantomime? That parents, the media, politicians would look at this motley collection and laugh ? He could have cried. Even worse, they were all in it, together, and he was hovering outside, the dweller in the threshold, permanently detached.

A tall guy with a beard was droning on, but these well-mannered revolutionaries let him drone, and a Guinness was a great idea. He just needed to get Jill's attention, and tempt her out to a pub. But then she turned, active, happy and fulfilled, with the grin of a kid having fun. No, she wouldn't want to bunk off, and he'd have to stick it out.

She drove him back. No Guinness, no stop at her flat, no she didn't want a coffee, thanks.

"Thanks for the lift."

"That's OK. Thanks for coming. What did you think?"

He bit his lip. "Not what I'm used to. It means a lot to you, this, right?"

"Oh yeah."

"Is that because your mum's a teacher?"

"Maybe. Or 'cos my dad's on the buses." She must know she was winding him up. "I'll see you, Terry."

A confident, restrained wave, then she looked over her shoulder, and edged into the traffic. She knew who she was, where she was going. He could see her mum, some patient heroine in an inner city comprehensive, raising this demanding daughter who would never put a foot wrong. He couldn't help wishing her a minor set back, just a bump or a puncture, but her tail lights cruised off smoothly until she was out of sight. Which left him a confused mess, and tomorrow was April the first.

CHAPTER EIGHT:

APRIL

April. The onset of spring, poetic symbol of fresh growth, and the start of a new financial year. This, Mick whispered to himself, in the devious recesses of his soul, might be the year he actually struck rich. He strolled to his pigeonhole.

Glossy brochures, of video cameras. Not holiday snaps, but security, for the use of. He had listened, with minimal enthusiasm, to Rod Spencer's big idea. The same old rubbish, appearances on the cheap. Mick, will you build us a set? Mick, can you fix my car? Mick, we need some display stands for Wednesday night – oh, and don't spend any money.

If it was real cameras, if he got the chance to play with a bit of meaningful technology, like the beauties they had at King Edward's well, that would be something else again. But this, making dummies for a dummy, this was just a chore. Still, he had screwed the editing unit out of Spencer, and that was making money, so he'd go along with it.

As he moved away from the pigeonhole he realised he'd missed something. Under the brochures lay a small white envelope, from the Inland Revenue. Why to him here, and not at home? He knew there was nothing to worry about, so he was calm as he opened it, which was just as well. Inside there was a demand for unpaid tax – five thousand, six hundred pounds.

Colin Parnaby was ready for a holiday. It was the last week of term, and just as well. Around him he could feel tempers shortening, nerves fraying. More staff were ill, a bug was going round the kids and everyone had had enough. Even Joyce showed signs of strain.

"Who's that girl sat out there?"

"Tina Clark. Apparently she's ill."

"But is no-one looking after her?"

"It doesn't appear so." The more doggedly he pursued it, the more disdainful her tone became. As he watched her, busy at her work, it occurred to him that she had her heartless side. He moved closer, cautious but determined.

"Do you know who put her there?"

Finally, she stopped work, adjusted her glasses with both hands, and looked at him over the top of them. "Oh yes. Mr. Spencer, in his wisdom, decided that she should sit there – and then rushed off for a very urgent meeting with some business-man. At FLATPAK, I think he said."

"Right, thank you." He breathed in, looked away, and strolled towards the window. He didn't want to get into a row about Rod's priorities. On the other hand, if Tina had to be taken home, it would give him a break. He could get to the bank, which was always tricky at lunchtime. There was the risk of kids going to the chip shop, smoking, needing to be intercepted, followed up, let-ters to parents. The more he thought about it, it seemed a good idea, although he didn't look at Joyce as he told her.

"Maybe I'd better take her."

"Are you sure that's wise?"

He gazed out of the window. "I'm not as bad a driver as you think."

"I didn't mean that." She paused, until she made him look at her. "Mr. Spencer's out of school, Miss Macdonald is teaching – that only leaves you for crises."

"Don't worry, there won't be any." He rubbed his hands, in an unconvincing gesture of enthusiasm." I've fixed it." He gave her a cheery wave, called "Come on, Tina" and sauntered down the corridor. Nothing happened. He turned back.

Innocent cherubic face, fair hair, a plaintive look, like Marilyn Monroe in the early days. "My bag's in maths, sir."

"Well, you'd better fetch it."

"I'm... I don't feel..." Big blue eyes, hands to stomach, modest glance at the ground.

"Oh, all right, then." Colin's goodwill was rapidly evaporating, and was not sustained by the knowledge that Joyce, typing furiously, had nonetheless caught every word.

He looked round the maths block for 10A4, but then remembered that Maths was taught in sets, so there was no way of being sure which room Tina had been in. He tried one at random. The teacher didn't know, but three pupils made helpful suggestions – three different suggestions. Tina's group was the third one that he tried.

After a five minute interlude he was back, holding a heavily loaded black Adidas bag.

"Thanks, sir." She flashed him a smile, much more animated than he would have liked, stood up without apparent difficulty, and quickly took the bag. Was she shamming? Was there something illicit in there? Should he have searched the bag? Should he search it now?

Joyce and Tina, knowing females in a world unfit for men, were watching him. With an effort he dredged up the chirpy tone, muddy and dripping. It did not convince.

"Let's go, then."

He led her out into the car park, indicated his car and settled her into the passenger seat. He got in, and drove towards the drive, where he met the Spencer gate. He fished in his pocket for the key. No key. He went round again, systematically – jacket right, jacket left, trouser right, trouser left, squirming to gain access to each one. Inside pocket, back pockets, breast pocket; gradually – and it took time – he recognised that his suit contained no less than eight pockets, and that the key was not to be found in any of them. Then he remembered that he had changed suits that morning, in a rush; the key was safe in yesterday's suit.

The mixture was one part relief, nine parts humiliation, as he scuttled back to Joyce.

"Sorry, I've left the key at home. Can I borrow the spare?"

"Are you sure this is a good idea?"

"The key, Joyce. Please?"

Sulkily she handed it across. He was not going to give in now. He almost ran back to the car, ignoring the twinges in his knee. He was just going to get this episode over, and then sit back in his office with a cup of black coffee and lock the door.

He fought with the padlock, which was cold and slippery from the rain. Eventually, it yielded. He opened the gate, fastened it open and hobbled back to the car. He tried to start it, and there was a brief cough, and then silence. Tina smiled at him. She watched carefully, as he turned the key, with increasing desperation. Eventually, it fired, and he moved slowly through the gap, past the gate.

Then he remembered that he shouldn't leave it open. The voice of Rod Spencer, proclaiming self-evident truth – "If we're going to leave it open, we might as well not have a gate." How true that was. Why had he agreed to the thing in the first place?

He was worried about the car stalling, and looked to Tina for inspiration. She hugged her stomach, and gave a little groan. He leapt out and slammed the door. Pain shot through his knee. This time, it took him only three pockets before he found the key.

The engine died just as he opened the lock. He shut the gate, pushed the padlock through the hole, and pressed the hasp to lock it again. It wouldn't go. He shoved harder, bracing himself against the tarmac, the padlock against the post, as his knee-joint growled complaint. The lock, having been opened, didn't want to close. Swearing faintly, he rammed it with all his might against the gate post. The key fell to the ground as the padlock closed. He looked across the wet, pitted tarmac, and the lights of classrooms seemed welcoming and warm.

"It's there, sir." Tina had wound down the window, and was pointing at a puddle. He paddled around it, picked up the key, took a couple of hasty, angry breaths in a vain effort to calm himself, and got back in the car. He turned the key, and pumped frantically with his right leg, ignoring the messages of pain. She watched, concerned.

"Is that the accelerator?" she asked.

Muptaz watched through the workshop windows, as Dale doodled on his folder. "What's up with Parnaby?"

"You know teachers. Always ratty at the end of term."

"So why's he taking Tina home?"

"Search me." Dale shrugged, and continued his portrait of a space-age earwig. "Maybe he fancies her. Or he's just had enough – wants to get out."

"You don't reckon she's been suspended? They've sussed what's going on - the alarms, the robberies?"

"Relax, Muptaz. If they want to suspend Tina, there's thousands of things it might be."

"Maybe, but just at the moment she's got her hooks into us." He paused, uneasily, between the window and the bench. "I'm not happy, I'm telling you."

"We're still selling, aren't we?"

"Yeah, but not many. You go round now and they laugh at you. Wally's one – the one Spencer sells – I reckon they've sussed them. They don't work."

"So? Serve 'em right. They should have left it to us."

Muptaz came back to the bench. "You don't get it, do you ? I'm not talking morality here. Markets, Dale, the bottom line." He glowered over his friend. "If the genuine ones don't work, why should they buy the fake? That's the point. Why should they give us money, for a lousy copy of an alarm that doesn't work."

Dale looked up, worried by the passion in his voice. Muptaz was the brains of this operation. Now that the operation was failing, now that Muptaz was on the edge of tears, what were they going to do ?

"So, what d'you reckon?"

"I reckon we get away from Tina, fast."

"Suits me. That Dennis does my head in. But that puts us out of business, yeah?"

"No. We diversify. We go into videos."

"Wally's editing suite, right?"

"Right. Only this time " – and there was a steely look in his eyes that Dale found both scary and reassuring "we don't tell no-one. Right?"

Lunchtime, and Ms. Macdonald smiled graciously round the geography room. It had been hard to arrange a meeting, but whenever she looked at this group, her chosen few, she felt a tremor of hope. Maybe some things would get better, after all.

"I just wanted to get you together at the end of term, to thank you for what you've done, and to ask about ideas for next term's work."

Teachers, it struck Valerie, were a very strange breed. When the Equal Opportunities group criticised the Careers talks, she knew for certain that Ms. Macdonald was furious. She'd sulked for half a term, had called one short and inconclusive meeting, and now she was thanking them for things they hadn't done. Why didn't she sort out what she wanted, and stick to it?

"Dresses, miss. Summer uniform."

Chris nodded grimly. This was a battle she welcomed. Men wanting girls to be in summer dresses, and then claiming that this had some connection with school identity and discipline. Were the boys going to slip into shorts?

"There's publicity, miss." It just came out. Valerie was watching, listening, idly thinking. She hadn't planned to start a crusade.

"Yes?"

"You know, miss. The brochures, the guides who show them round."

"You mean, are they boys or girls?"

"No, miss." No question, she should have kept her mouth shut.

"I'm sorry. I don't understand."

"I mean, what they look like, miss. Do people get chosen on their looks?"

Among Chris' chosen few there were a lot of bright, attractive girls. Some of them may have wondered about Valerie, whether she meant to eat that much, liked being dumpy, and whether this had any connection with what she said. Nobody spoke.

Chris toyed with an unexpected thought. It was interesting,

certainly, and she started to make connections with Rod Spencer and his projected video. It would be a vain and expensive shambles, of course, but maybe here there was further grounds for resistance.

"I think she's right, miss." Emma Sheargold, with her chestnut hair, perfect skin and honest eyes, was on the side of virtue. Nobody could argue that Emma was compensating for her own defects. "I think people judge far too much on appearances."

"Yes, Emma, I'm sure you're right. Thank you, Valerie." Chris flashed a brief nod of acknowledgement at the podgy thinker from year 8, and looked back to her diary. Must move on. "So, please keep your eyes open – we'll come back to this next term." She stood, and smiled benevolently, trying to suppress memories of Jean Brodie. " Thank you again, and could you please straighten the furniture – so we leave things tidy."

Down the corridor, the camera operator for "Rab Butler – Quality School" was saying nothing, but trying to plan his short-term future. He wasn't sure what he was going to do with two weeks' holiday, but collapsing seemed a nice idea. Pete Wrench was canoeing down the Wye, Sylvia was off to France again, and Jill Williams would spend a week at a conference of English teachers. Terry wouldn't have done that, not for a crateful of Guinness or a CD player crammed with the collected works of Van Morrison. No, he needed a break.

Colin and Joyce took the caravan to the Yorkshire dales, and had a marvellous time. They talked, went to pubs, pottered around the shops. Colin read a couple of books, went to a film, and bought himself a pullover. The kind of mind-changing experiences that normal people managed all the time, which didn't feature in his term-time week. If retirement were to be as sweet and easy as this, it couldn't come too soon.

The holiday raced, as holidays do, but it wasn't so bad to be back. Summer term, lighter evenings, better weather, only one to go - and with year 11 leaving early most teachers would shed a few lessons before half-term. A slight slackening on the pressure, lightening of the load. They would get by, again. Terry felt sure, as he ambled thoughtfully towards the staffroom, that survival was a more pressing concern for him than for any of his colleagues.

Unlike them, he had extra work – the Rod Spencer commercial. He corrected himself – maybe that should read, the Rab Butler commercial. Then again, maybe not. For Rod was writing the script, Rod thought he would do a piece to camera here, and Rod had ideas about how the ending might look.

Late in the day, Terry had realised he was dealing with a hydra. "The management" existed on paper as a diagram of a single, rational organisation. But only on paper was that true. In practice, it was a sprawling, permanent feud, and keeping Rod Spencer happy was no guarantee of Chris Macdonald's approval. Rather the reverse, in fact. The head was the key, since only Parnaby could make him permanent, but there was no obvious way in which Terry could gain his support. Maybe brownie points from Spencer might help, provided Parnaby liked the result and he didn't get up Chris Macdonald's nose in the process. Fairly straightforward, really, for a foreign office diplomat, provided you kept your mouth shut and never went outside.

The kids. That was the answer. Stop calculating the imponderables of pleasing management, and get something that kids could do well – an honest, thorough piece of work. That way, too, it occurred to him, it would be easier to justify spending lesson-time on the project. This was, after all, a hands-on experience of the media, a purposeful use of video in context, with a clear audience and purpose in mind. So why, if it was educationally valid, did this project invariably fill him with misgivings and a sense of doom?

He had nearly reached the staffroom, and the consolation of company and coffee, when he was arrested by a yell. "Sir!" Craig Hutchings, a wayward talent who had always lost his book, and always said that Terry had it, was actually holding the exhibit in his hand. He ran up, as Terry waited by the staffroom door.

"Sir, sir – my book."

"Yes, Craig?"

"You wanted to mark it, sir."

Terry straightened his shoulders, suppressed the wisecracks, and acted wise.

"I wanted to mark it last Thursday. Still, since you've brought it, give it here." He took the book, and slid into the staffroom with relief.

"Mr. O'Mara!" the relief vanished. Offhand, he could think of no occasion in his life when that greeting had meant anything but trouble. Now, it was Sylvia March, brandishing the note he had left in her pigeon-hole before school.

"This says you need Emma Sheargold this afternoon?"

"Sure. Is there a problem?"

"A minor one. I am, for my sins, endeavouring to teach her how to speak a foreign language. And for that, unfortunately, I need her in my lessons."

"I'm sorry if it's difficult. I'll do it another time."

"I'd be most grateful. Couldn't you do it after school? I'm sure a video club would be popular." In victory she was charming, smooth, polite, and Terry could see his free time vanishing into smoke.

"It isn't just for interest. This is for the school." Listening to himself speak, it sounded pathetic, unconvincing garbage.

"I don't understand?"

"Mr. Spencer has asked me to do it. A commercial, for the school."

"Ah, marketing ! Well, of course, I can see how that must take precedence over anything so peripheral as lessons. Forgive me, I'm an old-fashioned Philistine, from the days when we used to teach. But tell me, when we have attracted these droves of new pupils, will they also be taken out of lessons to create more commercial videos, or will there ever come a time when they just learn?"

The bitter sarcasm dripped from her lips, and he was helpless to argue because he agreed. "I'm sure I couldn't say. Just forget it, please. I'll find another time." And corporate man stumbled from

171

the fray, annihilated, to get a salving brew. Mick had got there first.

"It's tough at the top, son."

"Thank you, Mick. A sympathetic ear is just what I could do with, right now."

"Don't let it get to you. Those of us on the side of progress must not depair."

"That's what we're doing is it, making progress? You, me and Rod?"

Mick sipped his coffee and paused, with a crafty grin. "I don't know about Rod, but I do know about me. And you, young man, could be right in there with me."

"Is that something I ought to be pleased about?"

"No question." He winked, and stroked his nose with a knowing index finger. "Believe me, young 'un, you and me, we have it made."

"Aren't you forgetting something? Tax demand?"

"Very funny. I've got my suspects for that and I tell you, when I know, they're going to suffer." And they both paused, as Joyce Davies walked into the staffroom, carrying two piles of paper, and headed for the pigeon-holes. They watched her feed them in, one pink and one yellow into each.

Mark Hutchings looked angrily round for his car keys, as Sheila watched him.

"But you can go, can't you?"

"I can, but I don't see why I should."

"Look, Sheila, it's a swine of a week. I've got a council meeting on the Monday, a management session on Wednesday and there's a good chance the chairman will want a word after golf on Thursday." She stood, arms folded, as he continued the hunt.

"Life's a bitch, ain't it? All this drinking you have to do."

"Sheila – "

"So yet again it will be Sheila the witch who goes into battle. I'm telling you, I shall swing for that March woman. If you'd heard her on the phone – "

"You haven't had my keys, have you?"

"You left a pile of stuff in the kitchen."

"Terrific. Look, I'm grateful, really," and he tried to look it, as he moved into the kitchen. She followed him, more slowly.

"Oh yes, now you can see daylight you're grateful. But what about Craig? It's him this is supposed to be about."

He found the keys, put them in his pocket, and checked his hair in the mirror. "Craig? I don't get you."

"I know. You don't get it at all. Where is he in all this, Mark ? What does he think he's doing?"

"Search me."

"I do. Every day. And I find nothing, absolutely zilch. He's your son, and you just haven't a clue where he's going. And, surprisingly enough, nor has he."

He moved to the door. "I'm sorry, love. I have to go."

She looked away. "What I don't get is why anybody thought the feminist movement had many any difference at all. Not a scrap. Not the slightest, bloody scrap." He watched her, and looked for something to say, to make it better. There was nothing. Stealthily, he went out of the door.

Each teacher got a yellow one, and a pink one, and the combined wisdom of the staffroom tried to measure the damage.

"Well, Mick, what does it say?"

"We've had it before, Jackie. It's Chris' thoughts about Record of Achievement."

"She put those out last Christmas."

"That's right. But then Rod put out his reflections on the National Curriculum at least a year ago, and we've got those again as well."

"Déja vu, all over again." Sylvia sat, with a weary sigh. "Is there some management drive to clear the rainforests before the year is out?"

"Come on, Sylvia. Chris wants us to think positive."

"From the sound of her missive, I am forbidden to think in any any other way. 'Comments must be expressed constructively, recording actual achievement.' Fine. Dennis Waite has entered my room, and sometimes he has sat down. He hasn't listened, he hasn't spoken French and he's never done homework, but I shan't record those. They're negative. Some days, he has sat down."

Jackie tried to melt the ferocity of the judgement with a smile. "It can't be that bad, surely?"

"I was in the lessons. Remember, we linguists don't have quite the freedom you English teachers are allowed. We have things to teach, you can make it up."

Before Jackie could voice her outrage, Marion Harper joined in. "I quite agree. So far as I'm concerned there's nothing positive to be said about Dennis Waite. And he's not the only one."

Mick tried to be fair. "He does have extra-curricular interests, mind."

"How could I forget ?" Sylvia was flying now. " 'Have you organised an event which involved planning, problem-solving and decision-making ?' Certainly. Dennis can take credit on all three counts. The break-in at Shellworth Cricket Club was a smooth operation, and Dennis succeeded in removing three crates of beer without spilling any."

"Is Rod's any better ?"

"Come off it, Jackie. Idealism's all very well, but act your age. Rod's paper is a circular from the planet Zarg."

"If it's based on the National Curriculum, that's not surprising. God only knows how parents are supposed to understand it."

Jackie pondered for a second. " You know, it almost makes you grateful for parents' evenings - we can try and talk sense instead of writing rubbish."

"Oh yeah, I can hardly wait. Roll on Tuesday."

After school, Terry had an appointment in Jill's room, handing in his homework. He checked his own tables, noticed that there was less mess than there used to be, and found the file he wanted straight away. He was so efficient it was almost boring. But it was getting better, and he knew where more things were. No longer did he dream of the perfect zappy lesson, the one-off performance that set off fireworks. Now, he thought in packages, chunks of work over three or four weeks, even half a term. He took more notes, tidied more often, panicked less about things he thought he'd lost.

This new improved O'Mara picked up a folder, took it to Jill's room and opened it, knowing the stuff was there. He handed over a sheet of paper with neatly copied questions. He watched her as she read them through.

"What are periods?

Why do boys have to ask girls out?

Why don't girls have to move furniture?

What is a clittorriss?

Why are some dicks bigger than others?

They say they don't want it but they do really."

She shook her head slowly. "I didn't know it was this bad."

"Yes, you did. You hear it every day: 'get 'em off, slag, you dumb bitch.'"

"It still looks funny, typed out like this."

"Yeah. I thought I'd do a worksheet, copies to head, deputies and governors."

The alarm on her face was worth it. "You're not serious?"

"Na, but it's interesting, right? There's a lot of little boys in there, just terrified. Mind you, I know how they feel."

She looked at him warily. "Now you are joking."

"Honest, Jill, I feel sorry for the poor little blighters. Everyone's telling them they've got to be manly, sexy and decisive, and they just haven't a clue. Not a clue."

"So, where do we got from here?" Crossed arms, businesslike tone – there has to be a lesson in this.

"God knows. I was hoping you'd be telling me."

"No way. I've given you the anonymous questions bit – though I did pinch that from Jackie. But what you do with it, well…could you just go through them, saying what you think?"

He stared, incredulous. "Probationer teacher, talking about penis sizes and the location of the clitoris? Not me. I'm just a temporary stopgap."

"You think it's easier if you're permanent?"

"I think it feels easier if you're permanent." And they were both surprised by the speed and force of his reply.

Jill thought about it. "Yeah, fair enough."

"It's so bloody complicated."

"You think it used to be simple – when men were men?" The ironic twinkle in her eye was also a peace-offering.

"There's just so many ways of getting it wrong."

"Like opening doors, you mean?"

He remembered, and looked carefully, trying to measure the degree of her scorn. It was hard to tell. "Yeah, that too. I mean, if I offer you a drink, after parents' evening, say, that doesn't mean I'm going to rape you, does it?"

"What does it mean, then, Terry?"

"It doesn't mean anything. Just a friendly gesture. Mates in a pub."

And now she was involved. "So if you and I go in a pub, who's going to buy the first drink?"

He shrugged. "Me, I suppose."

"Why ? I'm older. I make more money. Why you?"

"I don't know. Custom, I suppose."

She seized on it, leaning across the table like a chess player about to take a piece. "Blokes' custom. Stay in charge, call the shots, keep her under obligation."

"It's only a drink."

"Maybe. Only flowers, only a meal out, rings, hotel rooms – he pays, he's in charge. That's what it means. So he's entitled to some return."

"And you think that's what blokes are thinking?"

"Hold on. I didn't say blokes were thinking that. I didn't say they were thinking at all. But that's what's going on."

"Christ." He stopped, hit by a vision. "There's a lesson there."

"What you and me, arguing in front of the kids?"

"No. Situations. Buying drinks, offering lifts, asking back for coffee."

"The Gold Blend advert."

"Yeah. What does it mean? If A does this, what does B think ? Agony column for teenagers, etiquette between the sexes."

"Like, who puts on the condom? "

"Hang on. I'm not up to that. In lessons, I mean."

She put her hand on his. "It's OK. I'm not taking the piss. This is good, Terry, it's really good. You go home and work it out."

"Well, thanks, miss. "He got up, and pushed the papers back in his bag. "So, can I buy you a drink tonight, without blackening my character ? Oh, God, there it goes again."

But she was helpless, caught in a tidal giggle.

"The legendary O'Mara foot, planted in the mouth."

"Sorry, Terry. I've got a parents' evening."

"I know that. I meant afterwards."

"I don't know. I'll see how I feel." But she seemed to be thinking about it already, as he went to the door and left her in her room.

Parents' evening. By the stage was a huge seating diagram, matching the rows of tables and chairs like some pedagogical game of battleships. On each table was a carefully printed name card. The old, faded ones announced Mr. Summers, Miss March, Mrs. Fairbrother. A brighter, newer batch proclaimed the coup two years ago in which Ms. Macdonald and Ms. Williams had achieved their independence. And the hastily handwritten cards of a different shade proclaimed that Messrs. O'Mara and Wrench had recently joined the staff . Rod Spencer and Chris Macdonald would both have agreed that this was shoddy, but neither would have accepted responsibility for remedying the fault.

Behind each name card – like a quiz contestant – sat a polite teacher, better dressed than usual, ready for the fray. Could these eager, immaculate professionals, Terry wondered, possibly be the same weary cynics that had slumped in the staffroom at four o'clock?

Handicapped by the tottering pile of books, folders and markbook that threatened to spill beyond his grasp, he negotiated his way to his place. On his left were Jackie and then Jill, already deep in conversations, and Brian Summers was on his right.

Keeping an eye on the new boy, maybe – ready to pick up the pieces?

Terry bluffed his way through. A few parents were accompanied by their children, some looked identical, and some helpfully announced their child's name as soon as they arrived. There were glaring, unspoken battles between parents who had booked appointments and parents who had queued, as two sacred value systems battled for precedence, but basically he got by. He smiled, he offered platitudes, he leafed confidently through the books and folders, and he charmed them out of the trees.

But he was waiting. His year 9 group included Craig Hutchings, and that meant Mr. Hutchings and Ms. Thorpe – Sheila of the drama group, of the Chico Mendez audience, of the Christmas invitation to which he had never replied. Back in the inspection Jackie had said she had been looking for him, but they had managed not to meet. Until now, when she was heading down the aisle alone, with Terry in her sights.

"Mr. O'Mara – or can I call you Terry?" She put out a hand he could not ignore, and smiled meaningfully.

"Er..fine." He retrieved his hand, sat down, and started flipping through the books, looking for Craig's.

"I suppose we ought to talk about Craig's English – at least for some of the time." She laughed, a girlish titter which seemed ridiculous. She was streetwise, confident, detached; why did she need this silly act?

Terry, meanwhile, was going to be safely, neutrally competent, sticking to the work agenda, but that would be difficult without Craig's book. He went through the pile from top to bottom, and halfway through thought that he might have gone too fast. Perhaps if he went slowly, in two piles, left to right, he would have more chance ? It had to be there. He remembered Craig handing it in outside the staffroom. Sheila Thorpe was watching him.

"He's probably lost it. He usually has."

"No, I've got it. I know I have. Well, um, his writing's not bad, but it's a bit basic."

"Masculine, you mean?"

"He could do with a bit more detail when he's describing people."

"Oh, you're so right." She laughed, and threw her head back, shaking off the reins of male dominance. "His dad's the same. Fine, except with people. You want workaholic macho efficiency, the hard sell, then Mark's your man. But anything requiring sensitivity, a touch of warmth, then…well…"

First he heard the quaver in her voice. That made him look closer, and he saw the tears well up. Oh Christ, he couldn't handle this.

"Mr. O'Mara?" Jill stood patiently at his side, with an exercise book in her hand. "Sorry to interrupt, but I could see Ms. Thorpe was here, and realised you would need Craig's book. Thank you for showing it to me – it was really interesting." She handed it to Terry – with a trace of a wink? – and was gone.

"She's nice. You've got some decent people here."

"Yes. Yes, we're lucky." How the hell had she got it? Still, rescue was rescue, in any language. He zoomed about the book, pointing out a witty poem, an essay that might have been better planned, some carelessness with punctuation. He definitely owed Jill Williams a drink.

Sheila was looking at him. "You never came."

"I'm sorry?"

"At Christmas. I invited you for a drink."

"Yeah…I mean, no, you're right. I'm sorry. You know Christmas, it's chaos. Besides, I had this call from home, Belfast, had to go."

"Not family trouble?"

"No. My fiancee, actually.Well…"

And that was enough. He watched the wheels click over, the cogs slot in. It was a lie, but she was buying it, and that made it all come good. No problem.

She got up. "Well, thank you, Terry." Again the handshake, but this time it was quick and formal. What felt like a long pause, as she recovered her poise, the nerve to live with herself, dispense with the dreams. He stood and watched her go, no longer a

179

terrified victim. Now she was gone, he felt sorry for her. One more loner, looking for a bit of love.

The pub was packed. Two hours of solid talking does wonders for the throat, and half of the Rab Butler staff seemed to have wedged themselves into the saloon bar of The White Horse. Mick was in party mood.

"And a point of Guinness for Paddy O'Reilly, moy Oirish friend."

"Ah, you're worse than the kids, so you are. Ta, Mick."

"Do they give you a hard time, then, with the IRA connections?"

"Not more than twice a day."

"You're not the only one, you know," said Jackie, beaming, glass in hand.

"So which part of Belfast are you from, darlin'?" With the drink, in a group, safe with her, it was so easy. Why couldn't she just ditch her feller and move in?

"There's other oppressed minorities apart from the Irish, you know. You don't have a monopoly on prejudice."

"Not yet, maybe, but we're working at it. That, and the melancholy."

Mick bored his way in. "So what's your problem, kid? The feminist whinge?"

She stuck out her tongue. "Feminist nothing. I'm a Polack. How would you fancy working in secondary with a name like Grabowska ?"

"Wall has its problems too."

"Yeah. Reminds me of a limerick."

Jill was sat in the corner, with a lager and a quiet smile. Which Mick took as a challenge. "You're not saying much . Aren't you putting in a bid?"

"Me, I'm streets ahead." Terry had worried, but she wasn't fazed at all. "My best was the graffiti in the boys' toilets – Williams is a wanker."

As the laugh died, Mick steered Terry into a corner.

"Doing OK, then? You and Jill?"

"Don't ask, Mick. If I want something fixing I'll ask Cilla Black."

"Any competition?"

Terry looked instinctively round the bar, until he found the tall, cheery figure of Pete Wrench, telling a joke to the other PE staff. He nodded.

"You're joking? Muscular Pete?" Mick's heavy frame shook with laughter.

"He's all right, is Pete."

"Oh, sure. Good lad. But gay."

It was hard, in a pub, to be sure you caught every word. Terry screwed up his face, desperate to be sure. "What did you say?"

"You heard. Problem solved. Go on, get in there."

Terry sipped his pint, and grinned, but he'd tried being a dummy, with Mick at the controls. No, he was not going back to aerobics, which was just as well, since by the time he turned back, Jill had gone. Jackie patted the seat next to her, so he sat down.

"How was your evening, then?"

"Not so bad, really. I saw a lot where there was nothing much to say, and there were a few I wanted to see that never came."

"That's standard. How about Sheila ?" She was too happy, too relaxed, to bluff well.

"I get the feeling I'm being set up."

"No." She wasn't a good liar. "I'm just nosy, me."

He gulped the last of his pint, and put down the glass. "To be honest, I felt sorry for her. You know?"

"Yes. Yes, I do." She nodded, and looked at him. "You know what, O'Mara? You'll do."

"Well, thanks. Can I get you another?"

"No, it's my round. Guinness?"

He nodded, and she rose to fetch them.

"Hang on a minute." Stern interruption from Mick Wall, blocking her way.

"What's up, Mick?"

"It's only fair to warn my innocent young friend here – Terry, just because she buys you a drink, you don't have to do anything you don't want."

181

He grinned, and Jackie belted him, calmly but hard, and went to get the drinks. Terry did a slow rewind of the evening, and when Jackie came back he was ready.

"Ta. So tell me, how did Jill get Craig's book?"

"It was in the staffroom. She scooped up her things, and it was there. She only found it tonight."

"So it was just an accident?"

"Sure. What did you think?" She tried to read his face. "Did you think we were winding you up?"

He didn't know what to think.

"Jill? Oh come on, Terry. If she was winding you up she'd have kept it, right? No, if we were setting you up we'd do it properly. Hang on to the book, cassette recorder under the desk, photos of you and Sheila – the works."

He stared at her in horror.

"It's OK. We didn't. We're nice. Mostly. I mean, Mick really does need to practise filling in his tax return –"

"That was you?"

"Ssh. Me and Jill. He thinks it was the kids. But the book was an accident, and getting it back to you proves it. Take my word for it, she's innocent."

Innocent? He was the one who was innocent. Or maybe gullible was better. He didn't know a thing. How could a bluff, cheery joker like Mick Wall know Pete Wrench was gay, and Terry have missed it ? Were there other things he had missed?

"Night, Terry. See you tomorrow."

He waved, as Jackie went off cheerily, unworried, home to her husband. Leaving the isolates, the single people, to their lonely beds and thoughts. What about Jill? What was she thinking, tucked up in bed? Celibate? Lesbian? Workaholic? And in any case, so what? Lubricated by Guinness, the internal theory generator purred into overdrive.

Sheila Thorpe was miserable, Pete Wrench was gay, and Jill was the way she had chosen to be. Mick and Jackie were married, separately, but in such different ways. So whatever happened to the 'normal' world, where people had jobs, men were in charge and all the grown-ups lived happily ever after? Had he watched too many films ?

And had Terry the actor, the lad who makes things happen, become a permanent spectator, staring at the screen? It was over a year since he'd slept with Lavinia. Slept with anyone, come to that. No big panic, sudden resolutions or vital parts withering away, but a year ago Terry would have dismissed that possibility with a laugh, sure that nobody with anything about them, let alone him, could possibly be that sad.

Yet as he walked home, with the soft drizzle sprinkling down through the beery haze, Terry didn't mind. There was no big chance he'd missed, challenge he'd chickened out of, obvious mistake. Either Marion Harper or Sheila Thorpe would have been total disaster; some things were worse than nothing. This was the way it was. He needed the fresh air, the time, to sort his thoughts. He was certain – well, near enough certain – of one thing only. Whatever else he didn't know, whatever the eccentricities of other folk, he , Terry O'Mara, was a five star deviant of the weirdest possible kind. That wasn't much to go on, by way of consolation, but he was reassured that on this particular evening it didn't worry him as much as it might have done before. Van, as usual, got the last word: here comes the nah – ight.

CHAPTER NINE:

MAY

Rod Spencer tensed forward, alert, like a cat stalking a nest. This was THE BUSINESS, the reason he was here. The senior management team was talking budget. The quality of education was notoriously elusive, but money was something you could count.

Colin was worried. He didn't like dealing with his own money, let alone the school's, where there were far more noughts and a greater chance of doing damage. He didn't understand all of Rod's printouts and projections, but he followed enough to see that the future was black, or rather red. The kids they had and the staff they had to teach them didn't match, and there was no way of balancing the books. Well, there were several ways: they could stop cleaning the school, they could buy fewer books or – easily the quickest way to save cash – they could sack teachers.

Chris was watchful. Quiet, attentive and restrained, but watchful nonetheless. Rod Spencer always needed watching, but where money was concerned he was lethal. She had heard the gossip, how King Edward's governors had voted a massive pay-rise for their head and deputies, and she knew that Rod had heard it too.

If there was a quiet, legal way to raise her salary, she wouldn't fight that hard; the car was making strange noises, and a holiday in the Bahamas would suit her fine. But she was canny enough to know that at Rab Butler, this year, such extravagance was a dream. Whether Rod Spencer shared this realism was much less certain. So as they sat near Parnaby's window, in the usual uneasy triangle, she was not at all surprised to hear Rod say

"I know that on paper, it doesn't look too bright, but I think we have some room for manoeuvre."

"You mean we don't have to sack anyone?" Colin sought, innocently, for a reassurance only an idiot would accept.

"I wouldn't go that far. We'll need some rationalisation on that front, maybe some part-timers, but elsewhere I think we can move forward."

"Elsewhere is where, exactly?" It was a brutal, grammatically clumsy challenge, but he knew what she meant, even if Parnaby didn't.

"Well, in the area of management incentives, I think there are some interesting developments. At King Edward's, for instance–"

"You're joking."

"I don't quite follow you..."

"What he is suggesting, Colin, is that we not only sack staff but simultaneously give ourselves a pay-rise. Tactful, don't you think?"

"It's not as simple as that..." Rod's hands fluttered, trying to wave away this threatening clarity. "We need a sound financial long-term strategy– "

"I'm not sure I agree." The speed and confidence of Colin's intervention was unusual, and surprised them all. Long-term, for all sorts of reasons, didn't interest him. "I think we go a year at a time, and we try to hang on to all the teachers that we've got."

"All of them ?" Rod was appalled.

"Who do you think we should sack?"

"There's no need to be emotive."

"Sacking's an emotive business."

Rod was plaintive, looked hurt, held out his hands in an inno-cent appeal, a childlike assassin. "But this isn't personal. We're saving resources for the benefit of the school, to give our pupils a better education."

"Are we?" There was no trace of malice in Parnaby's question, but an anxious tremor, the questioning of a liberal who seeks to do the decent thing. "Is that really what we're doing? I wish I could be sure."

Rod was sure. His clenched fist battered out the message, thumped the cliches into position. "We need quality control. In all honesty, we have to admit that some of our teachers are substandard."

"Of course they are." Chris also knew the gambits, and worked coolly through the subsequent moves. "But which ones are we going to sack? What if the worst teachers are in shortage areas? Languages, for instance? Can we afford not to replace them, if we lost a language teacher? Be honest," and she paused deliberately, as if allowing him time to adjust to an unfamiliar concept, "is this quality control, or financial culling?"

And now the child was truly hurt. He looked at Parnaby, challenging the ref to do his job. "I must protest. My views are being caricatured here."

Colin was old and wise enough to know the value of diversion. "What I want to know is, can we keep Terry O'Mara?"

"Yes" from Chris. "No" from Rod. Simultaneous, confident answers.

"I know the arguments. He's temporary, last in, first out, drama is being squeezed and we can always con somebody into doing a bit of English."

"Exactly."

"But he's very good with kids. He's lively, he's keen, and I want him to stay."

"Right. Education. That's the business we're in."

"But it is a business, and we have to balance the books." He might be outvoted, but Rod clung tenaciously to his principles, and glared at each of them in turn, determined they should face financial facts. "If O' Mara stays, someone else is going to go. So, who will it be?"

His challenge hung, awkwardly. Chris, pushed to the wall, could make a couple of suggestions, experienced part-timers who were pleasant enough but not indispensible. But it wasn't her move. Colin was thinking retirement. That was the easy way of saving money: get someone to retire, and don't replace them. But he was the oldest member of staff. If he went, and wasn't replaced, Rab Butler would save £40,000 a year. They would also have to find a replacement head – either Rod, or Chris – and do without a deputy. All three of them considered the possibility, in silence.

"I'll kill him." Dale stamped across the playground, as Muptaz tried to reach him, calm him down, cut down the chance of a scene.

"Hang on, mate."

"He's two-timing us." Dale was breathing heavily. "He's had the tapes and we haven't got the cash."

"We haven't got it yet." For Muptaz, there was always an answer. Not straight away, maybe, but catch your breath, calm down, wait.

"Grow up. We'll have left by the end of the month, and that's what he's waiting for." His hatred, like a laser, crossed fifty metres of the playground in a second. He could see the beams hit Dennis' gut, and knock him to the ground. "I'll fix him, the thick, black, two-timing sod."

"Dale?"

"Yeah, I know. Nasty racist comment. I'm sorry, Ms. Macdonald, I take it back and I promise to love everybody from now on. But I'll fix that bastard Waite."

Muptaz put his arm round Dale's shoulder and steered him round, looking away. "You've got to be careful."

"I'll be careful."

"One, there's the race thing. Two, we're older than him, and we'll get done for bullying. Three, the whole trade is illegal. These videos are from Wall's equipment, that he got from Spencer. They're not going to like that."

Dale shook his arm off, and stepped back. "I'm not stupid. But we're in this business, and we're selling lots of tapes, and Dennis isn't keeping to the deal. It's not right. That's all."

"And there is one other thing." Dale bobbed restlessly, watching Waite, impatient with the chat.

"What's that, then?"

"He'll murder you."

Joyce stood by the side of his desk, holding a box. "Haven't you signed those cheques yet?"

"Sorry. Something came up." It always did. A school of somethings seethed below the surface, like monsters of the lagoon.

"And you've got this. A present from the government. " She plonked the box down on his table. He flipped up the lid, and saw a pile of glossy leaflets, telling parents how standards would rise. "And Mrs. Chalmers is waiting."

"Well, of course. A perfect day." He straightened the mess on his desk with a perfunctory shuffle, more psychological than effective. She had not moved.

"But that isn't all."

"It'll have to be. I just don't have the time."

"That's truer than you think." He looked up, surprised by the steel in her voice. "It's May. By May 31st any teachers who are resigning need to have put in their resignations."

"You don't have to tell me that."

"I think I do. This also applies to teachers retiring."

"Ah." And back it came. The nightmare, the budget, Chris and Rod, talking to the authority, the governors, about a possible replacement. He couldn't face it. It was easier to entertain the prospect of simply ticking on, even of confronting Joyce, than to actually commit himself to a date when he would retire. On the other hand, the peace, the relaxation of being out of all this...

"I'll think about it."

"No, please. Don't think about it. Just do it . Please?" She hurried out and it struck him, guiltily, belatedly, that she was on the verge of tears.

Terry shoved the papers and files, any old how, into his bag. He'd got better, no question, but some days he was still a mess. One day he'd be organised, everything would have a place, and maybe he'd buy one of those black attache cases, rectangular leather replacing saggy canvas. One day. When he had a permanent job, some kind of future. For the moment, improvisation would have to do. Vamp until ready.

"Can I talk to you, sir?"

Emma Sheargold, anxious innocent face, and rich brown hair that just demanded to be stroked. Any time, my dear, any time. What must it feel like to have this effect on him, on any bloke ?

"What is it, Emma?"

"This video, sir. I don't like it."

You and me both. The whole thing stinks. But I have to have a job, and keeping Rod Spencer happy is a possible route.

"What's the problem?"

He could think of several. It was a lousy script, which didn't require proper acting, for a dubious cause. If he were Emma's dad, he'd disapprove; if he were Emma, well,...

"Why me, sir?"

"I don't get you."

She was embarrassed. She braced herself, stood tall, drew breath and repeated the question. "Why did you ask me, to do the video?"

"You're very good. You're confident, you're keen – and I knew you could do it."

"And that's all?"

"Yeah." Apart from, you're a joy to work with, sexy to look at, and a strong recommendation to every warm-blooded male under eighty. But he didn't think he'd say that bit.

"Oh, sorry. I'll come back." With a clatter, Linda Jones announced herself, and started to retreat.

"It's all right. Come in."

"I can do you later."

"No. Do me now. We're just finishing – aren't we?"

Emma nodded, bit her lip, and picked up her bag. "Er, yes. Sorry. Thanks, sir."

Linda watched her go. "Nice kid, that."

"One of the best."

And now the ground was clear, she swung into her routine,

straightening chairs, putting up the ones that had been left, talking as she worked. "Some of them, treat you like dirt. So full of themselves they don't think we exist. Mind you, teenagers. Must be hard."

"You're right there." He sat at his desk, watching her work, reviewing his own adolescence. That period of gloom and confusion, the cloud of uncertainty, unspecified dread, which had loomed even more heavily over him then than it did now. Some things got better. "How're you keeping then?"

She looked across briefly. "Not so bad. I was off four weeks last term, but then it was cold. I should be OK, in the summer. Better be, if I want to keep my job."

"They're not cutting back, are they?"

"When it's cleaners, they're always cutting back. I had these four rooms when I started here. Now it's them and the corridor and the hall, plus the foyer if Marie's not here."

"Same amount of dirt, eh?"

"Same amount of dirt. Twice as much graffiti, and a ton of chewing gum. I reckon in some of these lessons they do nothing but chew. Oh, I shouldn't say that, should I?"

"You could be right." Did kids chew in his lessons? He didn't know. Didn't really, if he was honest, care. Until now. He'd try to keep his eyes open.

"Right then, I'll be off." He gathered the last of his papers, and stuffed them in the plastic bag. "I'm sorry it's such a tip."

"It's all right." She surveyed the debris. "I'm used to it. You're not the worst."

Chris Macdonald checked through her documents, one last time, surveyed the empty desk, the immaculate office, shut her attaché case and went to the door. Five years ago a morning off, going on a course, would have seemed like a perk. She walked across the car park. Away from the kids, away from the school, catch up on the professional gossip.

Now there'd be a bit of that, but a lot of the other. The other being sex education. Interesting enough topic, in itself, but not when the government got their hands on it. Now they'd be looking at the umpteenth draft circular, prepared by idiots, for the consideration of professionals, whose considered, careful, expensively gathered views would then be returned to the idiots. Not, in her view, a promising model.

She went through the routine. Unlock the car, start the engine, drive to the gate. Get out, unlock the gate, open it, cursing Rod Spencer all the while. Drive through, park on the other side, stop, get out and shut the gate, lock it, and get back into the car. And then, at last, she could drive off. There were days when Chris, a careful, cautious planner, longed for a life without security.

But that was dangerous talk. Security was in fashion, government policy, the compulsory ingredient. Teenagers were at risk from AIDS, and drugs, and glue-sniffing, all of which carried a heady whiff of risk; so her job was to put these kids off, without admitting the existence of homosexual attraction, extra-marital sex or pleasant sensations from drugs. And without offering an opinion of any kind, other than a blind, passionate faith in the unique perfection of the married state, a faith which for Chris was not borne out by experience; neither by her own, nor by the parents of pupils with whom she came into contact. Still, that was the politics of education : never mind reality, feed the myth.

It was too much for the powers that be to understand what it was like to have a tearful teenager confide in you, worried about her period, terrified of her parents or hating their guts, desperate for a little bit of love. But if you weren't careful, helping such kids could put you in trouble with the law.

Simon was not much help. True, he suffered from similar pressures, but they had little opportunity to compare notes, now that he had been sucked into the maelstrom of OFSTED training. He was about to become a qualified inspector, which meant that he spent increasing amounts of time away, brought mountainous piles of paper home, and worked later into the night. None of this made him any easier to live with, and as for old-fashioned sympathy, companionship, support – forget it.

Damn. The fuel gauge was winking at her, and mechanical

breakdown was an extra problem she could manage without. She pulled into the next garage, which was like they all were nowadays. Self-service, glossy, automated, flowers outside, cans and cassettes inside, but this one also had a book display. In disbelief, she read the titles – "How to recruit Good Managers", "How to Overcome the Manager's Objections", and – predictably – "Pressure at Work." Spencer's bedside table must look like this; were there really enough passing motorists who wanted this garbage with their petrol? Lots of little Rods pulling in for forty litres of diesel and a top-up of management theory?

She smirked, as she paid and walked out, but she didn't laugh. Chris didn't laugh that often, these days. She had moved on, moved up, been to the courses, got a better car and bought good clothes. Compared with many, she'd done OK. But when she looked back to the early days, starting teaching, she remembered Mick Wall and the fun they'd had.

Mick would never do. He was losing hair and putting on weight; he was lazy, sexist, selfish, and no self-respecting modern head would appoint him to anything. He was in a professional cul-de-sac, and might not be bright enough to know it. When Chris looked back, to the pub crawls, the chip shops, the games of cricket in the staffroom, she could see it was silly and childish and irresponsible, irrecoverably past, but she also knew that in the process of growing up something had been lost, a taste of laughter that she would never have again.

"Why the doughnuts, Jackie?"

She placed the plate on the table, at the heart of the meeting, and shrugged. "Oh, I don't know. Just a prize for being alive."

"Fair enough. Thanks a lot – do help yourselves." Brian Summers followed his own advice, took a large sugar-filled bite, and reflected on his fortune in having such a generous and imaginative colleague. He'd never have thought of it, but already the meeting was transformed. "OK, let's spend some money."

Terry expected some enthusiasm. Instead, each member of the department accepted a copy of the sheet Brian was issuing, and grimly scanned the columns of figures. Half of the money they had would go straight away, on stationery. Just giving kids something to write on seemed to cost a fortune. He recalled the thousands of sheets which had been anointed with two lines of scribble, and then consigned to the bin. That was just in his classes. Multiply that by six, and the bill was huge. Or maybe you shouldn't; maybe that kind of waste wasn't going on in the other rooms; maybe these quiet, dour professionals were conserving resources, rationing the paper, and funding his profligate ways. Not a comfortable thought.

"We need a lot more readers," Jackie offered.

"Yes, but there's set texts as well."

"And the tests. Don't forget the tests. Lots more copies of Shakespeare."

"The exam syllabus changes next year. We'll need a whole lot of new stuff."

Jackie looked from face to face, increasingly incensed as the gloom set in. "So all the money goes on texts, and we pack up proper reading?"

"Near enough." Brian didn't say it with any enthusiasm, but that's what the figures implied, and it was a long time since he'd had her energy and fight. He looked at Jill, who had not yet spoken. Surely his other star could offer something, a glimmer of hope? She wasn't keen.

"Jill?"

"Well, you can get some good stuff second-hand."

"Where?"

"In the market."

"But we can't use an order form there."

"Could I buy them and get a receipt?"

It was his fault. He'd asked, and she'd offered. But he knew where this led. Wrangling with Joyce about school money and approved suppliers and keeping the books straight. On the other hand, there was no nice, legal way of building up the stock. Jackie was certainly keen.

"Come on, Brian. Just thirty quid or so. See what we get."

"We could have a jumble sale."

Jill turned to Terry with total contempt. "That was a joke, right? This is serious stuff, Terry, even if we are talking peanuts."

It was too late to soften the blow, but Jackie tried to soothe the bruise. "Anything special you want, then?"

Terry shrugged. "No, just something kids can read. Boys especially. If you can get them second hand, fine."

"Sylvia, could I have a word?" Rod's invariable opening, to which it would have been delightful to offer a negative response. She settled for neutrality, staring blandly at him, saying nothing.

"In my office?"

Question, expecting the answer yes. If it's only a word, then we don't need the trek to the office. But he's management and I'm a peasant, so here we go. She looked at her watch, followed him down the corridor, into his office and sat down.

"About next year. The timetable."

"Yes?"

"How do you feel about commercial French?"

She settled into the chair. This was fine, just trivia.

"I don't like it. It's a bastard form of learning, neither good French nor good commerce. And I'd be very surprised if it's of the slightest economic value on either side of the channel."

"Ah, now that's a shame."

He waited for her to retract. Waited in vain. She took in the details of his soulless cell, the family photo on the desk, the bright colours on his computer screen, continually, mindlessly changing. What a life, to retreat to this.

"It's a shame, because we've been working on the possibility of putting on such a course, and we thought you might be just the person to launch it."

"Could I ask the precise composition of 'we'?"

He fluttered, floundered, panicked, like some teenager challenged to define the optative mood.

"You said 'we'. I just wondered who was proposing this idea." And she smiled, very sweetly. Because, the subtext ran, it doesn't sound like Parnaby or Chris Macdonald, so maybe it's just a little Spencer whim which can safely be ignored.

"I'm sorry. 'We' is the governors' curriculum working party – planning for the future." He didn't spell out the details: tapping the governors, keeping them happy, making them feel important. Getting them used to Rod Spencer as the man who made decisions, the man in place when the time came for Parnaby to go.

Sylvia had heard enough. She had her hands on the chair, ready to ease it back and excuse herself, when Rod resumed. "Actually, it was Sheila Thorpe who suggested it. Apparently, she used to teach something similar."

"I'll bet."

He sat up, startled by her change of tone. "I beg your pardon?"

"She wouldn't like to teach it now, I suppose?" Sylvia smiled again, and Rod laughed, unconvincingly. Was this sarcasm, or did she suspect a plot ?

"Is that all right, then?"

She looked at him, hard, unpitying. "Do I have any choice?"

"Well, we wouldn't want you to take on anything unless you were committed to it."

"Really?" Her features lightened, and he began to sense that he might have gone too far. Sometimes, his good nature was a curse.

"In that case, I think it's an appalling prospect, and I would only consider being timetabled to teach it if the sole alternative were boys' metalwork and PE on a Friday afternoon."

You could always tell a fight. The purposeless sprawl of breaktime activity was abruptly focussed, as a hundred casual conversations and games broke up; little kids chattered urgently, and ran to get a view; older kids sauntered towards the attraction, feigning indifference; and the whispered refrain of "fight… fight…fight" drew you, as if by magnetism, to the shouting, gasping animal centre of it all. Wearily, programmed to respond, Mick went to break it up.

"So you still don't know?"

Terry, installed in The White Horse at lunchtime, hadn't planned for his future to appear quite so stark. Rick McManus was chewing the remains of a chicken satay. He was also running courses from his power base at King Edward's, and sitting on a goldmine, while Terry clung to his temporary status, unsure of what September might bring.

"I could get you something here."

Had he heard right? Back to King Edward's? And how exactly could Rick manage that?

"Not teaching. I'm not the head. Well, not yet." The wide boy's wink suggested that this was only a matter of time. "Technician. You could come and do my filming. You can work a camera, right?"

"Yeah. Well, we've been doing this school video..." Terry hadn't liked to confess to Spencer's venture, a Mickey Mouse operation by McManus standards, so he was surprised by Rick's response.

"Oh, put it there, mate. A fellow sufferer. Believe me, I do know how you feel."

"You're doing one too?"

"Yeah. It was a real pain." He put down the final skewer as he crunched the last piece of chicken "The crew amble around, they're never on time, and they want you to run every lesson six times over."

"When you say 'crew', that's a proper TV crew, right?"

"Sure. One of our governors is a shareholder in Mercia TV, so we have to get the best." He picked out a crisp, and used it to scoop up some of the sauce. " I've never seen anything like it. That camera cost twenty-five grand."

"But it wasn't a barrel of laughs?"

"Right. The staff went spare, the director kept changing his mind. I'm not kidding, we had this woman in doing supply, filling in for a guy with a nervous breakdown, and he insisted on filming her."

"But why?"

"She was a dish. Gorgeous hair. Brunette. No use as a teacher,

196

but very tasty. Nicole Kidman, near enough. And all over the county there'll be dads slavering away, desperate to send their kids to King Edward's so they can get a look at her on parents' evening."

"Yeah. Yeah, know what you mean." Yet again, that unsettling feeling. Rick has got there first, done it better, even if it's only exploiting lust. Also, he was still working away at the satay sauce, and Terry was starving. "So, what are you offering? Best boy? Continuity girl?"

Rick scooped another crispful of sauce, and settled to his favourite task. Making the pitch.

"The money wouldn't be as good as teaching, but you'd get away from the kids. Anyway, there's no future in drama, and you don't want to be marking English essays the rest of your life. How about it? We could have some laughs."

And that was true, but what surprised Terry was how little that mattered. He didn't want to go back to King Edward's, didn't want to leave Rab Butler, but most of all he didn't want to accept that he was finished as a teacher. And the solemnity of that resolve came to him as a shock.

"I don't know. I'll think about it, Rick. Let you know."

"Up to you, mate. But don't hang around."

"You've got someone else?"

"As director of marketing", and the grin as he lifted another crisp confirmed that this was a pisstake, " I get to make a number of appointments in this expanding field. If you weren't interested, well – it could be Cheryl."

"Can she work a camera?"

"Tut, tut, Terry. Showing your age. Cheryl has many talents, and working a camera is certainly one of them. Or it will be, after the weekend."

"So you wouldn't want me anyway?" Why couldn't he just pinch one of the crisps, or even ask?

Rick took a long pull at his Guinness, licked his lips, and looked at Terry. "I might. I know it's pushing it, business and pleasure. Might be simpler to keep it between us lads. It's yours if you want it. Anyway, how about you and your…er.. responsibilities?" Rick was staring at him, very hard, very nosy, the poker player's eyes searching for a sign.

Terry drained his glass, and looked casually round the pub. "I told you. Finished with. All over, Rick. Done, dusted, over and out."

"You don't sound too sure."

"I'm very sure. I'm not going to be a dad, Lavinia and I have said our goodbyes, and she's got someone else."

The last crisp, the last of the sauce. "All cut and dried?"

"Well, cut. It's funny, Rick." He rested his elbow on the bar, and gazed at a beermat. "You know, we go round, playing the hard man, pushing for what we can get…."

"Go on."

"Yeah." He looked up, at the sharp suit, the silk tie, the cool, attentive face. "Oh, never mind."

"Come on, Terry." McManus nudged him gently. "Don't leave me gasping, mate."

But the memory of Lavinia returned, too sharp for betrayal. "No. Maybe some other time, when we've got an evening. Make a night of it, eh?" He moved away from the bar. "I've got to get back."

Each area of the staffroom, even smokers' corner, was aimed at Mick's bearlike frame as he reported on the fight. "So, anyway, there's Dennis pumping away like a prop forward on speed – I mean, you know our Dennis. If someone says 'fight' then that's what he's going to do."

"Strong lad, is Dennis. He can't half put the shot."

"It's a shame nobody has managed to teach him anything else. He certainly can't speak French."

"The English he came out with wasn't that great. Mind you, Dale was pretty far gone."

"Dale Adams – year 11? Looks like a rodent?"

"One of my stars. Well, he was till this lot happened."

"He's leaving in a fortnight."

"If Uncle Colin doesn't throw him out first."

"We've another two years of Dennis, anyway."

"If he lasts the course."

"But what was it about, Mick ? How do those two get to be in a scrap?"

And now Mick's relaxed expression was clouded by doubt. "That's the funny bit. When I got there, Dale was puffing. 'You black bastard' he says." Mick looked round, to check the audience. Jill, the one black member of staff, was at a meeting. The sudden chill came not from her, but from Chris Macdonald. She had come in only to post messages into pigeonholes, and she had never liked smokers' corner, whether or not it reeked of nicotine, but now professional zeal overcame her lingering distaste. She was looking at the pigeonholes, carefully extending the time required for her errands, but memorising every word. She was hooked, and they were hooked, waiting for her response.

Brian Summers stirred the pot. "Go on, then, Mick."

Mick Wall settled himself deliberately in the chair, thumbs in his belt, hands straddling his paunch. Take your time, make them wait.

"Well…he calls Dennis a black bastard, and Dennis calls him a little puff – "

"That's two-all so far."

"Oh no, they're not the same. Black's racist."

"Doesn't puff count as sexist, then?"

"Chris, is puff as bad as black?"

"Is little as bad as bastard?"

The look which Chris Macdonald directed into the smokers' corner was a shaft of ice. They looked up, innocent, at the humourless, upright deputy in her charcoal suit. Except for Mick, who continued as if she were not there.

"And then Dale says, 'You owe me, Dennis. Fifteen quid. When are you going to pay up?'"

"And then what?"

"Then he hits him."

"Mr. Wall," she sniffed, "I take it that you've reported this incident – or is this solely for staffroom entertainment?"

"Oh no, Muzz. Macdonald I've told Mr.Spencer – unless, of course, you'd prefer to take charge?"

Mick and Chris faced each other across a silent staffroom, whose older members could easily recall them laughing, drinking, holding hands. But not today.

Jill was soft. No other word for it. With the causes she cared about – NUT, Amnesty, Friends of the Earth – she found it hard to say no. She wasn't keen on the way Chris Macdonald ran her Equal Opportunities Group; there was something elitist, managerial, a bit joyless about it, but when she came up, claiming an urgent phonecall and asking her to take over, Jill had said yes.

They were decent kids. Better than that: bright, keen, critical girls. All girls, and that wasn't a problem. She'd seen enough of silly boys, sneering youths, superior men to know that for many girls the one real chance of being heard was to have the floor to themselves.

She thought back to the Leicester comp, the noise, the aggravation and the gossip, and her taking refuge in a home full of books. The jeers of kids who didn't do homework, didn't read books, didn't see the point. And fighting her way over the hurdles, knowing they shouldn't count – girls are thick, you won't get the grades, teaching is a waste of time. And all the way up, the urgency to get everything she could from the staff that cared a damn. It was better now, more open, more rational, more chance of support. So she didn't begrudge these kids half an hour of her time.

"Anything else?"

"Yes, miss."

Emma, quick, certain, confident – and then strangely bashful.

"Well?"

"The video, miss. Mr. Spencer's publicity thing."

As a notoriously precise English teacher, she couldn't have found a better phrase.

"What about it?"

"I think it's sexist, miss. I think they've chosen us –"

200

"Chosen you, you mean."

"And why you? What's so special about you?"

"Hang on a minute, Melanie. Go on, Emma."

"Well, miss. I can see it's an opportunity. A chance to do something, put a point across. But it's not our words, we're just told what to say. And I think they've chosen us, you know, the people in it..." Nervously, her mouth closed and her eyes dropped down.

Poor kid. Yes, Emma, you're gorgeous, and that's the first thing that almost anyone says about you – man or woman. And if Rod Spencer wants you in his sordid little promotional video, you're right that it's not your brains he's after. But how do you tell the other girls that? How do you say that you're dishier than they are and it's not right?"

Jill looked round the tables at a dozen girls, assorted shapes and sized. "Is anyone else involved?"

A couple of sarcastic laughs.

"I wouldn't mind, miss. If we got the chance."

"It's always their lot."

"It's not fair."

"Maybe not, but don't blame Emma for that. Don't forget, she was the one who brought it up. The point is, what do you want to do?"

"I think we should all be in it."

"Don't be silly."

"Or none of us?"

"What, no-one in the school? That's mad."

"No. No-one in this group."

Jill smiled grimly, acknowledging the old, impossible choices. Just us, or the world? Stay in and dirty, or pure and out? If we don't do it, who does, and does it matter? Is the gesture we make for the others, or for us? Tough questions, and the answers were hard.

"You can't decide for the whole school. If you all agree to boycott the video –"

"Someone else'll do it."

"Yeah. Mary Farmer, I bet. You know what she's like."

"We're not just going to slang people."

"No, miss, but you know what'll happen. We're aware of the issues. Emma can see the risks – at least she's worried about it."

"Is she?"

"You know she is. She raised it."

"But she's got no say. It's just teachers – men teachers."

"Why don't you do it, miss?"

Jill laughed. "Oh, sure. I can't even take pictures on the beach."

"Couldn't you talk to Mr. O'Mara?"

"He's not in charge."

"No, but he's filming it."

"Well, of course I could talk to him. But this isn't about me. What are you going to do?"

A brief pause, by the end of which they were all looking at Emma.

"Maybe that's not fair. You think about it, Emma, OK? You're the only one actually in it, so you'll have to decide. But thank you for bringing it up. You're right to think it matters."

Emma nodded, grateful, anguished, less sure than when she started. Given a moral dilemma, what did you do?

"We'll have to stop there. Can we straighten the chairs, please, before we go to registration?"

Records of Achievement. Like anything else in education that was official, it was polysyllabic and hard to understand. But it wasn't all bad. Some staff, Terry found, had time for it, had even worked to develop it, before the government made it compulsory. The only snag was, he was facing his year 10 tutorial group and he hadn't a clue what to do.

"Now, on these pieces of paper –"

"Haven't got one, sir."

"Just wait a minute, Johnny."

"Yeah, shut it, Navarro."

"Shut it yourself."

"You going to make me?"

"If you like."

"That's enough!"

It was sad, that you had to throw an Olivier just to get started.

"You need to know where you're going."

"The top. Heading for the top, that's me."

"Yeah. Top of the dole queue."

"Where are you heading, sir?"

"That's a good question, Tina, and I don't know the answer, BUT –" and, as he'd planned, the sudden shout stilled the titters at birth " – I'm going to think about it, and I'm going to write something down." Muted, sarky oohs and aahs, of exaggerated excitement, but they were listening.

"Can we see it, sir. What you write?"

"No. This is private. Me, thinking for myself."

"But you'll see ours, won't you, sir?"

"Why can't we do it just for ourselves?"

"Because you wouldn't do anything, dumbo."

"How do you know? You calling me a dumbo?"

"Want to make anything of it?"

"OK, lads. That's enough testosterone for today."

"What's testosterone, sir?"

Oh God.

"You need to set yourself a target, something you plan to work on, something you're going to achieve, in the next couple of months."

"I don't know what you mean, sir."

"Does it have to be in school?"

"I know what I want to do."

"Yeah, but she won't let you. Will you , Janice?"

"What's it got to do with you, Fartface?"

"No, you don't need to talk about it. It's a lot better if you think about it for yourself, and write something down. I'm going to take them in, because as your tutor I want to look at what you've put –" the expected chuckles, rebellious mutters, slanderous insinuations – "but I shan't tell anyone else what you've put, and I'll keep them for you to look at later. You need to plan what you'll do next, the target you've set yourself. So, write that down and you won't get into bother."

"That's a promise, is it, sir?"

"Johnny – write it."

And strangely, in the silence that followed, he did what he'd said he would. He tried to work out his own future, set himself some reasonable targets by the end of term. No, he didn't need to ask anyone out, get anyone into bed or buy a new car. Yes, he did need to keep his nose clean, maintain control of his classes and get himself a job for next term. Simple, really.

The kids didn't find it easy. There were the predictable anonymous fantasies from boys lusting after film stars, a couple of dreamers who thought they'd go from being semi-literate to Oxbridge candidates, and a few who knew what they wanted. "Getting a part-time job...I'd like to do my homework better...I want my mum off my back...I want to go out with Barry...All I want is my sister out of my bedroom PERMENENT!". Tina wanted to drive a car, and Emma was looking for a good drama group, to replace the video crap – though it was Terry who added the final phrase.

"Mick, could I have a word?"

Rod's timetable discussions were going badly. As he went on his rounds, offering teachers deals that they could not refuse, he increasingly felt like a failed insurance salesman. Surely somewhere was the happy customer, eager for good news, but it wasn't Mick Wall.

"Yes, Rod."

"It's about the timetable. In my office?"

"Fine."

Mick wandered in, surveyed the computer, the wall charts, the furniture and the space. How did a prat like Spencer get acres of carpet while he ended up with a broom cupboard?

"It's about next year. I think the time is right for some innovation."

Alarm bells rang loudly in Mick's head.

"On the technology front. "

Somewhere a siren was screaming.

"I've called it TT . Technology Tomorrow…" He smiled indulgently, as though the provision of a snappy title were the primary effort involved. The peripheral stuff, like designing, teaching and assessing the course, could safely be left in the hands of minions. Mick was a minion.

"Maybe I'm being a bit thick here. Is there somewhere this course is being taught?"

"Well, not yet. That's why it's an innovation. Curriculumwise, you'll be at the sharp end."

"It sounds painful." Mick sketched a mental diagram of a sharp end, and where he would most like to stick it.

"But you have to see it as an opportunity."

"I do?"

"Oh, definitely. All over the country teachers like you will be breaking new ground." A nervous smile, and he clumsily spread his arms, like a trainee MP, to convey the scope of this exploration. "There'll be courses, conferences, packages of materials – and you'll be there."

"I don't want to be there."

"You say that, but –"

"I not only say it. I mean it. I don't want to do it."

"I can understand why you might have reservations at the start."

"I'll have reservations all the way through. I don't need this."

"But we need it." Spencer's clenched fist signalled power, determination, cloth ears. "It's an opportunity that the school can't afford to miss. And it's also an excellent occasion for staff development."

"You mean it will hasten my nervous breakdown?"

"No. Promotion."

The bugger meant it. You didn't get Rod Spencer making jokes about promotion. Mick shifted uneasily, trying to settle, wanting to go.

"This is a new course, for September, that we're talking about in May. Right? In the old days, when we put in our own courses, they'd never let us do it that fast."

"I've been talking with the governors, and they're keen."

"Don't tell me. That idiot Hutchings."

"You have to take a positive attitude to this."

"Why?"

"It's the only way it will work. This is an exciting new development, a chance to do good work, and at the same time something which may advance the development of your career."

"In which case, " Mick replied, "why does it feel like a cock-up?"

Terry sidled up to Jackie in the staffroom.

"Can I ask you a favour?"

"Depends. Is it interesting?"

"Not really." He sat next to her. "You teach Emma Sheargold for Literature, don't you?"

"Yup. One of the best."

"Quite agree. She's one of my acting stars."

"So what's the problem, O'Mara ? Doesn't she fancy your casting couch?"

"Hey, that's not fair. If I came up with a line like that I'd get crucified."

"Quite right too. Your lot have been dishing out filth for a millennium; now it's our turn." She settled herself, and grinned at him. " So, what's the favour?"

"This video I'm doing for Rod Spencer."

"Ah." Her eyes raked the ceiling.

"Don't be like that. Sure, it's not the greatest opportunity since "Gone with the Wind". I've never pretended it is."

"Emma doesn't fancy it?"

"No. Well, that's the funny bit." He picked a speck out of his eye. " She seemed OK, and now she's not. Something's changed her mind."

"And you want me to find out what?"

"Yeah, I reckon." He went for it. "Maybe, even, change it back again."

"No. Sorry, Terry, but no."

206

"It's no big deal, I know, but Rod asked me to do it…"

"Just because he's a deputy doesn't mean he's right."

"Christ, I know that, but you are talking from the luxury of a permanent post."

"I'm sorry?" She sat back, and looked at him critically. "Oh, no. You really think that getting this video done will get you a job? Rod likes you, he tips the wink, you get to stay? Is that it?"

"I don't know, Jackie. I really don't know."

Kindly, sexlessly, she put her hand on his. "You are in a mess, aren't you?"

"Oh, that's for certain."

"Fair enough." She smiled, almost motherly. "but it's not fair to load that on to Emma, right?"

"God no, I wouldn't say anything to her."

"And if she's made up her mind, that's up to her, right?"

"Yeah. I'm not going to do anything evil. All I'm after is just a miracle – a baby miracle, that's all. Please?"

"I'll put you through to Mr. Parnaby now."

"But Joyce –" He gestured, but she would not be denied.

"Mrs. Adams would like a word. Mrs. Adams, you're through."

"Mr. Parnaby?"

"Speaking."

"Mrs. Adams here. I wanted to say, how grateful we were, about the way you handled that business last week, over the fight…"

"That's quite all right, Mrs. Adams. There's no point in being vindictive. Dale's achieved a lot here. He should do very well."

"Yes." A pause. "Yes, I think you may be right."

"Er, was that all?"

"No, there's something else. I've been clearing out his bedroom, in case there were books he hadn't returned, that sort of thing."

"Oh yes?"

"I don't know if they're yours or not, but there's some video tapes, and I know that they're not ours."

"Well, we do use them in lessons, but it's unlikely we'd send them home."

"That's what I thought. Dale said he was given them, as a reward for good work, but I thought that sounded a bit funny. You don't like to doubt your own, but...well, I just thought I'd check."

"I see. And Dale says he got them from here?"

"Yes, Mr. Parnaby."

"And er...how many tapes are we talking about?"

"A hundred and sixty eight. That's what Dale says. I haven't counted them myself."

Saturday morning in town, and they'd earned a breather. Jackie got the coffee while Jill went through the spoils.

"Hey, we haven't done badly. That Doris Lessing's a bargain, and there's a couple of Margaret Atwoods."

"We are talking school here, are we?"

"Of course, Jackie, what did you think?"

"You might just be getting carried away with what you fancy reading yourself."

"Me?" and they both collapsed. "But you need a few heavy-weights, at the top end, and we've a fair bit of the easier stuff. Buddy, Kes, a couple of Jobys, another Buddy." She finished going through that pile, and looked up into Jackie's inquisitor stare.

"Where d'you reckon these are from?"

"Market stall. 20p a go." Jill's voice was deep, steady, and her face expressionless.

"No. Before that."

"Well..." They both knew. Jackie opened one of the copies of Buddy. Inside was a stamp "This book is the property of King Edward's School".

Jill was a kid again. "I didn't know."

"I'll bet that makes you an accessory."

"Well, d'you want to give it back?"

"To the stall? Or the school?"

"Either."

"Course I don't. Though we ought to, strictly speaking..."

An uneasy silence, weighing morality, capitation, rivalry, effort.

"Hey, Jackie. Do you reckon I should ask King Edward's to buy them back off me, 20 p. a go?"

"No, you mustn't do that." Jackie was remorseless. "Ask fifty, at least." And they cracked up again.

It was over. It was boring, and he'd got in another girl for Emma (Mary Farmer, who wasn't half as good), but the bloody video was finally done. Terry slurped his coffee that break with deep relief.

Mick Wall approached him, waving a yellow slip.

"So what's going on, young 'un? Whose side are you on?"

"You tell me. Sit down."

Mick lowered his bulk on to the next chair. "I have here a missive from the langorous Chris Macdonald."

"Well, Mick, far be it from me to give tips to the master. I'm sure you'll manage fine. But you will remember foreplay?"

"Very funny. What it says is 'Boys' Attitudes to Gender'."

"Yeah?"

"And it also says – 'Have a word with Terry O'Mara if you're stuck. He's done some good stuff with year 10'."

"Let me see that." And he read it through, flattered but confused.

"So what are you after, Terry?"

"Me ? I'm just keeping my tutor group quiet."

"Don't give me that. It's a con, isn't it ? You reckon that if you set up as one of these New Men, it'll help you pull the birds. Am I right?"

"No, Mick, that wasn't the plan. And if it had been, it was no damn use at all. Really, I swear to God." And looking at each other, it was some time before they noticed Jill lingering in front of them, with a pile of books.

"Do you mind if I sit down?"

"Sure. Move up, Mick."

"Some other time, eh, young 'un? I'll – er – see you." Delicately for his bulk, Mick started to edge away, and then wrecked the effect with an outrageous wink that could have been seen from the far side of the playground.

"It's OK, Mick –"

"No it isn't. I want a private word." She didn't wait for him to respond. "First. There's some readers. Your share of the loot from the weekend." She handed him the pile of paperbacks, some of them fairly battered. He flicked quickly through.

"Why do they all have address labels in the front?"

"Don't ask. Now, the main business. " She sat primly, with her hands in her lap. "Emma Sheargold, and the video."

"It's OK. It's done. No problem."

"Do you mind if I go on?"

"Yeah. Sorry."

"Jackie said you were asking why she wouldn't do it."

"Yeah. Yeah, I was."

"I think she's a bit embarrassed about it." There was a rhythmic, nervous stress on "embarrassed" that surprised him. " I get the feeling she thought the motives for casting her were dubious."

"As in sexist, superficial male choice based on looks, sex appeal to other males?"

"You could put it that way. In fact, yes, you should."

"She's right. She was well out of it."

"It wasn't me, Terry. I didn't put her off."

"That's OK. I didn't think you did."

"I just didn't want you to feel got at. I mean, I know it's lousy, with the job being temporary, and that…"

"It's OK, Jill. No sweat."

"Fine. I'll go and get some marking done." As she stood, her face dropped, shyly. Did the cool, unflappable Jill Williams really suffer from embarrassment?

"Hang on. There's something else."

She turned to face him. "What's that?"

"Tutorial. Me and the boys. You and the girls. Have you been talking to Chris Macdonald?"

She smiled, slowly, with pleasure. "Um, yeah. Yeah, I think that might just have been me. Casual, you know, saying how you were all enlightened – well, for a man – and worth having on the staff. Why, was I wrong?"

"Thanks. Thanks a bunch. My mission now, should I choose to

accept it, is to initiate Mick Wall into the joys of talking with boys."

"Mm. Sounds lovely. That's almost another limerick." She was radiant. How could he have thought she didn't have a sense of humour? "Never mind, Terry. I'm sure you'll do it brilliantly. See you."

CHAPTER TEN:

JUNE

The Whit holiday passed, and exams began. A six-week break was in prospect, and the rain was lashing down. But as Colin Parnaby watched the puddles from his office window, he smiled contentedly. It was summer in his soul.

For he had finally made the move. He had put his resignation in writing, and submitted it to the governors. Better than that, he had discussed the succession with Mrs. Chalmers, and they had agreed that neither Rod Spencer nor Chris Macdonald should occupy his desk. So the straining Rab Butler budget would be stretched to accommodate a successor, and he would be free at last.

Joyce was a disappointment. Having endured the systematic nagging, the contempt for his lack of resolve, he felt he was entitled at least to acknowledgement, if not congratulation. He got neither. Joyce noted his resignation with ill grace, as if his eventual, reluctant capitulation could be taken for granted. Worse, there were hints that it might turn out to be a mistake, that their mutual dream of retirement and marriage might not be such an idyll after all. Now it was definite, he started to think in detail about their future life – houses, cars, her mother – and to wonder whether he was launched on a brave new voyage of discovery, or simply burning his boats.

In the subterranean squalor of the editing suite, Rod Spencer ignored the dusty gloom of his surroundings and focussed on the screen. This was his first foray into film, and it wasn't bad at all. Well, so it seemed to him, and Rod had so organised his life that he did not encourage more objective evaluation of his work.

It was, in fact, a competently shot, poorly scripted, one-dimensional plug of utter banality, but since this was what he was after it could be accounted a success. More to the point, it was on time, which meant that copies could go to governors, the media and even prospective parents before the month was out.

In his study at home, far from prying eyes, Rod had a flow chart of his assault on the citadel of power. The marketing campaign of the winter was matched by the video in the summer; approaches to the governors on the timetable would be supported by a presentation in the autumn; he already had the overheads, all he needed was the invitation. "Future Development of the Curriculum", maybe; it should be enough to paralyse Parnaby, who these days was looking increasingly a pushover. In the unspoken depths of his deepest plotting, Rod reckoned he'd be gone within a term.

There were the new courses, identified, titled, almost timetabled, requiring only to be taught; the replacement of the computer hardware, with the addition of a software licence that must be a snip at a mere four hundred pounds. He had effected economies in the budget – a leaner cleaning operation, capitation rationalised by formula – and he had the draft of a new management plan. This programme had its costs. He had spent hours with governors, in meetings and in informal dinners; and he had granted some paltry, harmless favours (the sponsored homework diary, logos on exercise books, the ice-cream concession for Sports Day), but it was cheap at twice the price. By Christmas, surely, the succession would be secure.

At last, the sun came out. Chris strolled round the grounds, imagining Parnaby retired. What must it be like, to look around and think "this is all mine" ? Mine to run, organise and reinvigorate – but also my price to pay, my can to carry: the place for which I take responsibility, listen to complaints, eternally pick up the pieces. Chris picked up enough pieces as it was; there couldn't, surely, be that many more that were Parnaby's alone.

She looked round at the kids, who also seemed better for the sun. No huddling in doorways, sheltering from the elements until the caretakers deigned to emerge from their heated den to unlock the doors. Now they could dawdle, sit on the grass, drink in the sun. A pastoral scene of innocence, except that the girls had to wear these bloody summer dresses, while the boys remained the same. Maybe next year.

Smokers' corner was meant to be secure. You could sit there, moan, drink a coffee, and they were supposed to leave you alone. But now, in his lunchtime, Brian Summers sat in a comfortable chair, and was being harangued.

"Brian. We have to talk to you."

"Urgently. And in private."

He looked from Jill to Jackie, and back again. Most of the time they were great. He liked to joke about "my girls", knowing that while he did the crossword they would be printing materials, filing resources, running workshops and magazines. The distribution of labour suited his psychology, and although a purist might argue that their relative pay scales failed to reflect justice, it wasn't a perfect world. Even he could not evade responsibility for ever.

"Fine. Tomorrow lunchtime any good to you? "

"Not as good as now." They stood, ready. They were not going to go away.

"In the English office?"

"That will do fine."

They sat around the table in the office, with Brian maintaining the illusion of leadership. "Right. Now, what can I do for you?"

Jill grimaced. The refrain of impotent man throughout the ages. Unfortunately, in this case it applied.

Jackie was ready. "It's about Terry. He's only temporary, and I know he's not trained. Now in normal circumstances we'd insist on an English graduate – "

"And we know you would too."

"But it's unlikely we'd get someone else."

Now he knew where they were going he relaxed, eased into head of department languor, the reasonable man beset by constraints. "That's true. Rod took us through the budget before half-term. It's not good, I can tell you. We may not get all our capitation."

"That's outrageous! You've got to fight him on that –"

"Jill?"

"Sorry. You go on."

"The thing is, Brian, we reckon Terry's doing OK."

"So we want to try to keep him."

Brian sagged, relieved. "Well, if it was up to me –"

"That's the point. It is, a bit."

"Well, not really. Senior management, budget, the governors..." The litany of abdication. All these important forces weighting me down – *that's* why I'm so useless.

"You can tell them. Talk to Colin, before they give Terry the push."

While Jackie made the case, Jill watched him, warily. "Well?"

"I'm on your side, really." He squirmed, trying to look at his watch without making that too obvious.

"Fine. And you will say so?"

"Soon. To Colin. Loud and clear." It occurred to him, slowly but with increasing discomfort, that she was talking to him as if he was a slow learner.

"Do it to them, Brian. Before they do it to you."

"Is that a quote from somewhere?"

"Don't worry about it. Just do it. We need him."

"Sir?" A slow, sexy drawl. And a searching look as she walked up to face him, put her hands on the table behind her, and hitched herself up to sit on it.

"Yes, Tina."

"Why didn't you ever get married?"

The touching innocence of the teenager, that anyone over twenty was dead and buried. Terry saw the hands on the hips, the

215

blonde waves, the challenging blue eyes, and hunted in his brief-case for nothing at all.

"To be honest, Tina, I'm none too sure. It's something that might yet happen. I'm not fifty for a couple of years yet."

She giggled, more than the joke deserved. "Do you fancy any of the teachers?"

"I don't think I'll answer that."

"Ms. Grabowska's nice. Is she your type?"

"OK, Tina, it's time you were going home."

The legs still swung, idly, as she worked through the field. "Or Miss Williams. But she's moody, maybe a bit tall. Sad, I'd say."

"That is more than enough. Go on. Where's your bag?"

"Don't need it, sir." She edged gently off the table. "The sort of homework I do doesn't go in bags." She moved away, between the desks, towards the door, but then turned to flash him her weathergirl smile. As a tutor who fancied keeping his job, he didn't want a fuller account of how Tina spent her leisure time.

As she went out a grey-haired cleaner came doggedly through the door.

"Mr. O'Hara, is it?"

"O'Mara."

"Near enough." She put up two chairs in the back row.

"Sorry. The kids forgot."

"It'll come. When you're new to it, you've got other things on your mind."

"That's true." He watched her pick up bits of paper, sort loose books on the side. "Where's Linda?"

"Didn't you know? They sacked her. I'm Elsie, by the way. Cutting back, they said. I reckon it was because of the illness. She had a lot of time off last term. "

"So she's out of a job."

"They're boggers like that. But she'll cope. She's working for her cousin, on an ice cream van. Though the hours aren't as good. Still, something's better than nothing."

"Right." Terry fastened his bag. Just at the moment, he didn't welcome conversations about job security.

"You were lucky with her. Her health's not great, but she's a good worker, is Linda. Though she's let you keep this in a tip."

"Well er…yeah, I suppose so. I'll…er…sort it out, eh?"

"You'd better. I've still got my usual rooms. I'm not tidying your papers on top of that."

" OK, Elsie. I'll work on it."

Pete Wrench was touring the staffroom, clipboard in hand. Sports Day was on the horizon, and he was checking jobs. A necessary errand, one part courtesy to two parts pressure.

"Hi, Mick. OK for Sports Day?"

"Sure. Wouldn't miss it for the world."

The pen moved happily down the list."Crowd control again?"

"Sorry."

"What ?" He was young, innocent, shocked to find a snag.

"No can do. I have acquired other responsibilities."

"What does that mean, in English?"

"Rod wants me to film his sponsors." Mick gave a glum shrug.

"Oh, great."

"Well I wouldn't go that far. But it should make gripping viewing."

He should give up, move on, try another teacher. But Pete was persistent. "What about Terry? I thought he was the camera-man?"

"Young Terry helped us out with the video.This is different."

"I see." He started to go, then turned back. "No, I don't. It doesn't make sense. If Rod wants a memento of Sports Day, he could get a kid to film it. And if I don't get enough judges, then it won't happen at all."

Mick felt for him, recognising a fellow victim, like himself, shat on from a height. He hugged Pete round the shounder. "Sorry, son. You could always have a word with Rod."

"Right. He could do crowd control, instead of you."

Mick looked at him kindly, unwilling to puncture the dream. "Ask him. I'm sure he'll leap at it."

In his office, Colin Parnaby was sat in a comfy chair, gazing out of the window as the slaves arranged the hurdles.

"Just think. My last time."

Joyce fussed round his desk, straightening the papers, and returning his coffee cup to the tray. "You can come back next year, if you like."

"Don't be like that."

"I'm sorry. I'm as bad, really." Boldly, without invitation, she joined him and sat down. "It's getting used to the idea. A bit like sex. All that build-up and suspense, and then, well, it's happening."

"Yes?"

"I still can't decide between Italy and Portugal."

He stared, baffled. "Are we still talking about sex?"

"No, the honeymooon. What do you think?"

"I'm happy to go anywhere. Really."

Her mouth was clamped in irritation. "Mmm. I knew you'd say that."

"Do you want me to decide?"

"I don't know." She shook her head, unable to look at him. "If I knew the answer to that, I'd tell you." And then she clasped her hands together, and did look at him. "Colin...we are going to be all right, aren't we, without this work to do?"

The phone rang, and she went across to the desk. "Yes?..." she held the receiver out to him. "Miss Thorpe, wants to talk to you about options."

He held his ground, and mouthed "Rod?"

"No, he's out talking to some business people. Probably her husband, come to think of it..." Parnaby, increasingly uneasy as he imagined Sheila Thorpe listening to Joyce's description, tried a tiptoeing mime of tact. It was wasted.

"Sorry, I'm supposed to say partner, aren't I? It always reminds me of tennis or dancing, and they're very different, I'd have thought. Still...do you want to take it here?"

He nodded, anxious to stop her, but reluctant to take the call. He walked across to his desk, took the receiver and sat down. With a slight, ironic wave, she left him to it.

"Hello, Colin Parnaby here. How are you?"

"Since you ask, Mr. Parnaby, I'm angry."

"I'm sorry to hear that. What can we do for you?"

"You could alter your option pattern, for a start."

"That may be a little tricky." He shuffled in his seat. "What appears to be the problem?"

"I'm a linguist. I'm anxious that Craig should have the fullest possible opportunity to grow up as a good European..."

He worked, quite hard, to reconcile his impressions of Craig Hutchings with this unlikely model. He couldn't get anywhere near.

"...and I now discover he can only do one language."

"Yes, that may be so."

"But why is that?"

"It's partly to do with Craig's progress in French." Or lack of it, he nearly said. "And there's also this new course, Technology Tomorrow. Rod Spencer tells me it's quite promising."

"So my son is a guinea pig?"

Well, certainly closer to that than a good European.

"Not at all, Mrs. Hutchings...I mean, Miss Thorpe... Ms. Thorpe. The government are very keen on Technology, many other schools require it."

"I see. And does the government require a generation of linguistic illiterates who have no knowledge of any culture other than their own?"

This spelt out Parnaby's personal suspicions with uncanny accuracy, but discretion held his tongue; there was no need, or opportunity, even, for him to speak.

"So far as I can see my child is being compelled to take an untried course in a subject whose very nature, let alone its future, is thoroughly suspect."

"I'm sure Rod Spencer would be happy to explain."

Dimly, the memory returned. Wasn't it Mark Hutchings, Ms. Thorpe's other half, who had proposed this course ?

"Oh, I'm sure he would. Rod Spencer would happily explain why grass was red, if he thought it would suit his career. Unfortunately, this will not enable Craig to take two languages at GCSE, and thus move on to 'A' levels. Perhaps King Edward's will take a more enlightened view."

Parnaby was philosophical. It was a new experience, having someone hang up on him. He got a lot of VIP calls, self-important parents who didn't want to bother with anyone lower than the head, but it was rare for any of his callers to simply slam down the phone. With a kind of detachment, conceivably related to the imminence of his retirement, he conceded that he was impressed.

The door opened quietly, and Joyce slid back in, bearing a fresh cup of coffee. "That woman is an uncultured bitch."

"You're not supposed to be listening."

"You've still got to get through till the end of July, and you won't manage that without me to look after you." She put the coffee down.

"You think so? You could be right. Wasn't it Mark Hutchings who put Rod on to that Technology course?" He sipped, to check that it was hot enough, and almost burnt his lip.

"It's hard to tell. He's been greasing up so many governors I can't keep track." She turned to go.

"Joyce, that's not nice."

She stopped at the door. "No, but it is true." She flicked through her mental filing cabinet. "Yes, you're right. It was Hutchings."

"So why is she complaining? You'd have thought they could sort that out at home."

She looked at him, in disbelief.

"You don't understand, do you? You really don't understand."

He smiled, nervous and jolly. "No, Joyce, that's why I'm asking."

She shook her head and said nothing, but walked slowly out, and shut the door behind her.

It was a good life. Terry sauntered round the grounds, nominally on duty but just enjoying the sun. The decent weather seemed to have a benevolent effect all round – teachers less ratty, kids less aggressive. It was dry enough for the serious criminals to vanish into the woods, leaving only the nervous, the passive and the law-abiding safely within teacher vision. If this was teaching, he could cope. He found a flat patch of grass, at the top of a small rise, where he could sit down, sip his coffee and still keep kids in view.

"Sir?" He turned, to find the tall figure of Emma Sheargold standing behind him. No question, these summer dresses made a difference.

"Can I ask you something?"

He looked up and round, awkwardly, and nodded. "Go ahead."

She settled herself gracefully on the grass, next to him, as he tried not to watch. If he was a politician, the News of the World would be filming every move.

"Do you think sex is over-rated?"

He nearly dropped his coffee. It must be News of the World . If it was Tina, he'd fear the worst, even if he couldn't see the microphones, but Emma was innocence itself, bordering on shame.

"I'm sorry, sir. I knew I shouldn't ask."

"No, no. It's OK. I just wondered what brought that on?"

"It's my mum, mainly. Since she and dad split up she goes on about how she doesn't need him, doesn't need anyone."

"Yes, well, there's different ways of living. Some people manage better on their own."

She looked at him, checking that he was listening, did care, could be trusted. "And then there's Tina, and her crowd, going on as if you're not really alive unless you sleep with a different bloke each month."

"That's just Tina." And then came the memory, of wise agony aunt Jill, teaching him the facts of female life. "Well, anyway, it's the way Tina talks."

"You think she's just talking, sir?" The intensity of her look rang warning bells; mustn't say anything that shouldn't get back.

"I wouldn't know, Emma. Do you know? Ever been to her house?"

She said nothing, but her denial was vehement. Just because we're in the same class doesn't mean we share the same world.

"Me neither. But I'd guess her house isn't much like your house. Different families do things different ways, watch different pro-

221

grammes, eat different food. And then it all changes, as you get older. You see things in a different light ."

He looked at her, and smiled, and listened to himself. How did he ever end up, sitting on the grass, sounding like a trendy priest?

"What matters to you varies. It might be your family, your friends or, later, the job you do." Or the girl that you get pregnant, but he didn't say that bit. Pompous preacher he might be, but he was right. What mattered, changed. What he cared about now wasn't what he cared about in The White Horse with Rick McManus, only a year ago. Slowly, in the warmth of the sun, he felt himself getting wise.

"You just have to work out what's best for you. We all do. I mean, nobody's handing out answer books for this kind of thing. I haven't got the secret of life."

She stood up. "I know that. I'm not stupid."

"That's true. Stupid is one thing you definitely are not. There, that's a good English teacher's sentence for you."

"Thanks, sir." She brushed bits of grass off her dress.

"That's OK. No problem."

Then she stopped, and looked at him. "But you know, sir, there's one other thing."

"What's that?"

And now she was strangely hesitant, twisting her fingers. "I don't want to be rude, sir."

"You wouldn't know how. Go on, what is it?"

"You weren't boring or anything – "

"Well, thanks."

" – but you never answered the question."

"You mean I have a choice?" Marion Harper's beautiful vacant face was tilted up towards Pete Wrench. He, like her, was powerless.

"Not really. Still, you'll get some fresh air, and there's a couple of lessons you won't need to teach."

"Yes, there is that. Wednesday, 9C, Dennis Waite. Alright, I'll be there." Pete had had more enthusiastic replies.

But not many. It wasn't going well. Without warning there seemed to be an undue amount of doctor's appointments, urgent fillings, hay-fever sufferers who'd prefer to stay in the results tent, if he didn't mind too much. None of them were actually against Sports Day, they just weren't keen to do the work which would enable it to happen.

"Sylvia, could I ask you a favour?"

"You can certainly ask. I don't promise that I'll agree."

"Friday afternoon, Sports Day. Could you be a field judge? Javelin."

She looked thoughtful, but she might be messing him about. "That's the spear-like object they impale in other pupils' feet?"

"It's like a spear, but they don't impale. Not with you in charge."

Despite herself, she smiled. "Flattery will get you a long way. But not the whole way, I'm afraid. On Friday I am due to see the senior moderator for oral examinations, or I'd be delighted to help you." She swept away, smiling, and he didn't believe a word.

"Cheer up, it may not happen."

He turned to face Jill's smile, but couldn't return the warmth.

"OK, then. What are you doing Friday afternoon?"

"I'd assumed I was helping with Sports Day, but if you're offering an alternative I could be tempted."

"No. Stop there." He ticked her name. "Track judge, OK?"

"Fine."

"Terry. You OK for Friday?"

"No problem. Drinking bout, tickets for Wembley, Van Morrison concert?"

"You're close. Sports Day."

"What am I doing?"

"Shot. OK?"

"Sure."

"Thanks. You're a star." Another tick, mercifully without hassle, but still a long way to go. Pete scanned the staffroom, and moved disconsolately on.

Terry sat down, next to Jill. "What's up with Pete?"

"Sports Day blues. Not all our colleagues are as enthusiastic as you."

"I didn't think I was that keen."

"Keen enough. Anyway, how's it going?"

"Mm. Not bad." He thought briefly, and savoured the joy of a straight, neutral conversation, without the undertow of sex. "You know, Jill, I could get to like this job. If they let me."

"And that surprises you?"

"Yeah. It sounds daft. But I drifted into teacher training, teaching practice, might be a teacher, might as well teach."

She nodded. "I know what you mean."

"You? Don't give me that. I'll bet you wandered round in a nappy, looking for a piece of chalk. Anyway, wasn't your mum a teacher?"

"My mum lectures in history, at Leicester University. It's hardly the chalkface."

"Get away." The loud clanging noise inside his skull was the collapse of further assumptions, but he tried not to let it show.

"Why does that surprise you?"

"No reason. I just…no. So, how does she meet your old man – don't tell me she forgot to pay her fare?"

"Do you dream in clichés?"

"Is there any other way?"

She explained. "My dad's a big union man. The university runs extra-mural courses, oral history, workers' rights, OK? And my mum's one of the lecturers. So – here I am."

"Poor kid. You never had a chance."

"That's right. Doomed from the start." She rose, and picked up her bag. "Still, there's worse jobs than this, even if the bell has gone. Come on."

Colin surveyed the mounting reams of paperwork on his desk, with considerable distaste.

"I think I'll just take a look around."

Joyce followed his glance through the window. "But they haven't started yet."

"All the same –"

"All the same, this lot needs doing, and this afternoon is an ideal opportunity."

He put on his stubborn look. "If the rest of the school has to stop for Sports Day, then the head ought to stop too."

"The head doesn't stop any time. You do twice as much as the rest of them. And when they've all gone home, you'll still be looking at these."

Together, they looked at the pile. It didn't diminish, or move. It was waiting for him. But he wasn't ready to give in. "Somebody needs to keep an eye on things, look in on the troops. It's good for morale."

She stiffened, and looked back, suspicious. "I thought Rod was doing that."

"Well, yes...." He trailed off, looked down, shuffling out of scrutiny.

"What was the row about, then?"

"It wasn't really a row. We were short of people." He sighed. "I told Rod he'd have to do his bit. He wasn't happy."

"He doesn't have to be. But I don't want you miserable, and you will be if you don't make a start on these."

"All right, you win." He looked at his watch. "I'll do half an hour, then I'll go and take a look. It's a dangerous time, Sports Day. Everyone out there, anything could happen."

In the staffroom, last-minute preparations were rather less rational.

"The smooth-talking two-faced bastard – I swear I'll kill him one of these days."

"Not happy, Mick?"

"Rod doing your appraisal?"

"If only. I'd tell him a thing or two. He's got me on crowd control."

"I should be more than happy to relinquish the javelin." Sylvia, having had her arrangements disrupted at short notice, got little sympathy. They had to do it; why shouldn't she?

"I'm sorely tempted, but I think I'd better not. Just at the moment there's only one place I want to stick it."

Jackie, not trusting an English summer, toyed with a sunhat. "But what's the problem, Mick? We've all got jobs."

Brian knew it would be freezing, and put on another jumper before adding his coat. "Don't wind him up. Rod told him he could play with the video camera, and now he's changed his mind."

"I thought Terry was the cameraman – ooops. Sorry, Jackie. Operator."

"Don't worry. You're nearly ready for the twentieth century, now it's gone. No, Terry's done his filming. He's running off the copies now."

Mick, still disgruntled, was finally ready. " Are we right, then?" Half a dozen teachers picked up their stopwatches and clipboards, and left the staffroom for the challenge of the great outdoors.

Down in the depths of the editing suite, Terry stood over a steaming video. It wasn't that dramatic a role. Just linking up two VCRs and getting one of them to tape off the other, but Rod wanted a hundred copies by the end of the week and this – crude, slow, repetitive – was the only process that the budget could afford. Rick McManus would have laughed himself sick.

"Excuse me, sir?"

"What is it, Tina?" He shouldn't be here, she shouldn't be here, not good news at all. As she moved gingerly towards him, he realised that Emma Sheargold was not the only actress in his class.

"I don't feel too well, sir."

"But you're running in the relay."

"I'm sorry, sir. I don't think I'll be able to do it. Emma says she'll do it if I can't."

I'll bet she does, thought Terry, as he watched carefully for symptoms. The earnest face, eyes not quite brimming with tears, lips slightly apart – this was getting silly. "So, what are you going to do ?"

"I thought I ought to sit and rest a bit, sir." Clever. Not wanting to go home, not wanting to cause trouble, just sit around like a quiet martyr and maybe I'll get better. As he clumsily put out the hurdles, he knew she'd be over them in seconds.

"There'll be no-one to look after you. They'll all be out on the field, like I should be – God, is that the time?"

"I could be by the office, sir, if you gave me a note." She was good. The line of least resistance every time.

"Mrs. Davies has her own work to do."

"It's all right, sir. I won't be any trouble. Honest." At an audition for Christmas tree fairies, she'd have walked it. She might be lying and she might not, but it would take a better teacher than him, one with time to spare, to find out. Earnest and appealing, she held the gaze.

"All right." He searched his pockets for a pen. Stood up, ransacked his trousers, looked at Tina. She mimed helplessness, and looked admiringly round the suite.

"Come on, let's get you to the office."

Not bad. Not bad at all. Pete Wrench surveyed the teeming activity of Sports Day, and pronounced it good. Not high class athletics, maybe, but decently organised, reasonably on time and enjoyable for most of the competitors. The staff were a different matter, but since his summit meeting with Parnaby he had at least got the numbers he wanted. And they were all in place with the single, odd exception of Rod Spencer. He was meant to be available for crises, and although at the moment there were no crises visible, Pete had a tidy mind and he didn't like loose ends.

"Mr. Wrench?"

Mrs. Cartwright, usually a dinner lady but today a purveyor of ice-cream.

"Everything OK?"

"The site's fine, but we seem to have competition." She pointed over to the far side of the field. A bright, attractive tent, with a fancy awning and rows of coloured pennants. At a test match, Pete would have said it was a hospitality tent; at Rab Butler's

Sports Day, which he was helping to organise, he didn't have a clue.

"Sorry, Mrs. C. I'll have a look."

"I wouldn't mind, but they've got more flavours than we have. Their prices are a bit high, but even so."

"Don't worry. We'll sort it out." Or Rod Spencer will, when the pillock finally shows up.

Sharon and Valerie sat on the grass, auditing discrimination.

"The boys had to shift the hurdles."

"Is that good or bad?"

"I don't know, but it's a difference. They do 1500 metres and we don't."

"I wouldn't complain about that."

"This is a scientific survey, not a grudge. Maybe the boys get a rough deal."

Valerie pondered the possibility. She was not convinced.

"How did you get on, anyway?"

"Fifth."

"That's good." For Sharon, enthusiasm oozed naturally. "You were tenth last year."

"Yeah, but last year we were keen first years, and there were twelve runners."

"How many this year?"

"Just the five."

The aggressive satisfaction in her tone unnerved Sharon, who didn't know what it was like to be useless at PE. "D'you fancy an ice-cream?"

"No, I don't like their strawberry. Pink plastic."

"Not the kitchens' . That tent over there, they've got rum and raisin, tutti frutti, all sorts."

"Go on then, get me an all sorts. I like liquorice."

Terry was having a good time. Putting the shot wasn't subtle, but it was good to see kids – especially big, heavy kids – doing well at something outside lessons. A burly third year girl with a permanent scowl got near a school record, but the star was Dennis Waite. His big, muscular body slid across the ring, and with a grunt he propelled the bomb into a graceful, slow parabola.

"Nice one, Dennis. Better than your last."

"Am I still winning, sir?"

How could he not be, after his own throw? What was going on inside that head? "Sure. By a mile. Well, you know."

"What time is it, sir?"

"Nearly half-two. Why?"

"Er, nuffing. I'll be back in a mo'."

As Dennis slid off, Terry recalled the news cuttings, the gossip, about him and Tina. Nicking car badges, nicking cars, rumours of teenage sex. But maybe that was just teacher talk, nasty middle-aged professionals scared and jealous of kids.

Tina. Illness, the note that wasn't, sitting by the office, and he'd left the suite to do it. Mick's priceless equipment, exposed to view and unlocked, with everyone out on the field. And Terry, probationer, temporary, looking-for a job Terry, was responsible for it all. He left a startled year 10 pupil illegally in charge of the shot-put circle, and started walking back.

He saw in the distance the figure of Rod Spencer flailing wildly, as if trying to communicate a scientific formula through semaphore. But Terry had his priorities straight, mimed overpowering dazzle from the sun, and carried on, back to his duty and the school.

It was all going wrong. He watched Terry O'Mara disappear with a raging sense of injustice. Nothing in the plan was wrong, each stage of it was entirely reasonable, and the overall package was neat, even beautiful. So why was it falling apart?

The deal with Carter, offering sole ice-cream rights for Sports Day, might have been new to an innocent like Wrench, but in the world of commerce it was commonplace. Maybe he should have cleared it with the PE department, but they were busy enough with the arrangements for events.

Having got Carter here, with the lure of giving him free film of his own stall in operation, Rod had lost his cameraman – thanks to Parnaby. He had brought the camera out, but he wasn't confident of his own ability to work it, which was why he needed O'Mara, just at the point when O'Mara decided to walk off. First impressions, as so often, had been correct; he wasn't reliable. After early enthusiasm, he'd cooled over the video, and it would be no great hardship to let him go.

And now there was the truck. Not just the dinner ladies, flogging their second-rate ice-cream, but some kind of cowboy operation in a white lorry, drawing droves of kids. Mick Wall, that was the answer. If Mick couldn't do the filming, he could at least stop kids from buying ice-cream at the wrong outlets. Rod grabbed a kid, and sent a message to the loudspeaker van.

Terry noticed the truck, and half wondered what it was doing, but he couldn't afford to be deflected from his task.

"Go on, then. Ignore me."

He recognised the friendly smile of Linda Jones.

"Why don't you stop me and buy one?"

"You look as if you're doing OK without me. All right, give us a choc ice. I'm sorry about the job."

"Not your fault. How're you doing with Elsie?"

"OK. She's not as good as you."

"Not as soft, you mean. That's fifty p, to you. Special rates." There wasn't the time to argue, nor to analyse the wink she gave him, so he paid and hurried on.

He was earning his pay today. Mick Wall was good with crowds, and he liked the sense of power, but you had to keep your wits about you. Slide off to the toilet, feign injury, done my event and need to get changed....He had long since adapted an advertising slogan, rough and ready but it seemed to meet the need. "The answer's No – now, what's the question ?"

Once the kids knew he meant it they settled for a truce, but that wasn't the same as conceding defeat. If he turned his back, or let a few slip through, they'd have kids heading home, back into school and everywhere.

And now there was that cretin Spencer, waving frantically and holding on to an ice-cream. Fat chance. If Mick turned round to buy himself an ice-cream he'd lose them in a flash.

"400 metres intermediate to the start, please. And could Mr. Wall report to Mr. Spencer at the hospitality tent."

All over the field he could see the teachers laughing. All right, you idiot, you've asked for it. Mick Wall stumped angrily across the track, knocking sideways the leading competitor in the girls' 800 metres. By the time he had picked her up, checked the damage, and watch her closest rival break the tape, twenty-seven spectators had vanished from the field.

Terry hadn't thought about what he'd find. The door might still be open, or the caretakers might have locked it. Luckily, he still had the key. And there was Dennis, standing on guard, too dozy to notice his approach.

"OK, Dennis, where should you be?"

"Shot, sir."

"Right. Get back there, now." Dennis hovered, torn between warring bosses. "Now, Dennis. Or it's serious trouble." A further moment of indecision, but only one boss was in vision, so he trundled off.

The door was open, but Terry was surprised to hear voices inside.

"What, just unplug 'em?"

"Or bite through the wires if you'd rather. Come on, you dickhead, we don't have much time." The voice was unmistakable, contemptuous and calm.

"You're feeling better, then, Tina?"

"Christ!" The tall youth glared at Terry, looked askance at the ice cream, barged his way past and ran. He was well over six foot, and Terry didn't move. It was Tina he wanted.

"Hello, sir."

"Hello, Tina. Come along and talk with Mr. Parnaby."

"It isn't what you think, sir." Already, the eyes, the lips were at work. A lifetime of wheedling strategies were whirring into play. She hadn't got much, so she was used to using everything she'd got, anyway she could. Look away, look away.

"What I think, Tina doesn't matter. You talk to him."

With a pang of regret, he dropped the choc ice into the bin. First things first. He was terrified she'd run. You daren't grab them, lay a finger on them, even.

But he'd caught her in the act of theft. Big stuff, maybe expulsion stuff. Whatever, way out of his league. It was a huge relief to know that the right thing to do was to pass it on, pass it up, not try to sort it himself. Mercifully, she was doing what he said. So far.

By the time Mick reached the tent he was out of breath. He used to play five-a-side on Friday nights, but that was a long time back. Now he was a 36 inch waist, going on 38, and the puff was hard to find. Patience, too, was in short supply.

Spencer stood straight, tall and outraged. "Where are those children going?"

"They're bunking off, because it's my job to control them, but you've called me over here. I hope you've got a good reason."

"I shall be the judge of that. Mr. Carter " – a grotesque, theatrical nod, to indicate the large, unhappy man in the inner recesses of the tent – "has been promised a unique franchise as a vendor for ice-cream at this event."

"Right. But no-one told the dinner ladies, or Linda Jones. Shame."

Spencer was flummoxed already. "Linda Jones?"

"The cleaner who got the boot." Somewhere in his hasty journey, Mick had lost caution, self-preservation, the last remaining scraps of respect for authority. It was a heady feeling, which almost made up for the frustration he felt as he watched more kids vanish behind the perimeter hedge.

"I'm not sure that you recognise the gravity of this situation."

"Yeah. That's possibly true."

"I have been personally responsible for arranging this franchise. Mr. Carter has my guarantee that he is the sole supplier at this event, and you must realise that the presence of two competitors threatens to make me look foolish."

There was a long pause, while Mick in turn considered, and rejected, three possible responses.

"Mr. Wall? You do understand what I am saying? I expect you to remedy the situation, without delay."

Mick relaxed, and smiled broadly. "Oh, that's no problem."

"I don't follow you."

"Nor do the kids. In fact, they're going in the opposite direction. Nobody's going to sell much more ice cream this afternoon. Market forces, I think they call it. Voting with their feet."

"But what about me? Mr. Carter? I put my reputation on the line..."

In pubs, in the staffroom, for many years to come, Mick would recount the tale, and celebrate this moment of saintly restraint. He settled for the single monosyllable:

"Pass."

"Joyce, she' ll have to go home. I've sent a letter, but she's not to come back until her parents have been in – and maybe not then. I'll need someone to take her home. Is Chris around?"

"She's still at the sports, adding up the scores."

"Rod?"

"I haven't seen him all day – no, here he comes."

Rod strode purposefully down the corridor, to be blocked by Parnaby.

"Tina Clark. Needs to go home."

"But there's an urgent – "

"It'll have to wait. She hasn't got a bag, she can go now."

"I'm not going with him."

"Well, you're not staying here."

Rod was a tangled mess, limbs writhing, outrage seeking to be voiced.

"Mr. Parnaby – "

"When you get back. Please?"

Tina sat, arms folded, staring up in defiance. "I don't trust him."

"You, young lady, will do as you are told."

Tina, Colin and Rod all stared at a new, freshly formidable Joyce.

To the surprise of them all, Tina slowly rose. "If he lays a finger on me, my dad will kill him."

"I wouldn't choose to touch you with a disinfected bargepole."

Tina and Rod glared at each other, and then stomped down the corridor, towards the front door. Parnaby scuttled into his office with relief, while Joyce tactfully looked down at a file of accounts she had already checked.

Only Terry O'Mara, relaxing in the staffroom with a hard-earned cup of tea, saw the final act of the drama unfold. A silent movie, he could fill in the dialogue for himself.

Tina, sulky, sullen and jerky, clumps her way to the car.

Rod, equally sulky, opens the door, gets in, and opens the passenger door. Tina refuses to get in. Rod gets out, gesticulates, shouts and points, eventually forces her in. In a court of law, Terry wouldn't have confirmed that physical force proved decisive, but he'd much prefer not to be asked. There is a brief exchange, during which Tina indicates allegedly injured parts of her anatomy, and the car moves off, to stop at the gate.

Rod gets out, with exasperation locates the key to the padlock, and opens the gate. As he fastens it, his car moves forward, juddering, through the gateway. He watches in disbelief as Tina Clark, sitting in his driving seat, steers his car down the drive and into the path of some sleepy, startled traffic, triumphantly honking his horn. The car's progress is hesitant, bumpy but continuous, as the driver contrives to prevent it from stalling. It occurs to Terry, ever the concerned tutor, that Tina, whatever her faults, has achieved her short-term goal.

CHAPTER ELEVEN:

JULY

July began with a heatwave. Second half of summer term, no year elevens in school, exams almost over and holidays in sight. A few year tens strutted their stuff, practising for next year, but no-one was very impressed. There were clear skies, bright sunshine and a warming glow, as assignments gave way to assignations, and the serious work of tanning got under way. By tacit agreement, the demands of school work shrivelled in the heat, homework became a rarity, and a sense of exhausted well-being spread almost everywhere.

The exceptions were few, but powerful. In the offices of Rod Spencer and Chris Macdonald, the icicles of ambition hung darkly down, protected from the benevolent rays of the sun. Colin was definitely going, and the governors were due to appoint his successor, so why this nonsense of smiling and relaxing uniform?

The other eccentric, who would have been grieved to see himself placed in such company, was Terry O'Mara. Parnaby was his fragile insurance, the nearest guarantee he had to a future. Parnaby liked him, wished him well, would not have the will – or stomach – to sack him. But Parnaby was going, and what chance had Terry got in this managerial age that the new head would have the time or inclination to afford a teacher of drama?

The smart career move would be to look at alternatives, check the adverts, apply to another school. Budgets were in flux all over the land, with teachers leaving, giving up or being sacked. In this chaos there might well be a school desperate to fill a gap, as Rab Butler had been, only twelve months ago. But things were not the same. Terry was not the rootless vagrant of last year, indifferent to what came. He had got used to this, as a place, a group of people, a pattern of work, and he resented doing anything which confirmed he'd have to leave.

So he fretted, made jokes on the surface but beneath the patter he was careful. The cards would be close to the chest, and he would keep his nose clean – which in his case meant buttoning his lip. He realised in disbelief that he couldn't remember wanting anything as much since the early days with Lavinia. And look what happened to that.

He planned his lessons, marked his books and watched his tongue. If his own effort and control could keep him in this job, fine. If not, he'd get legless and go begging to Rick McManus, in whatever sequence was required.

Joyce liked the summer and enjoyed her garden, but Colin was getting her down.

"Why don't you take that jacket off?"

The window of his office was open, but it gave him no relief.

"What?"

"You look terrible. Like a turkey facing an oven."

He turned briefly to her. "Actually, that's how it feels." And then he buried himself again in his work, a martyr to administration and the heat.

She stayed, standing, a yard from his desk. "So, take the jacket off. And the tie."

He sat back, weary but determined. "I can't do that."

"Why not?"

"Parents could come in at any time."

She sat in the desk opposite his chair. "Of course they could. They always could, and you may not have noticed it, but just now ninety per cent of them are wearing shorts and T-shirts."

He looked cunningly at her. "What about the other ten?"

"The other ten are stuffy, sweltering and awkward."

"Right – and looking for trouble. And if they come in and I'm not wearing this, they think they're not getting value for money."

"So our taxes are to provide a tailor's dummy?"

Yes, oh yes, he wanted to say. "Sometimes, maybe."

"If you took the jacket off you could easily put it on again. Most of them don't barge through the door. We usually get a bit of warning."

"You're right." Slowly, mechanically, he took off his jacket without standing up, and draped it over the arms of the chair. She waited for action on the tie front, but that was asking too much.

"You're not going to be so difficult, are you, when all this is over?"

Smokers' corner was content. Sprawled in chairs, no need yet to be facing kids, and savouring summer holidays in advance.

"Where d'you fancy, then, Mick?"

"Easy. Greek islands."

"Sounds good."

"Perfect, mate. This little taverna, overlooking the beach. Shady, cheap, with Dmitri on hand to bring me what I want. Just start to drop off, a little nod in the sun, and he brings another bottle of retsina."

"Are your kids all right in the sun?"

He sat up, shocked. "Kids? who said anything about kids?"

"You're ditching them, then? Just you and Karen?"

"Karen nothing. Michelle."

And this was new. Teachers used to routine, knowing where they stood, familiar with the facts of life, had got used to Mick and Karen.

"So, who's Michelle when she's at home?"

"She never is. Worst luck. Michelle Pfeiffer?" He looked round, innocent, savouring the groans. "You asked me what I fancied, so I told you. Actually, it's me, Karen and the kids, for a fortnight at Scarborough. Again."

The howls of derision, disappointment, of having been had, were almost a compensation for the dream. Given a six-week break, a taste of freedom, where was it going to go? The luxury of imagination, comfort, peace. Till the bell goes.

Jackie turned to Jill. "No magazine this year, then?"

"No. I am not doing a magazine."

She meant it. To Terry, a silent spectator, the ominous tone and granite stare spelt trouble for the Grabowska-Williams partnership, but Jackie seemed unfazed.

"Just wondered."

"Fine."

"I'm not complaining. It was me said I wouldn't do it last year. Believe me, I've been there. I just thought..."

And it was gone. Like an ice cream dropped on the prom, you'd never know it was there. Melted away, mates again.

"Bloody Rod Spencer." Jill grinned, maliciously. "Because he was sniffing around, showing off, chatting up the advertisers, there was no way I was going to back down."

"But now he's applying for the headship – "

"Right. It's just down to me, and it won't happen. I said, when year 11's gone, and it's summer, and we get some breathing space, I might do another magazine. Well, no year elevens, it's definitely summer and I'm still waiting to breathe."

"You mean it doesn't get better?"

She turned to Terry, and laughed. "That's right. Mayhem all the way. But you'll get used to it."

"I hope so." He bit his lip, and she realised what she'd said. Always a tricky time, the end of term.

Rod Spencer sat at his pc, calling up his application for Priory Hall. Five years ago even he would have known he stood no chance. The local authority never gave headships to incumbent deputies; if you wanted promotion you had to move. But now governors ruled, not authorities, and governors had minds of their own. Not always rational, but definitely independent, and quite a lot of governors were scared of the unknown, happier to bank on a face they knew rather than risk trusting the charms of a stranger from outside. And who at Rab Butler had done more to exploit the goodwill of the governors ?

The further he explored, the more confusing the political map became. Rod knew which parties they came from, which firms they ran, and he had a rough idea of the cliques within the group. But he had learned that Mark Hutchings and Sheila Thorpe did not aways vote the same way, and Mrs. Chalmers, though conservative, had some strangely radical ideas.

Which was illogical, but not enough to disturb his equilibrium. As his screen unscrolled the numbered paragraphs of "Education for the New Millennium" Rod was in another world, of ambition satisfied, promotion finally secured. For a moment he pondered briefly whether this would make him happy, whether to run Rab Butler, with Chris Macdonald as his deputy, would be a situation he would relish. But this was a niggling, unattractive thought, to be rapidly despatched like some minor delinquent from year 8, safely out of sight.

"Can I ask you something, sir?"

Terry was in his room, marking, looking at scripts. The sun streamed through the window, and without looking up he could picture the slender outline of Emma Sheargold standing by the door, with long, chestnut hair trailing down.

"Sure." Which was his invariable response, and had been all year, except that now he was being extra careful, keeping his cards close to his chest, buttoning his lip.

"It's not about work."

"Oh, right." He moved past her to shut the door, knowing that this was a risk, but also unnecessary. There was no lock on it, and Elsie could come in at any time. Elsie and a confidence did not belong together; you could have one, or the other, but not both.

He was careful to move back to the other side of the desk before he sat down. "Well, Emma, what can I do for you?"

It came out quavery, though he tried to sound neutral. The shade of Rick McManus laughed at his naivety. He was done for.

If Emma ripped her school uniform and rushed out of the room, he could be out of a job for life. He didn't think Emma was that sort of girl, but then the other teachers didn't think other girls were that sort of girl, which was why they were now unemployed. She watched him steadily, as if she were following all this.

"This summer, sir. The holidays."

No. Definitely no. You're very nice, but you're too young and it wouldn't do my professional prospects any good at all.

"We're going camping in Ireland, sir."

"That's – your family?"

"No, sir. Me and Martin - sorry, Martin and I."

"You make it sound like the queen." No, Terry, don't joke. You've mentioned the queen, which means behaving proper, at just the point when this girl is going to ask you for advice about contraception – which you may be breaking the law if you supply. So, no jokes, right?

"Look, Emma, are you sure I'm the person to help you here?"

"Oh yes, sir. Who else could I ask?"

"Um...well... Ms. Macdonald?"

She shook her head vigorously. "No, sir. Nothing against her, but I'd rather ask you."

"This Martin. Do I know him?"

"Oh no." She was chirpy, factual, relaxed."He's a friend from where we used to live."

"I see." Meaning, I am totally blind, helpless and in the dark.

"Not a boyfriend. Just a friend. But we get on really well. He's someone I can talk to. You know, really talk. He's not bragging all the time, trying to prove how hard he is."

"Sounds a nice lad. So, how can I help?"

They had to tell their parents. That was the first line. Any sniff of sex and she had to talk to her parents, and if she refused he wouldn't listen to another word. She'd think he was crazy, he thought he was crazy, but he mustn't throw away the job. Or the chance of the job. In September, if he was back, permanent even, he could explain.

But for now, it was monastery time.

"What it is, sir..."

"Yes?"

"Do you know any good places to camp? In Ireland, I mean?"

Chris Macdonald sat at home, going over her application. It had been a pleasant surprise that Simon not only took an interest, but encouraged her to use his Apple Mac. On top of that, he brought "a pack of stuff from work" – brochures, videos and programmes.

"This is state of the art, believe me."

She leafed through the catalogue, from "How to achieve your Goals" to "Negotiate like the Pro's". It was a fairyland, inhabited by bright young men in suits. One of these grinned back at her, proclaiming "I am a high content speaker who motivates." The only woman on show was a suited zombie showing "How to Present a Professional Image."

Chris felt sick. If this was high level performance, she was happier lower down. All this gloss, assertion and expense, just to run an ordinary little school like Rab Butler? If this was real life, which planet did Colin Parnaby occupy? And were the prospective heads of schools like Rab Butler really forking out part of their wages to purchase this televisual junk?

Simon was relaxed. "Sure, fifty per cent of it is waste – but you don't know which fifty per cent."

"I can't believe that five percent of this stuff is of any use at all."

"Well, give the programmes a try. Spencer would kill for some of these. They say Rowley's applied, should have a good chance. Though I'm backing you, of course."

She stared through the wink, trying to count the layers of irony, but he was unperturbed. The generous professional, the supportive husband, the adviser bearing gifts – he was having a ball.

She sat in front of the screen while "Write the Irresistible CV" revealed its riches, confident, humourless and totally convinced of its effect. He was right. It was exactly the sort of thing Rod Spencer would have loved.

And that was a problem. To herself, if not to Simon, she was prepared to concede that it was Rod who provided the motivation; the fear of Rod taking over from Colin, the sense of Rod down the corridor, polishing the latest draft of "Education for a new Millennium."

On paper, there was no comparison. Chris had the objectivity to know how the two documents would read, and hers was clear, concise and informative. Anyone who preferred Rod's vacuous self-assertion would need their heads examining. On the other hand, governors were involved. In the interview, too, she felt that she would have a better sense of what other people were after, of how she was coming across; Rod was so bloody insensitive.

And yet...he was busy, he had poured time into governors' meetings, governors' sub-committees, and somebody there might appreciate that commitment. Chris had not put in those hours, by deliberate choice. She knew what Rod was doing, but for her it simply was not worth the evenings, the irritations, the company – just to curry favour in the hope of a distant reward.

And now, as the possibility became more certain, the reward much closer, she wondered whether it was a reward at all, whether she should even bother to apply. What if it were simply resentment of Rod, a bitter protest against the obscenity of working under him, that were driving her to apply? That would be vengeful sexism of the narrowest possible kind, and she resented him for making her even contemplate the thought.

Mrs. Chalmers warbled cheerily into Colin's office, and a different kind of head might have been unsettled by the way she eased into his chair.

"Strictly speaking, of course, you will have no say in the appointment."

Colin signalled affably that he was happy to disclaim responsibility.

"However, we shall of course want you to meet the candidates, and give them the benefit of your experience. There is also the delicate question of the deputies."

She talked flowery, but acted blunt. She had paused, and seemed to be waiting for his response, but surely they had had this conversation. Rod and Chris were nowhere, needn't bother to apply. Or had she changed her mind?

"Yes?"

"As you know, their applications will not be successful. We both agree that to appoint either would not be in the best interests of the school."

So clear, so confident. He admired her directness, although he would have preferred a more passive role for himself in her account of the decision. But he controlled the urge to stammer any qualification.

"I feel it would be kinder not to give them an interview." She pronounced the sentence calmly, with no hint of uncertainty. She had thought about this, and her mind was made up.

He was staggered. Over the years, when headships came up, incumbent deputies invariably got an interview. They didn't get the job, but they got an interview. A courtesy, it was called.

"What do you think?"

"Well, obviously, they'll be disappointed…"

She waved the flannel away. "Obviously. But the disappointment will be greater the further they progress, and if we're not going to appoint them then it's no kindness to pretend that we are."

The logic was impeccable. Do it, get it over with; the bull is coming this way so grab it by the horns. All Parnaby's instincts took him in the opposite direction, but there was a heady excitement in seeing how differently things could be done. Even so, the day they actually got the news was going to be sticky, however it was delivered.

"Mr. Parnaby?"

"Er, yes. Sorry."

"You do agree?"

"Yes, Mrs. Chalmers. I'm sure you're right."

"Good. We'll see them now."

Outside his office, Joyce was panicking. An observer would have seen the tidy desk, heard the ripples of a Mozart piano concerto, and assumed business as usual. But although Joyce had posted

243

the letter of resignation, seen the advert and sent off the details, she could not feel at peace.

There was an uneasiness about Colin, a good-natured distaste for conflict and decision which bordered on the evasive. Evading Rod and Chris she could understand, and often abetted, but she worried that he might also be evading her.

They got on well enough, had enjoyed the holiday, and weren't going to throw teenage tantrums, but what did they have in common beyond the life of school? Take away six hundred kids, forty odd staff – very odd, some of them – and what would there be left? She took a hankie out of her bag, and blew her nose.

She could never quite be sure. There was that strange end to the inspection, when he'd been closeted for three hours with Mary Prendergast and a bottle of vodka. He'd never really talked about that, apart from looking exhausted and being relieved for the name of the school. She was discreet and patient, and had not made waves, but she was inquisitive just the same. Still, there was no great urgency, and he might choose to tell her later. They had, after all, the rest of their lives to come.

"Go on then, Brian, what is it?"

Jill watched as Jackie pushed the folder across the table.

With comic deliberation he balanced it on his right palm.

"Feels like a B."

"Don't be silly."

"On the other hand…" A clumsy transfer here, from right to left, and the fingers of the right hand moved in, like calipers. "1.3 centimetres. Probably an E."

"Brian, will you please be serious?"

He giggled like a kid. He loved working with these two, especially when they trusted his judgement. Moderating folders was a tough, professional job, and they all knew it, so he could pretend to mess about.

"Jill reckons it's –"

"No, don't tell him. We don't agree, that's all he needs to know. So what is it, Brian?"

Fooling done, on his mettle, he skimmed expertly through the folder. Bright, argumentative essay, bit dodgy on paragraphing; a decent enough comparison, but short of detail.

"I'd say – D."

Jill was calmly, infuriatingly smug. "Told you."

"But he's worked ever so hard."

"Jackie, you said to ask Brian."

"I know I did. And I know he's right, really…it's just…."

"Yeah. I know."

"Any other problems? Jill?"

"No. I'm happy about the rest of mine. It wasn't so bad this year, was it ? Last year it seemed to go on for ever."

"Last year it did go on for ever." Jackie gathered her files together. "Ian was still here - remember?"

"Oh God, Ian." Briefly, Jill mimed despair. "Whatever happened to him?"

Brian shuffled his papers together, and put them in his briefcase. "Well, thank you, ladies, for another efficient session."

Jackie smiled. "Our pleasure. I can't think of anyone I'd rather moderate folders with than you."

"Don't get carried away. He'll get bigheaded."

Brian stood, with a sneaky smile. "No, everything in moderation."

"Oh Brian, that's terrible." Jackie put a hand on his arm. "Just hang on a bit, can you?" He sat down again. "You didn't think of asking Terry?"

"Hardly. He only teaches lower school."

"But what about next year ?"

"Exactly." They both looked at him, wanting more. "We don't know about next year. Nor does he. Nor does anyone. It's no favour to Terry to suggest he'll be around next year if he ends up not being. Right?"

Jackie was not giving in so easily. "But you did talk to Colin?"

"Yes, I told you I would."

"And?" Jill could be abrupt, verging on rude. Under her stare he felt uncomfortable, recalling the aimless, shifting conversation in which he and Parnaby had convinced each other and themselves that they were both doing the right thing, without actually deciding anything.

"He couldn't give me a definite answer."

Jackie' warning look caught Jill's grunt before it became offensive. "So when will he know, Brian? What can we tell Terry?"

"At the moment, nothing. It could go either way." This time they didn't stop him as he got up, and walked out of the English office, but it saddened Brian Summers that he did not leave with their full approval. It was almost as if, in some way he could not quite define, he had let them down.

In The White Horse Rick was waiting, cool and casual in a cotton trader shirt. How had rugby wear, traditionally sweaty and torn, come to epitomise aggressive, sharp success? There with two full pints in front of him.

"You were sure I'd come, then?"

"Sure enough." Rick nodded and sipped. "Crisp? I thought you might be buying. "

Terry nibbled the crisp, took a sip and looked around. It was a quiet night, good chance for a man to man chat. "How's that, then?"

"You tell me. New job? New girl?" As Rick fixed him with that foxy look he realised that there was something about this guy he didn't like. Pleasant enough company, potentially a useful contact, but he had a streak of selfishness that was beginning to get him down.

"Sorry. No real news."

"So, you want me to get you a spot?"

Snag was, he might. He hoped not, but he might. And if there was going to be a time when employment meant a favour to Rick, even at King Edward's, then he'd need to be careful. This was not the time to reveal his brand new moral scruples. Whatever you say, say nothing, one more time.

"Parnaby's going, but they haven't appointed yet. It'll be up to them"

"Rowley. English adviser. The smart money says he'll get Rab

246

Butler. He's keen on drama – you could be in there." Rick gave him a playful punch, but that wasn't the cause of the nauseous sensation in his gut.

"Tall feller? Greying, with glasses?"

"That's the one. Bit of a smoothie, but supposed to be sharp."

"I think we've met." Rewind to the INSET meeting, back in the Christmas term. Fast forward through boredom, rebellion, shooting off his mouth. A three hour workshop, zapped in two seconds.

"Didn't hit it off, eh, Terry?"

"He was running this course. I thought it was crap."

"So?"

"So he asked me what I thought."

"So you told him." Rick shook his head, in disbelief at this naivety, and stared at his shambles of a friend. Unkempt hair, unravelling pullover, faded jeans and trainers stained with mud. "You poor colonial git. You need a minder, to keep you out of bother."

"Are you offering?"

He licked his lips appreciatively. "No. I'm pretty useful, but I think this one is beyond me. Pity about Rowley; they say he's good."

"Alright. Don't rub it in."

"So, you want the technician slot." Hastily, cannily, he corrected himself. "If it's still there?"

"If it's not there I can't have it. No, I don't want to give up on Rab Butler till I know for sure."

Rick put his glass down and looked him up and down, as if appraising Terry's health. "Well, what's happened to you, then? Or should I say who? Cherchez la femme, as my French mistress used to say."

"No-one special. It's the job."

He looked around, with mock concern. "It's OK, mate. This is not an interview. You can say what you think. Besides, with a vacation coming up, who needs a vocation?"

Terry tried to hide his impatience. "Yeah, OK, Rick. Whatever."

"No offence, mate. If she's that good, fine. I just didn't recognise the sex- starved little paddy who got his lady up the spout. You were going to tell me about that, remember?"

And he did, all too well. Late night drinking sessions with Rick, mutual rounds of nostalgic strip-tease, confessions of lads at play. And yes, a year ago he would have told him everything.

"So go on, then. My life with Lobelia."

"Lavinia, idiot."

"That's the one, Lavinia Idiot. With a little baby O'Mara on the way. Or not. Finished, right?"

"Yes, Rick. Finished." No way would he show McManus the lead lying at the bottom of his heart. "Do you want another?"

"No hard feelings. I do know how you feel."

"You and Cheryl?"

"Yup. Me and Cheryl. Like I said, we have a vacancy."

"Same again?" And as he collected Rick's glass and moved to the bar Terry felt an exultant, evil surge, the joyous reassurance that even Rick was subject to sod's law. He had a job, was permanent, raked in the shekels – but he too was just another drinker, breaking in a brand new broken heart.

"Cheers. You're a pal. Now, you and... Lavinia." He said it very carefully, emphasising each syllable. The new concerned McManus, treating his ex-girlfriend with respect. "You said there was something different?"

"You what ?" He might get plastered, but he never missed a thing.

"It wasn't what you'd expect. You told me, last time. You said you'd tell me the full story next time we got ratted. Well, here we are. Not ratted yet, but on the way..."

"Yeah, it's coming back." Had done straight away, in fact. Was sitting there, at the front of his mind, waiting to be spilled. "It's nothing special, mind."

"After this, it had better be."

"The thing about her was...what made it all so different." He stopped, and gave him his Irish joker grin. "You don't want to hear this."

"Terry, I'm gasping. Get on with it."

"OK, if you insist. But don't say I didn't warn you. The thing with Lavinia was, that made her different from all the other girls – she was utterly, totally ambidextrous."

He managed the laugh, and timed the nudge, and had Rick laughing with him, till the moment was buried and the conversation staggered on. It was neatly done. He kept the blur in his speech, the matey illusion of vagueness, but the memory was there in his brain, clear as an engraving.

Him and Lavinia. No, Lavinia and him. That was it, the guilty secret Rick would never know. Terry the laddo, the wild young man, had got his girl pregnant and blown his career, but it wasn't him that had done it. Biologically, maybe. He had played his part. But it was Lavinia made the moves; Lavinia asked him out, Lavinia got him into bed, Lavinia saved him from having to use his brain. Just keep talking, Terry, smile away, and leave the rest to me.

She was in charge, and had been from the start. There were lads who'd call that magic. All the way on automatic pilot – can't be bad. But for Terry it was shame, even then, and all the more so now. Still, it was shame on the far side of the Irish Sea, and if Lavinia could get herself back up then he'd no reason to fret. He'd pick up his own pieces, and try to do better next time. If there was a next time. But nobody – McManus least of all – was going to have to know.

Joyce ran down the list of candidates. "It's like Wimbledon."

"Mmm?" Parnaby, as so often these days, was not quite with it.

"You start with a list, and then it comes down, and down – to one."

"The singles champion. Well, if I was a candidate I wouldn't get it." He spoke as if this was a bold remark, challenging disagreement, but they both knew it was true.

He worried her, more and more.

"You don't wish you were staying, do you?"

"Good God, no. I'm just saying, they look for different things."

She picked up a stray paper clip, and put it in the drawer. "Such as?"

"Marketing the school, links with industry, management."

"What about teaching?"

"No, they don't look for that. It's the teachers do the teaching, not the heads."

She looked at him, sadly. "So. Who's the favourite?"

"They seem to think Rowley's a good chance, and Roy Bannister. Janet Smart, maybe, the HMI. I think she's a pal of Mary Prendergast's."

"Oh really?"

"Yes." He tried to affect coolness, and failed dismally. "You remember – the inspection team."

"Yes, I thought I knew the name. Although I didn't see anything like as much of her as you did." She left the pause resting on the desk between them. Parnaby shuffled some papers, without affecting their relationship to each other, and looked out of the window.

"So, tell me about Miss Smart – or is it Mrs.?"

"Miss, I think. She used to be an inspector, but under the new arrangements her face didn't fit. I'd say that was a recommendation."

Joyce still looked puzzled. "But why should she want to come here?"

"It's a good school." For a couple of seconds, he faced her incredulous gaze. "Well, it's not bad. Maybe Mary told her nice things about us."

She had spent a working lifetime cultivating discretion, but her hrumph and abrupt departure left Parnaby in no doubt that, marooned on his little island of optimism, he was once more on his own.

Business in the staffroom sweep was brisk.

"Rowley's coming down fast. 5-2 now, and Bannister's 6-1."

"Smart?"

"Yeah, she's a promising little filly."

"Just for information, Mick, Janet Smart is older than you are."

"Is that right? 7 -1 at the moment, but that's probably generous.

So, Brian, are you backing the English candidate?"

Summers moved away from the pigeonholes, with a large screed of paper. He peered sceptically at the odds. "That's two questions. One, do I want Rowley as head? Two, will I give you some money?"

"OK, you're the English teacher. So what's the answer?"

"The answer is that neither question fills me with much enthusiasm, but to the second it's definitely no." Wearily, he sat down. " Have you seen this timetable?"

"I thought Rod was in purdah. Or should that be mourning?"

Jackie was in forgiving mood. "You know, I almost pity him. I can't see why anyone would want to be a head, but if you're desperate and don't get it...well, must be tough."

Mick was all heart. "Perhaps we should get him some flowers."

"Not till you've seen the timetable."

"Is it worse than usual?"

"Much. I reckon he sulked for a week, put the computer on automatic pilot, and then just threw whatever came out into the pigeonholes."

"So what's wrong, Brian?"

"We've got year 11 last thing on a Friday afternoon, he's split the year 9 classes, all year 10 is on Monday, Tuesday, Wednesday, and my free periods are all on a Thursday."

"But apart from that, it's brilliant."

Jackie leaned over to look at the detail. "But what's the question mark?"

"That's....well, it's undecided."

And just as they wondered why Brian's tone had changed, they realised Terry had come in. Sylvia plugged the gap.

"Never mind. A week to go. Toujours les vacances."

"Yeah. As I paint the bedroom I shall think of you supping - where was it?"

"Saumur. By the Loire."

"So mure, but yet so far."

"Hey, Mick, you're quite the linguist, yeah?"

"Just because I go to Scarborough, Terry, does not mean I can't manage the occasional bon mot."

"Is that bon mot while you wait?"

"Huh ?"

"Mot...M.O.T. Do you want diagrams?"

"Oh grow up, you two. I can't wait for Christmas, when the new crackers come out." Idle summer banter, with less than a week to go. The signs of relaxation are all too evident as Chris enters the staffroom.

"I don't know if you're all free, but the bell has gone. Lessons should have started by now." A firm glare round, and exit.

"Oops. Somebody's missed a headship."

"Did you have money on her, Mick ?"

"Well if I did it's not going on flowers, and that's for sure."

Parnaby strolled slowly round the grounds, waiting for the verdict. He had done the same seventeen years ago, when he had been appointed as a head. He couldn't stand the ritual sitting around, exchanging pleasantries and conventional estimates, when inside everyone was screaming for relief. So he cheerily greeted the candidates, smiled and left them to scream.

It was a pleasant enough little world, especially in summer. Nothing special architecturally, little lego blocks crammed together, but the grass around the school and the blue sky gave it a natural feel. He had visited inner city schools, grey concrete slums surrounded by high walls, which gave off the aura of a jail. Here you could see the smokers standing outside the tights factory, the fields beyond, the sense of a horizon which hadn't been contained.

Critics would call it limited, a fantasy world insulated from the pressures of real life, but to him it seemed pressured enough. It was a blissful, almost immoral thought that this September he would be forever safe from having to speak to irate parents, angry staff, recalcitrant children.

He would miss it. He liked the place, the predictable confines of the ordered day, the timetabled week, the calendared year, forever coming round like some natural cycle of the seasons. And although he looked forward to retirement as some kind of release, as all his colleagues seemed to nowadays, the imprisonment he was leaving was more familiar, less threatening than the freedom into which he would pass.

Perhaps they might ask him to stay. Not for ever, but just for the term or so, before the new head took over. Maybe they wouldn't be able to start straight away. It would save having to choose between Rod and Chris as acting head. If they asked him he'd be tempted, although they wouldn't ask unless they knew he was available.

Joyce wouldn't be keen. No, that wasn't right. Joyce would be bloody furious. She would…he found it hard to imagine the worst of Joyce at full flow. So far, even on holiday, their relationship had thrived within the inhibition of their roles; without that, God knows what she might do.

He turned back to look at the school and she was there, standing by the door, waving frantically. The smoke was rising from the chimney, the entrails were ready for review. Rab Butler was about to get its new head.

Kids had gone half an hour ago, but in the staffroom Jill was busy sorting, emptying cupboards, piling books, purging junk.

Terry sat, nursing a mug of tea, and watched her work. "You're allowed to knock off, you know."

She stopped, briefly, to survey the debris. "Sure, but then I'd have to come back in the holidays."

"I thought you did that anyway."

"Only a bit." She hesitated, looked down and then up again. "Any news?"

"The head, you mean?"

"That. Or your job. Colin say anything?"

"It's up to the new boss."

She shook her head. "He's chicken. Nice chicken, but chicken. He could have given you the job, and let the new head live with it. Or at least give you another year, temporary."

Terry's thoughts exactly. "He's been fine", he said

"So what will you do?"

"At the moment, wait." He looked round, at the faded armchairs and the squalor on the floor. Had he really got attached to this? "Just hang in there, and hope. See what comes." He summoned a cheery, unconvincing smile.

"Well, good luck. See you around, Terry." And she grinned, the comfortable grin of a fellow worker, that Jackie got all the time and Terry had been waiting for all year. Maybe he could put the memory of it in his folder, his record of achievement as he left.

Rowley went off in a sulk, like someone invited to a bridge party who turns up to find a poker school. Parnaby was surprised by his own enjoyment of seeing one of the county's heavyweights tossed on to the slush pile.

Their choice was Janet Smart. A tall, bright lady in her early fifties, and a close friend of Mary Prendergast's. She was happy to accept Parnaby's offer of tea, and settled readily into one of his comfy chairs. Joyce's expression as she brought the tea had a whiff of sulphur laced with vodka, but he wasn't going to let that put him off.

"You have here the makings of a very good school." She smiled and sipped her tea. A fiercer analyst might have pressed her on the things which weren't yet very good, but he was happy to acknowledge her goodwill.

"Mary told me what to expect. None of that cutting edge nonsense, but a decent, friendly place, with nice kids and a lot of potential. The staff are a mixture, but at least they're not cynical. Most of them, that is."

He strove to put on his most optimistic face. "You're not worried by target-setting, tests and all that?"

"Oh no." He would have given his lump sum and half his pension for that deep, calm confidence. "You and I know, Mr. Parnaby, that we're dealing with people here. In the real world of kids and teachers and classrooms this school has many things right, and a good chance of improving the things that need to get better. What more could you ask?"

It was like a commercial. There she was, sunny and unafraid, instantly absorbing the place where he had struggled all this time.

"That's very cheering. We sometimes take it for granted, don't think of ourselves so highly. I'm sorry, I've got used to saying "we"."

"Don't apologise." She sipped her tea, then put it down. "I'm not a fool. I don't think it's perfect. But there are some good teachers here, who can take us a long way. I may need to adjust the workings of senior management but then," a little smile, almost coy "you wouldn't expect me to stand still, now would you?"

He waved the possibility away. From the evidence of the last five minutes, standing still would not feature on this woman's agenda. Just what precise form of alchemy would transform Rod Spencer he couldn't be sure, but he guessed it would probably work. It would be nice to stay around to watch.

"There was just one thing, if I may ."

"Of course. What is it?"

"We have a temporary appointment, Terry O'Mara, drama teacher, just finishing his first year."

"Yes?"

"I didn't like to prejudge his future. I thought that ought to be left to my successor." He tried to make it sound calm and wise, but this was difficult, as he watched her anxiety rise.

"So what does he think is happening?"

"He doesn't know."

"Well, we can't leave him dangling, can we?" It was a commonsense observation, accompanied by a challenging look that pierced him to the professional core. Could he really have left it all this time ? "I shall need a staffing structure, current financial statement and next year's timetable."

Oh God. It was definitely time to leave. He rose "I'll just er...have a word with Joyce."

It was an eerie feeling. Terry didn't come out of the office singing, dancing or crying. There was just this warm distant glow, deep down, that said he had a job. A proper job, a permanent post, like real teachers. The new woman seemed pleasant and supportive, like Parnaby, but a lot sharper. If she said she was going to keep him, she wasn't going to change her mind.

Uncharacteristically, Jill was hanging around. Not reading, not zooming into action, not sorting out her files. If she'd been a teenager Terry would have said she was dossing, or waiting to chat up a lad, but she was a teacher, so it must be something else.

"Hi."

"Hi, Jill."

"Any news, then?"

He toyed with the options. "Yeah. As it happens, I have."

She walked towards him. "Well, come on, then. What's happening?"

"I'm staying. I've got a job." He felt his voice go husky as she came up and hugged him. Nothing sexy, just two mates with good news.

"Oh, that's great." She stood back, taking it in. "I'm so pleased. Jackie's gone, but we can have a drink, yeah? Celebration."

He drew a deep breath. He too stood back, and looked at her. "I'm not sure."

"What's the problem?"

"Well, there's something..." He looked down at the carpet, bit his nails.

"And that is?" She looked closely, mystified. "Go on, Terry, what is it?"

He couldn't resist it. "Who's paying?"